RINA KENT

To your deepest, darkest fantasies.

AUTHOR NOTE

Hello reader friend,

If you haven't read my books before, you might not know this, but I write darker stories that can be upsetting and disturbing. My books and main characters aren't for the faint of heart.

This book contains themes of consensual non-consensual and child assault. I trust you know your triggers before you proceed.

Red Thorns is the first book of a duet and is not standalone.
Thorns Duet:
#0 Yellow Thorns (Free Prequel)
#1 Red Thorns
#2 Black Thorns

Sign up to Rina Kent's Newsletter for news about future releases and an exclusive gift.

A bet turned into a disaster.

Sebastian Weaver is the star quarterback and the college's heartthrob.

Rich. Handsome. Bastard.

Everyone's attention flocked toward him and all the girls dreamed to be with him.

Not me.

At least, not until he made a move on me.

See, I thought I was stronger than Sebastian's charms.

I thought I could survive being his target.

I thought wrong.

Little did I know that he will make my most twisted fantasies come true.

Fantasies I didn't know existed…

PLAYLIST

Infra-Red—Three Days Grace
Oh My My—Blue October
Paralyzed—LANDMVRKS
Can You Feel My Heart—Bring Me The Horizon
In the Dark—Bring Me The Horizon
I Don't Know What to Say—Bring Me The Horizon
Another Life—Motionless in White
Blank Space—I Prevail
Learning to Survive—We Came As Romans
Breathe Into Me—Red
Is it Just Me?—Sasha Sloan & Charlie Puth
Auslander—Rammstein
Tattoo—Rammstein
Sehnsucht—Rammstein
Heartless—The Weekend

You can find the complete playlist on Spotify.

RED THORNS

PROLOGUE

Akira

Dear Naomi,

I'm your new friend.

Or at least, I hope to be.

Teachers in school told me it's a good idea to have a pen pal to help improve my English. So I thought, why not learn from someone who's living in the States, huh?

You must be wondering, why you? Good question.

I observed you once. Don't ask me where, because I want to keep that a secret.

But back then, I noticed two things about you.

One, you have a beautiful smile that reminds me of peach blossoms and falling snow. Don't make me choose between the two, because I dig both. So imagine my surprise when I found both of those traits in something as simple as your smile.

Two, you're so real that if anyone attempted to get inside you, they'd probably drown from how deep you are.

I volunteer to take a tour, though. If you'll let me.

Did that come off too strong? Forgive me. I tend to do that with people I'm eager to learn about. And there aren't a lot, for your information.

You must be wondering, how the hell does this freak know my address? Which is another good question, but I'd rather not answer that right now.

Not because I'm a stalker, though you probably think I am at this point, but because I'm not even sure you'll see this, let alone reply.

Before I move on to the boring chore of introducing myself, let me tell you what compelled me to write this letter.

And yes, I know I mentioned the teachers, but we both know that's an excuse to get your attention, a lame one at that.

My real reason is: I want to get to know you.

The girl behind the rare smiles and the 'fuck the world' attitude. The girl who wears her black hair short and her lips pink. The girl whose headphones seem to be her only friend (what do you listen to, by the way?).

That might give me a few points on the creep meter, but I wanted to be honest with you. No secrets and no lies.

I promise I'm not a dick—not for long, anyway. And I'm not some sort of an otaku as you're probably thinking right now. If you don't know, otaku is a geek in English, or so I was told.

Now that all of that is out of the way, allow me to do the introductions.

clears throat

I'm Akira and I was born in Japan. Tokyo, to be exact.

In Kanji, Akira is written with the characters for 'sun' and 'moon,' so I'm sort of like the whole package, having both sunlight and moonlight. Am I a catch or what?

I'm a senior in high school, so we're similar in age and you don't have to worry about old geezers. Unless that's your thing. I'm not judging.

So now, the million-dollar question: Can you be my friend, Naomi?

Awkward silence.

More awkward silence.

Did that sound pathetic? Desperate?

Probably. At any rate, interpret it in your own way and let me know your reply.

If you don't want to, simply don't send back anything. I'll move on after a week or so.

But if you do reply, I'll probably do a year's worth of victory dances.

Just don't get any ideas about what this is. I can only be your friend, Naomi.

If you go and fall in love with me, I'll have no choice but to disappear.

And that's just sad.

And unnecessary.

Impatiently waiting,
Akira

ONE

Naomi

Three years later

EVERYONE HARBORS A SECRET.

Some are mundane; others are downright twisted.

Apparently, my whole existence falls under the latter, because my mom is keeping it hidden like it's some sort of national intelligence.

Or maybe it's international, considering where she came from.

I kick the pebbles in my way as I unhurriedly make my way to cheer practice.

Blackwood College is one gigantic building with an ancient feel to it. A few towers stand proudly at every corner as if they're the watchdogs of this place—or that's what I've thought ever since I enrolled here.

Once again, courtesy of my dear mama, who hasn't only made sure I study in rich people's private universities, but also that I play the part by cheering and being in the popular crowd.

Who even likes cheering in college? Certainly not me. I'd rather live my twenty-one-year-old life listening to hard rock and having as little contact with humans as physically possible, thank you very much.

I'm not an antisocial who thinks stepping over people is okay. I'm merely an asocial who likes to leave them alone in hopes they'll do the same in return.

No luck thus far.

I stare up at the building whose walls I'm privileged to be within. A building that's as ancient as this town, located on the outskirts of New York City. Old, corrupted money constructed what others consider a place of elite education.

Well, maybe it is. Or maybe I'd appreciate it better if I didn't have to wear tight, tiny clothes that reveal my belly and strain against my sports bra that I wear in a fruitless attempt to flatten my huge breasts. 'Huge' per the cheer captain's words.

Why don't I just quit? Excellent question.

The answer is simple and boring—Mom.

As much as I have a love-hate relationship with the woman who gave birth to me, I haven't forgotten how much she struggled raising me on her own all these years. When I was young and depended on her, she worked several part-time jobs and barely slept to keep a roof over our heads. So when she begged me to make an effort about being in the cheer squad, I couldn't shoot her down.

She just likes seeing me in the spotlight, I guess. She wants me to make it so we don't give the racist pricks any chance to look down on us just because we're of Asian heritage.

That's the only reason I'm still part of this nightmare.

At least, I hope it is.

My footsteps are heavy at best as I shuffle through the entrance to the football field. Clear sky extends for as far as I can see and the early fall's sun shines down on the terrain. Due to the great weather, the captain and our coach decided we'd practice our routines outside.

There's some important home game at the end of this week between our football team, the Black Devils—stupid name, considering the only thing devilish about them is their uniforms—and their biggest rivals from New York.

The cheer squad is lined up near the sidelines because, surprise, we're not allowed to disturb their majesties while they're practicing. It's already stupid that the squad exists for their benefit, but they have the nerve to treat us like we're their whores.

Most cheerleaders either fuck or date the football players, or they look at them as if they're Jesus in plural form.

Like me, all my female teammates are dressed in tiny black skirts that barely cover their asses and white tops streaked with black lines. The males are wearing black pants and white T-shirts. Now, if I were a man, I wouldn't have to put my body on display, but that would mean carrying the weight of all those girls during our routines, so, on second thought, no thank you. I'd rather show my belly button and kill my breasts with tight sports bras.

Can You Feel My Heart by Bring Me The Horizon is blasting in my ears one second, and the next, it disappears when my headphones are plucked away. I'm about to stab someone when my attention falls on none other than the captain of our squad.

Reina Ellis is tall, blonde, fit, and has deep blue eyes that she's currently judging me with. Oh, and she comes from money—not new like Mom's, but very old and influential.

So she's basically the whole package, as indicated by her nickname, Queen Bee, and has the personality to go with it.

She taps her foot on the ground while still holding my noise-canceling headphones—aka my saving grace—out of reach. "You're late, Naomi."

"No I'm not."

She grabs my wrist that has a smart watch on it and shoves it in my face. "What time is that?"

"It's Bree!"

"Oh, my bad." I offer a makeshift smile that only angers her further, turning her face a dark shade of red.

She actually has fair skin, but she spends a fortune to tan it, so whenever she's angry or frustrated—usually with me, because the others are too scared of her to speak out—she looks like a volcano at the point of eruption.

The best way to kill bitches? With kindness.

Honestly, I may have never let anyone walk all over me before, but it's these people and their constant bullying that's made me a bitch just like them.

Wait. Does this mean I'm one of them now?

God, no. This is only temporary until I graduate. Then I'll live in a basement and beg magazines to publish my sketches.

I only have to survive this last year and then I can chalk up the cheer squad and everyone in it to life experience.

My gaze roams around the endless haters' faces until I find Lucy's soft one. She grins at me discreetly, then instantly hides it, but it's enough to paint what resembles a smile on my lips.

She's shorter and thinner than me, but she has fiery red hair and adorable freckles that dust her cheeks. Lucy is the only one I'd call a friend in the midst of these shark-infested waters. Mainly because she doesn't belong to Reina's clique and is kind of a reject like me.

We've found company in our misery ever since we first met as high school seniors, and it's continued in college. Which isn't a surprise since almost everyone present studied with me in high school. Another prestigious private institution in Blackwood.

Mom and I relocated here during my senior year, and let's just say that immediately categorized me as an outcast. Hence Mom's idea about my being part of the popular crowd by becoming a cheerleader.

Reina starts giving instructions and Lucy's attention goes to her, and in response, mine does, too, even reluctantly. Our coach,

"Fine. I'm ten minutes late. So what?"

"This is your final warning, Naomi. Be late again and suspending you. Countless people wish to be in your positic and if you don't want it, there's no need to keep it."

As if I care. I want to say that but bottle it inside becau. of—drum rolls—my mother.

Making me part of this plastic bunch was such a low blow, Mon.

Maybe she's taking revenge because of how much I pestered her with questions about my dad while growing up.

Maybe I'll have an emotional scar from the cheer squad and won't be able to live my adult life sketching mangas in a dark basement.

Or maybe I'll find my father and live happily ever after. Though, it's a long shot for that one.

"Are you waiting for an invitation?" Reina cocks her head to where the others are watching the exchange with clear disdain— toward me, not their beloved captain.

I extend my palm. "My headphones."

"After practice."

"But—"

"And only if you don't slack off." She turns around and waltzes to the others with a gentle sway of her hips.

Awesome. Now, I actually have to make an effort.

I try not to drag my feet as I follow after her. Snickers and whispers break out among the cheerleaders at my expense. They have this wolf pack mentality where one will start the mocking sessions and the others follow.

I glare at them. "What? You have something you're too scared to say out loud, so you prefer whispering like weak little bitches?"

"The only weak little bitch here is you, Naomi." Brianna, the co-captain and a member of Reina's mini-me club, points at me. "Look at your fat hips. I told you to start a diet."

"No, thanks." I place a hand on my hip. "And these are nat- ural beauty. Don't be so jealous—it shows, Bee."

a middle-aged woman with long black hair and thin lips, barely says anything when her favorite captain talks.

I'm bored out of my mind, thinking about what food to grab later and if I should endure the witch hunt and the fat-shaming if I eat a slice of pizza in front of the squad.

Reina grabs me by the shoulders and hisses, "Focus or dream on about the headphones," before she tells me my position will be on the second line, the one right above the male cheerleaders and, therefore, I'll be carrying her and many of the others.

Yay.

Thankfully, I don't make many mistakes, except for nearly dropping Brianna on her face, but, oh well, accidents do happen.

At least I'm not distracted by the half-naked football players carrying whatever their coach gave them and running around the field.

I mean, yes, I want to watch male perfection, but I'd rather do it in secret behind my computer screen and not in an ogling, bring-attention-to-me kind of way, like the other cheerleaders.

If I do, it'll seem as if I'm interested in the football players, yet all I care about is the glistening of sweat on their abs that travels to other…places.

But I have this perfect poker face that no one is able to read behind. Lucy calls me unfeeling sometimes, but it's not that I don't *feel*. It's that I have immaculate control over showing my emotions.

I take after my mom, thank you very much.

So even when a whirlwind of emotions swirls inside me, no one can figure anything out by observing the outside.

Not even the one person I actually notice on the football team.

The one with sandy hair and sharp features and hard, glistening abs that could very well be used as a weapon.

The one who doesn't know half the campus exists, while everyone is taught his name the moment they step into Blackwood.

But that one? Yeah, I'm glad he knows nothing of my intentions, because I will get over him.

It's just a crush...if a crush can go on for this long.

No. I'm sure it's only a crush and only physical, because everything else is a big no.

At the end of the routine, I'm ready to go have my pizza and give the cheerleaders the middle finger if they say anything about my hips again.

As usual, all of them—Lucy included—kiss Reina's ass about how *perfect* the routine is and what a *queen* she is. Everyone except me, of course. What? She can handle some silent criticism.

Then everyone starts to leave, except her holy circle of vicious mini-mes. Brianna, no surprise there. Prescott, the male co-captain, and a few other cheerleaders who've managed to get Queen Bee's seal of approval.

This close circle is basically all about Reina's cult activities aka the secret dares that she makes them do because she's bored in her expensive mansion, and tormenting other people is apparently fun.

I'm about to pull Lucy away so we can go home and binge watch the latest true crime show on Netflix when Reina calls to her.

Lucy turns around, her cheeks red. "Y-yes?"

I sigh. I've been teaching her to grow into her confidence, but it seems that's going to be a very long process. Once shy, always shy, I guess.

"Stay," Reina says ever so casually.

My lips part at the same time as Lucy's. Reina didn't just invite her to join her cult, right?

My friend grins, her skin reddening with apparent excitement as she awkwardly makes her way to the captain's circle. Other members of the squad whisper, probably in both envy and hatred, as I try to make sense of the situation.

This...there's something going on. But what?

Or maybe there isn't and I'm just being paranoid?

But it doesn't make sense for Lucy to be part of Reina's close circle. She's shy and is mostly backup in the squad, just like me. We're the invisible ones, the ones who people like looking at when we're with the others but find boring individually.

All of Reina's other subjects are either as beautiful or accomplished—or damn rich—as she is.

Lucy is average on all of the above. Though, in my eyes, she's the prettiest.

I stride toward them, my steps wide.

Brianna slides in front of me, crossing her arms. "You weren't invited."

"As if I want to belong in your secret sociopathic witch coven." I extend my palm toward Reina. "My headphones."

She reaches into her bag and retrieves them but keeps them out of reach. "You were passable today, Naomi."

I snatch them out of her hand. "I'll call when I need your opinion of me."

"That will be soon, bitch." Brianna breaks out in laughter and the others follow, except for Lucy, and also Reina, who doesn't laugh or smile unless it's on her terms. She's a leader, not a follower, and makes that apparent in each of her moves.

"What is that supposed to mean, *bitch?*" I ask Brianna.

"Let's just say your holier-than-thou attitude will be gone once—"

"Bree," Reina cuts her off with a stern look before she directs me, "Off you go."

I narrow my eyes on her, then meet Lucy's gaze, but she gives me an apologetic smile. One that says she's staying with this band of assholes.

But then again, that's not a surprise. Luce has always loved Reina and her followers. If anything, this is like a dream come true for her.

Releasing a long sigh, I plug in my headphones and leave

while listening to *In the Dark* by Bring Me The Horizon. Ordinarily, I'd wait until I was off of the field, but I'm more desperate than usual to block their whispers today. Especially since I don't have Luce with me to lessen the blow.

Does this mean I'm losing her to the queen bee? She has everything and everyone she wants, why does she have to take my only friend as well?

Sharp tangs of loneliness flood the base of my stomach and leave a bitter aftertaste at the back of my throat. And it scares me. The fact that I have no one and am all alone terrifies the shit out of me.

But no more so than the idea of actually reaching out to people and being vulnerable just so they can hurt me. Both are horrifying monsters I think of every day.

Ever since the day I trusted someone and they violated my innocence.

I'm so engrossed in my thoughts and the loud rock music that I'm completely blinded to my surroundings.

That's when it happens.

I see the ball traveling my way at supersonic speed.

But it's too late.

My legs remain frozen in place as my eyes widen in preparation for the impact.

But instead of the ball, a flash of movement catches in my peripheral vision before a hard body slams into mine.

And not just any body.

The body of the football player whose existence I've spent years trying to ignore.

And failing.

TWO

Naomi

I TUMBLE TO THE GROUND.

Or rather, both of us do in a mess of limbs and groans and awkward touches.

More accurately, inappropriate touches.

Holy Jesus.

Please tell me I didn't just brush my fingers against his *thing* right now.

I quickly remove my hand while he's trying to get off me, and that knocks us both down again.

But this time, he's glued to me. His cut body covering my entire front and his naked chest on my breasts. Now, I'm definitely touching his thing—or my stomach is, anyway.

My cheeks would be flaming red if my emotions appeared on the surface. I never thought I'd feel the ridges of his body this intimately.

At least, not in this lifetime.

Jesus. His abdomen is as firm as the ground against my back, only it's soft enough to sleep on.

Or rub my face against it.

Or any other activity that includes touching it.

He plants his palms on the ground on either side of my head and pushes up a little. His stomach, thighs, and umm, his *erection*, are still pressed against me.

That's when I have my first full view of him.

Sebastian Weaver.

Star quarterback.

A former senator's grandson.

And dangerous.

It's not only because of his lethally attractive looks, because honestly? He could be the most beautiful man God has created. Okay, in the top five.

His face may as well have been sculpted from granite, all rough edges and with predefined expressions. Not in a serial killer kind of way, but in a 'hello, I'm your next fantasy' kind of way. His cut jawline and sharp nose add to the general perfection that God bestows upon only some of his creations.

His eyes, though, tell a completely different story. It's not solely about their light green color that resembles the shade of a tropical sea that I've only seen in pictures. But what's most striking about them is the fading light in their depths, almost as if he's mad with the supremacy he was given. Or maybe he considers it a burden.

Gee, if having his looks is a burden, we can switch.

Or not.

That would make me a guy and I'd have to carry the cheer squad.

Okay, wait. Am I really thinking about carrying the cheerleaders when I'm trapped under Sebastian's body?

A very hard one at that. No, I don't mean his dick is hard, though I think it's getting there, but all of him, from his chest to his thighs and even his whole face.

His dark sandy-blond hair falls across his forehead, creating a dreamy contrast against his sun-kissed skin and the light color of his eyes. Eyes that are currently narrowing at me as if I committed a mistake by merely existing.

"Move," he says in that slightly raspy voice of his, one that's meant to whisper dirty things in the dark.

Or maybe in the light. Who cares?

"What?"

"Either you heard me and you're playing dumb or you have hearing issues. Both of which I don't give a fuck about."

My small 'worship at his altar while ogling him' phase comes to a screeching halt at both his words and their condescending tone.

Who does this asshole think he is? He might be a little attractive—okay, a lot, whatever—but that doesn't give him the right to treat me like the dirt under his shoes. I wasn't born for that position.

I adopt my half-mocking, half-snobby tone that I usually use when talking to Brianna. "Uh, hello? You're the one who's pinning me to the ground."

"Because you're wrapping your leg around mine."

I lift my head and search around until my abdomen aches from the half-lifted position, and sure enough, my leg is definitely looped around his. And are his muscles twitching beneath mine or am I imagining things?

Way to go, me. One to nil, Black Devils.

But instead of acting like the idiot my brain is telling me to emulate, I don't release him. "That's only because of the fall. Don't get ideas in your twisted head."

"Maybe you're the one whose head is twisted since it went straight there." He grins, showing me his perfect white teeth, and while that's considered a friendly gesture, the emptiness behind it forbids me from considering it as such.

I've been well aware of Sebastian's reputation ever since I transferred here during my senior year of high school. One would have to be blind while simultaneously living under a rock not to recognize Senator Brian Weaver's only grandchild and Blackwood's favorite quarterback.

He's the definition of a cliché with his mesmerizing all-American looks, background, and skill.

Everyone believes his grandfather is preparing him for a career in politics as soon as he's out of college and that football is merely a stepping stone. The NFL is too small for his ambitions and his future.

But that's not what I first noticed about Sebastian. It was neither who his family was, what he played, nor even what he looked like.

It was always his eyes.

The way they're muted, like right now, as if he's falling into a role.

He plays the social game so well, I'm jealous sometimes. I wish I could fake it as convincingly as he does. I wish I could smile at people when all I want to do is hide.

"Let's agree to disagree." He's still smiling, but he's not attempting to conceal its fakery anymore. That's what people do when they're fed up. They let the masks fall and allow their true selves to show through.

And right now, what he's projecting is entirely different from what he is.

"So are you going to release me or would you rather feel me up some more?"

I move my leg with a jerk. "You're the one who's doing that."

"Yeah, yeah, and I'm also the one who caged myself against you. Do you hear yourself?"

"Yes, I do, and I make more sense than you… Why aren't you getting up?"

The empty mockery on his features slowly breaks as a gleam shines through. "Didn't you say I was feeling you? Might as well go with it."

"Are you insane? We don't even know each other."

"Why does that matter? It's only a natural chemical reaction between healthy adults."

"Are you a fucking animal?"

"*Monster*, to be more specific." The way he emphasizes the word 'monster' sends a chill down my spine and it's with effort that I manage to hold on to my agitation.

I slap my hands on his chest to push him away, but I barely manage to move the rock-hard muscles. "Get off me."

"Shhh. I'm not done."

"Done with what?"

"With you."

My toes curl and it takes everything in me not to knee him or something. I've always been bad at handling these types of advances, but especially if they're coming from someone like Sebastian.

I guess the rumors are correct after all. He'd really sleep with anyone, wouldn't he?

"Weaver!" a male voice yells and Sebastian begrudgingly gets off of me, the loss of his body rattling me more than I care to admit.

I jump to my feet, gathering my headphones and bag, thankful nothing was broken, and my attention shifts to the guy headed our way. It's Sebastian's friend, Owen, another buff football player, with darker skin and a shaved head.

Sebastian, however, doesn't make a move to leave, his feral gaze zeroed in on me. Embarrassment and a feeling I can't identify grab hold of me and I want to kick my leg in the air and run in an open field so I can breathe clean air and get rid of it.

"Want an autograph?" I snap, then regret it. I really need to learn how to control my temper and not throw a tantrum at everything. But I guess I constantly have this feeling that everyone is out to get me, and the star quarterback is no exception.

Especially with the taunting way he observes me.

He smiles again in that hollow way that might be a sign his soul was recruited by the devil. "I'll think about it and let you know."

"Think about what?" Owen wraps a hand around Sebastian's shoulder when he reaches us. "What's up with you and the Asian chick?"

I place a hand on my hip. "The Asian chick has a name, doucheface, and it's Naomi. Tell Siri to spell it out for you."

And with that, I turn and leave, the echo of Sebastian's laughter following me long after he's out of earshot.

By the time I get home, I think I've analyzed what happened back at the field a hundred times over.

Okay, that's a lie. It's been at least double that.

Despite being a cheerleader, I don't actually talk to Sebastian or play house with the rest of the football team.

Sure, Reina, Brianna, and the rest of the squad do, but I don't for the simple reason that…well, they expect sex. It's not rocket science and I'm not a whore.

So why the hell did I make myself look like one when I looped my leg around his?

Desperate much, Nao?

I text Luce to ask her to call me as soon as she's done with whatever satanic rituals for shape and beauty Reina makes them do. But I know she'll be too busy for me today.

Or ever, for that matter.

She practically sold her soul to the devil, and Reina will make sure to keep her occupied.

Our house, or Mom's pride and joy, as she likes to remind me, sits on a large piece of land in an upper-middle-class neighborhood. We even have a huge-ass garage that we barely use and a fancy pool that Mom can show to her friends when she invites them over.

She always plays the game of 'accept me!' and it's kind of frustrating. I'm way younger than her and I already understand that we, as minorities, just don't get accepted. At least, not by most of the racists plaguing this godforsaken town.

If I had a penny for every time someone's called me 'exotic' or said I have such 'strange' eyes or that my soft black hair is so 'unique,' I'd be as rich as my mama.

She knows all that, but she just refuses to stop trying, which is both courageous and sad, I guess.

Instead of going inside, I rummage through the mailbox, searching for a very familiar black envelope...

Yes!

I get out Akira's letter and smile as I open it. I even pause my core metal playlist. What? It means the letter is *that* important.

Juggling the rest of the mail in one hand and my bag on my shoulder, I open the letter from my pen pal.

And yeah, that sounds outdated, but his first letter got me smiling, and I needed to smile that day, so I wrote back.

True, I still know next to nothing about Akira, but it's not like I'm telling him my deepest secrets or anything. It's just something that I look forward to every week.

And maybe that's because I'm pathetic and he's one of just two people I have as friends.

Dear Naomi,

Should I stop that? Starting the letter with Dear Naomi, I mean. Doesn't it sound tacky to you? I was thinking about it the other day, and somehow, it does to me.

Anyway, now that my musings about the salutation are out of the way, I want to tell you that your story for history class is lame.

You should talk about Japan and the Warring States period. You know you want to. But you can deny it, I don't care.

Well, you were born in America, so you might not consider yourself wholly Japanese, but let me insist on this. Do something cool instead of that old, rehearsed topic.

My studies have been going well. Thank you for not asking. But then again, you probably think I'm a nerd and that studying hard is expected of nerds. *insert unflattering language here that basically means, screw you if you think that way*

Now, where were we? Right. My studies.

I don't like what I'm doing right now and I'm thinking about changing majors, but I don't know what I'll change to or if I'd be making the right choice.

Do you ever feel like you understand nothing and when you finally do, the doors are closed? It's like you arrive at life too late.

Or is that too melodramatic?

Anyway, I'm not going to bore you with my life's story. Tell me about you.

Are you still eating the hearts of the cheerleaders, or did you grow some balls and quit?

If that happens, don't worry, you can always be my Yuki-Onna. Or maybe I'm yours.

Sincerely,
Akira

I smile at the dork. He always has such huge illusions about Japanese spirits and their evilness.

He calls me *Yuki-Onna* because, according to him, I resemble her with my pale skin, rosy lips, and Asian eyes that are so dark, they're nearly black.

He says I have the beauty of the snow woman, a ghost who roamed the mountains on stormy winter days to lure mortals and kill them.

And since then, it's kind of become our inside joke.

I never thought this thing with Akira—friendship, as he calls it—would go this far, but I'm glad that I at least have him.

Even if I still don't know what he looks like.

I contemplated asking for a picture; however, not only would he refuse, but it would also kill the image I already have of him. A cute guy who's definitely an otaku and talks about porn more than necessary.

He's corrupted me.

My feet come to a halt inside the front door of our house. It has a wide entryway into the living area that's diagonal from the kitchen.

Mom stands in front of a mannequin, a pincushion on her wrist and a phone to her ear while she pins a piece of cloth to the mannequin's chest.

She might have become the CEO of Chester Couture, but she still obsesses over a mannequin at home, trying to come up with her next masterpiece.

I hide Akira's letter in my bag before she lifts her head. While Mom knows I have a pen pal from Japan, I don't like her touching his letters. We talk about porn sometimes and that's not a conversation I want her to be privy to.

"Honey." She motions at a glitter box and I give it to her.

I opt to go upstairs to my room and grin like an idiot at the thought of rereading Akira's letter and thinking of an equally sarcastic reply. It's a game of ours.

"Nao, wait."

I'm two steps in, but I turn around to face Mom. She has placed the phone in her slacks' pocket, putting a rare premature end to her conversation with her assistant, her lawyer, her accountant. Anyone who needs the great Riko Chester's time.

She was born in Japan as Riko Sato, but she changed her last name as soon as she got American citizenship when I was a kid.

Mom is a small woman but keeps her hair long, not short like I do, and she looks like my older sister, not the woman who gave birth to me. She has flawless skin and beautiful small features that she passed down to me. Though she's paler and has more dark circles than usual lately.

Her eyes are brown, but nowhere as big or as dark as mine. Which I guess is a feature I got from my father, who's sort of a taboo subject in front of her.

"How did school go?" she asks with a slight accent. Since she's first-generation, she doesn't really speak with an American accent as I do, but it's not for lack of trying. I guess being born speaking in a certain way stamps you for life.

I lift a shoulder. "The usual."

Mom reaches for her pack of cigarettes and steps back from the mannequin as she lights one, then takes a drag. "How about practice?"

"It was cool."

"Are you lying to me?"

"As if I could. You'd call the dean and get all the deets. Or maybe the coach, since she was there."

"Do not sass me, young lady."

"I'm not. Just making your job easy for you since, I don't know, you prefer asking others about me instead of actually attending any of the stupid games I bust my ass for."

"Watch your language. And it's not like I don't attend them because I don't want to. Some of us work, Naomi."

"Get back to it then."

"Nao-chan…"

My stomach flips whenever she calls me in that endearing way. It's like I'm back to being a little girl, when Mom was my world.

Until the red night shattered it.

She approaches slowly, releasing a puff of nicotine into the air. "Are you mad at me?"

"I don't know, Mom. Maybe I am."

She strokes my arm. "I'm sorry. I know I'm barely around lately. But it's all for you."

"No, Mom. No. Don't use the excuse that it's for me. It stopped being for me after you bought this house and secured both our futures. Now, it's just for you."

She drops her hand, and although it's painful and I want her to comfort me again, I'm well aware that it's useless. Mom will always do what she thinks is best, not caring about what type of results that brings to my life.

"One day, you'll understand it all. At least, I hope you will." She smiles with a hint of defeat. "Go freshen up before delivery gets here. I ordered Italian."

"What's the occasion?" While I'm secretly glad she's eating in tonight, I'm surprised she doesn't have some sort of a dinner set up somewhere with all the associates and business partners she has.

"Why does there have to be an occasion for me to eat with my daughter?" She smiles again, but it's still with that note of defeat, or is that sadness?

I don't ponder on it long, because she kills her cigarette in an ashtray and goes back to her work.

Me, however? I can't help the giddiness I feel at the thought of having dinner with her.

Maybe our little family isn't beyond saving, after all.

THREE

Sebastian

BEING BROUGHT UP IN A CERTAIN WAY PUTS SPECIFIC expectations on me.

I can stand out, but not in a negative sense.

I can live my life, but not where it matters.

My whole existence has been mapped out ever since I was born as the senator's grandson and have had to play the role that goes with it.

Maybe that's why I'm often tempted to allow my rebellious side to get the better of me.

Why I sometimes let it rear its head and show the world the turbulent side of me.

You know, basic rich kid problems.

After practice, Owen drags me and a few other team members out for drinks with the cheerleaders.

I'd rather be sleeping, but Owen would probably display my head on a stick for the world to see. I kind of need my head—and everything inside it.

Besides, drinks with them is better than being trapped under the senator's and his wife's tenacious stares. Yes, they're my grandparents and the people who raised me, but I don't quite appreciate them when they barge into my apartment any chance they get, even long after I've moved out of their house.

Instead of drinks, Owen goes all the way for a meal at The Grill. We like this place because it belongs to Coach's brother, Chad, and he's a big fan of ours. Not only does he give us one of his private booths where we're hidden from the rest of the patrons, but he also serves us his best meals.

As soon as we walk inside, accompanied by some of the cheerleaders, Chad grins and points at us. "Give it up for the Devils, ladies and gents!"

Owen and the others make a show of tapping their jackets, on which the team's logo rests. The cheerleaders hoot and the men make howling sounds.

Most of the patrons clap, and endless praise and compliments shower us.

"Let's win State, son!"

"Show the Knights no mercy!"

"See you in the NFL!"

"Our heroes!"

Yeah, that's far from the truth, but this town is too obsessed with football. It's kind of unhealthy.

And yes, my thoughts remain, even as I grin, shake their hands, and take random selfies. In the span of a few minutes, I put on the show I was taught to perform when I was a kid.

Always smile. Always be on your best behavior.

Always put on a mask.

By the time we reach the stairs, I've shaken hands and taken pictures with most of the people present. Let's just say that Chad likes us as much as we like his place. Since everyone knows we hang out here, the restaurant is almost always full.

He gives me a bro hug, then clutches me by the shoulders.

The smell of grease and pepper comes off him in waves. "My star quarterback."

"Not really a star yet."

"Oh, yes you are."

I grin. "I guess I'll show you this Friday."

"That's the spirit, son!" He gives me an encouraging slap on the back like Coach does.

People in Blackwood expect one thing from me—to be efficient. It comes with the Weaver name.

Those who belong to my family need to bring something to the table, whether it's grades, victories, a senatorial position, or a hotshot lawyer role like my uncle.

At any rate, I need to have something to offer.

After a glittery welcoming in front of the townspeople, Chad finally points us in the direction of our private booth.

Brianna, the co-captain of the cheerleaders, slips her hand through my arm as she paints on her own plastic smile. Hers is so overdone, it's fucking turn off.

There's an art in faking one's smile. A part of you needs to believe in it. A part of you needs to send signals to your brain that smiling is the best solution for people to leave you alone.

We sit around the table, the guys already mixing and matching with the cheerleaders. There are five of us and about seven cheerleaders, so Brianna and Reina sit on either side of me. But everyone knows the blonde, blue-eyed beauty captain is off the table.

She's engaged to one of our teammates from high school, and although he chose to study international law in England and hasn't returned in three years, she still wears his ring.

In a way, we're only keeping an eye on her so that no one gets close. At least, Owen and the others do. I'm interested to see the stern look on her face break, even if that means she finds another man.

Yes, I'm a horrible friend, but I blame it on small-town

problems. As in, there's barely anything considered fun around here.

And I'm not the type who can be allowed to have free time. If I do, my fucked-up tendencies will take reign, and that would just be...tragic.

To everyone else, not me.

Owen stands up, clearing his throat, and I groan. This is heading in a direction I can see from a mile away, but if I stop him, he'll pout like a bitch and be a general douche. I kind of need my wide receiver on my side, at least until the critical game.

He grabs a glass of beer and holds it high as he speaks in his dramatic tone, "I want to toast our star quarterback who gets all the praise—not cool, man—and to all the beautiful ladies who make us play like beasts. To the Devils!"

"To the Devils!" everyone else echoes and I tip my glass in his direction before I take a sip.

Owen finally takes his seat, but he leans into Reina's side. "Queen Bee, what are you gonna do for me if we win?"

She raises a brow while tracing the rim of her glass with her pink-manicured nails. "What do you want?"

"A BJ. If you give me that, I'll win all the games."

She smirks. "Maybe if you get drafted into the NFL, Owen."

"You think I won't be able to do it?"

"Show me what you got then."

"Oh, I will, babe. In fact, you'll love my dick so much, you might dump that loser Asher for it."

"Maybe I will." She smiles, and unlike Brianna, it's not plastic, but it's still as fake as mine.

A hypocrite does recognize a hypocrite after all.

We dig into our food—we order pasta while the cheerleaders settle for salad, as usual.

While I eat and indulge in the humor, I wait for the other shoe to drop or explode or whatever the hell Reina does in these types of situations. There's a reason she convinced Owen to drag us all here.

"Don't you think it's time for another dare?" she asks nonchalantly.

There.

The reason Reina has perfected her fake smiles and facial expressions. The real Reina hides beneath the surface and subtly toys with everyone around her.

How do I know? I do the same sometimes. The difference is, she does it for ambiguous reasons that don't usually benefit her. In fact, all the dares she's issued so far seem cruel but actually end up helping her victims.

In my case, I participate to get them off my back, not harm them. Unless they turn out to be annoying pests, which is when interference is necessary.

"Hell to the yeah!" Josh, one of my teammates, exclaims. "Loved playing a prank on our history teacher that one time."

"And I loved helping." Morgan, a cheerleader, winks and he licks his lips.

"We should take it up a notch, Rei," Brianna says in her slightly squeaky, hyperactive voice.

Prescott, the only male cheerleader present, takes a sip of his beer. "Or else, it'll get boring."

I can relate.

But at the same time, Reina's childish dares were never my thing. She's been amping them up from high school as if she's trying to prove a point.

Still, I need to keep up appearances and pretend that I belong to their holy circle. Partly because Owen becomes really grumpy when I ruin his fun. Partly because I have no intention of being trapped in my head.

That's not a very comfortable place, last I checked.

"I agree. We should spice things up a little." Reina meets my gaze. "Are you up for it, Bastian?"

I leisurely finish chewing, trying to figure out why she sin-
gled me out from everyone present.

It's a first, and I learned from the best to never ignore such
deviation from the ordinary.

However, I can't put my finger on the reason for it.

"Is that a yes?" she insists.

"Hey, Queen Bee. I thought *we* would be sex partners." Owen
pouts, hitting his chest. "I have a black hole right in the middle
of my heart."

"Pass," I say. "Asher would serial kill me if I come near you.
I still need my life."

It's not a lie. The ever-so-calm Asher Carson turns into a
violent motherfucker when it comes to Reina and often beat
up guys for merely looking at her the wrong way in high school.
Even though he's currently away, if he catches wind of this, he'll
barge back in as if he never left.

But I'm merely using that as an excuse.

The actual reason? There's no way in fuck I'd let Reina or
anyone else use me as a pawn in their game.

I'm a senator's son, thank you very much. We use people,
not the other way around.

"I won't be anyone's sexual partner," Reina addresses Owen
and me, but her attention doesn't waver from my face. "I have a
dare for you if you have the guts to take it."

"Yes, totally take it." Brianna strokes my arm up and down
in what she believes is seductive but is actually getting on my
fucking nerves.

"Of course, he'll take it." Owen puffs his chest.

"Our quarterback isn't a pussy," Josh exclaims, and everyone
else from the team hoots in agreement.

That seals it from my end.

I can't go against it now, not when all the team members have
accepted Reina's dares in the past. If anything, they thought it was
a privilege to be 'chosen.' I glare at the Barbie who's still smiling

with hidden triumph. She plotted this whole thing so I'd have no choice but to oblige.

"What did you have in mind?" I ask in the calm tone I've perfected so well.

"Fuck someone."

Owen snorts out a laugh. "What type of dare is that? Chicks drop their panties for him without him having to ask."

"Yeah, Rei," Josh agrees. "He gets the best pussy without even trying."

I raise a brow at Reina. "Is that really your grand dare? Fuck someone?"

"Not just anyone." Her smile slowly vanishes, allowing a shadow to creep in. "Naomi."

My smile falters at the same time as hers and I hope she takes it as if I'm mirroring her, not something else.

Images of delicate skin, huge dark brown eyes, and soft full lips come to mind. Those images play the way she stared up at me as a blush crept up her pale neck and cheeks, turning them red. The way her smart mouth retorted back at every turn as if she did it for sport.

And I couldn't help picturing stuffing those beautiful lips with my dick and watch her fucking squirm.

"Nao...who?" Owen asks. "Wait a minute. Is it that Asian chick who was making babies with Weaver on the ground today?"

"That's the one." Brianna gives a foxy grin. "But she doesn't like making babies. If anything, we think she might be a virgin."

"Holy wow." Owen chugs the rest of his beer. "The plot fucking thickens."

Josh waggles his brows. "Can I have her, please?"

I let my utensils rest on the table. "Why her?"

"It was random," Reina lies through her teeth.

There's nothing random about this. Everything Reina does is calculated and has reasons only she is privy to. Did she come up with this dare after she saw me with Naomi earlier?

"And that bitch needs to learn a lesson." Brianna takes a slurp of her green drink. "She thinks she's holier-than-thou when she's just a loser."

"And she always talks back!" Morgan says in a shrill dramatic voice. "She doesn't respect those who are higher in rank than her."

"I don't see why that's my problem." I pick up my utensils again and pretend to be digging into my food, even though I'm barely seeing anything through my hazy vision.

No, not hazy. Red.

Like fucking blood.

"Is that a no, Bastian?" Reina asks. "Because I can dare any of the other guys to do it. Maybe Josh. He seems so into it."

"Yes!" Josh jumps up. "My Japanese porn fantasy will finally come true."

I lift my head, lips thinning, but I slowly release them.

The only image that comes to mind is that of a beautiful petite woman who'll be destroyed to pieces by the end of this bet.

And if anyone's going to be doing the destroying, it's only fair that it's me.

I won't take it far.

Or at least, that's what I tell myself.

I wipe my mouth with a napkin, meeting all their gazes. "I'll do it. I'll fuck Naomi."

FOUR

Naomi

THE REST OF THE WEEK GOES SUSPICIOUSLY WELL.
Aside from the usual bitchy remarks and some cat-fights. Okay, the catfights were my imagination. Reina will have my metaphorical balls if I fight with other cheerleaders.

I tend to punch and that's apparently a lower blow than clawing and pulling hair.

The only problem is Lucy.

I was right to worry. I think they converted her to the dark side and I have to perform some sort of voodoo ritual to get her back. It's not that she's been ignoring me, but she's been keeping her distance more than usual. She doesn't give me run-on sentences just to convey the simplest things.

I kill my engine in the school's parking lot. We have to cheer for the stupid Devils in their important game tonight and Reina will probably grill our asses and throw them to Brianna and Prescott to chew on if we're late. However, we need to have this conversation.

"Hey, Luce?"

"Yeah?" She stares at the rearview mirror as she fixes her bright pink lipstick.

Her ginger hair is pulled up in a ribbon that matches the black and silver pom-poms we will be forced to use later. She also put on a ton of makeup to hide her beautiful freckles, which is a crime. But if I tell her that, she'll say I'm the only one who thinks they're beautiful, so I bite my tongue.

As for myself, I'm wearing my tight cheer uniform and left my hair loose. I put on black lipstick because, hey, it goes with the Black Devils' theme. Or at least, they'll think that.

I face my friend. "Talk to me."

"About what?" She's still too busy with the lipstick.

"About why you've changed."

"I haven't changed."

"Yes, you have. You're not yourself since you became a member of Reina's secret society club that's rumored to be best buddies with Satan."

The lipstick remains suspended in midair as she stares at me. "Just because you hate Reina and the squad doesn't mean I do, too. I thought we agreed on that, Nao."

"We did. You can worship at her fake altar with blinding glitter all you want, but I just feel like you're…not the same."

"I am. Are you sure you're not jealous?"

"Of Queen Bee and her satanic glitter altar? No way."

She laughs, hitting my shoulder with hers. "You're so funny."

"Objection. Sarcastic."

"Funny," she repeats. "I wish the others knew about your sense of humor."

"So they'd choke on it?" I gasp in mock reaction. "I didn't know you had such a strong grudge against them, Luce."

"Yeah, well, Bree still says hurtful things with no filter."

"Then she'll be the first basic bitch to choke on my sense of humor. Got it. I'm going to need to up the dosage with that one." I raise a brow. "What about Prescott?"

She tightens her hold on her lipstick, even though she's already done with it. "W-what about him?"

"You just stuttered, Luce."

"No, I didn't."

"Yes, you did. If his name alone makes you nervous, how about all those rendezvous at The Grill?"

"Those weren't rendezvous. We went with the squad and the football team."

My lips twitch at the mention of the latter. Since that incident with their stupid quarterback, all of them hoot and howl whenever I'm in their vicinity.

They all pay attention to me, except for the asshole himself. Not that I want him to, and I'm totally not thinking about his hard body pressed up against mine at night. Or during the day, when I sneak peeks at him while he's practicing.

Okay, this isn't the time for Sebastian fantasies.

Wait. No. They're not fantasies. Just unwanted thoughts.

"Lie all you want, Luce, but all I see is your heart eyes when you look at Prescott."

"Stop it." She blushes a deep shade of pink as she stares at her nails. "He doesn't even know I exist."

"Of course, he does, and no, he's totally not gay like doucheface Peter has been insinuating in locker room talk."

"I…know that."

"How do you know that?"

"I just do. But the fact remains, I'm a nobody to him."

"Then it's his fucking loss, not yours."

She stares at me from beneath her lashes and smiles a little. "How do you do it, Nao?"

"Do what?"

"Remain so unaffected, as if the world doesn't deserve your time."

"Because it doesn't. The less you care, the less you're attached and the freer your mind is."

"But wouldn't you end up…I don't know, alone?"

"Hey, rude! What's wrong with being alone? It's better than kissing someone's ass and sucking someone else's junk."

"I hope you fall in love one day."

"First of all, how dare you? Second of all, I'll leave all that Hallmarky shit to you."

"It can be HBO level, not Hallmarky." She winks and we both snort in laughter before we get out.

I take a sip of my Red Bull. So I know it's not healthy and all that jazz, but I need the extra energy before every performance. If our own queen bee or the coach found out, they'd probably tell Mom and that would lead to drama that I don't need in my fragile relationship with her.

I throw the can in the trash before we go through the stadium's rear exit and toward the squad's locker room.

It's a buzz of motions and people backstage. Some of the most dramatic cheerleaders—Brianna included, of course—are singing or murmuring some voodoo shit.

Reina is stretching her long leg over Prescott's shoulder as he flexes his arm. He's good-looking with a tall, muscular body. His olive skin and light blue eyes coupled with his black hair and thick brows give him a Middle-Eastern look that made Luce fall head over heels. I think her crush started during high school, but she hid it so well that I only found out about it recently, when I caught her writing in her journal about dreaming to make babies with him.

When I confronted her about it and told her to confess to him, the chicken shit actually gathered her courage and almost did it. But then, during lunch one day, Peter was egging Prescott on about if he was gay, but he said he just wasn't interested in dating.

Needless to say, my best friend went back to her small bubble and refused to even broach the subject again.

Luce is almost as good at hiding as I am. *Almost.*

The only difference is that I don't get caught. And I sure as hell don't keep a journal.

Unless my letters to Akira can be considered one?

Lucy lowers her head at the scene between Reina and Prescott and goes to stretch.

"He doesn't like her," I whisper as I stand beside her.

"I know that."

"I mean, imagine our own queen bee actually interested in anyone but herself? Wouldn't that be a miracle?"

"Nao," she hisses so I'll stop. "Reina has a fiancé."

She really is starstruck by our captain.

A presence creeps up on me and when I look up, I meet Brianna's malicious stare. "If it isn't the immigrant. Aren't you late?"

I roll my eyes. "I was born here."

"Oh, so your mommy is the immigrant. It's hard to keep track with all of you people coming here."

I twist my lips, but I keep them closed, because anything I say right now will just be taken the wrong way.

So I try to move past her.

Bree extends her arm. "I'm not done talking."

"Well, I am. If you have anything else to say, you can take it and shove it up your racist, xenophobic ass."

"Xeno what?"

"Oh, I'm sorry. Was that word too difficult for you? Google it or ask your daddy to give more money to the dean so he'll explain it to you after I file a racial discrimination report."

And with that, I turn to leave.

"I'm not stupid!" Brianna's shrill voice echoes from behind me.

"Yeah, sure. I believe you," I mock without facing her. "Good luck convincing everyone else."

"Slut! After tonight, you won't be running your mouth anymore."

I stop and turn around. At the same time, Reina and Prescott, who were watching the show with everyone else, close in on Bree.

The co-captain stares at her own Lucifer—Reina—and her lips tremble with clear frustration. "She called me *stupid*."

Reina shakes her head and just like that, the subject is dropped as if it never happened.

I stare at them, trying to decipher what just transpired, but Reina claps her hands, calling everyone's attention. "Time to go out there and show them what the Devils are all about. No one is allowed to breathe until the end of the game. No mistakes, no slouching, and no slacking."

She puts her hand in the middle and everyone else follows suit, Luce and I included.

Reina shouts, "Black!"

"Devils!" we all shout in return before we break the circle.

Then we're out there cheering in front of over thirty thousand spectators who came to watch the classic rivals go at each other.

Friday night lights are blinding and the entire fan area is black and white as balloons of the same colors fly toward the sky.

Loud pop music blares in the air as the male cheerleaders breakdance. Soon after, we line up midfield. The fans go crazy with our opening routine, all precise and perfect like Reina wants. And then she ends it at the top of the pyramid, a huge smile on her lips, as fireworks explode behind us like we're at some concert.

Me? I'd rather be listening to my rock music in peace, thank you very much. But hey, on the bright side, Reina will lay off our asses after this performance.

Silver fucking linings.

After we're done with our routine, we jump and twirl to the entrance where the players are coming out.

Our mascot, a panda with a pitchfork, is fighting with the Knights' mascot, some sort of a horse.

The Knights come out among their cheerleaders first, and then it's our team's turn. They bulldoze through the large banner with the team's logo on it, led by number ten, the quarterback, and seventeen, the wide receiver. They're all dressed in their black and white uniforms and helmets, and black lines are smeared under their eyes.

I swallow, pretending the sweat that's gathering between my brows is due to exhaustion and not the fact that I'm focusing way too hard on a certain number ten.

A lot of hollering and howling comes from the players, their battle cries filling the air.

But not Sebastian.

A haze covers his intense eyes, visible through the opening in his helmet. It's like he's in a different zone and no one can reach him.

Or touch him.

This side of him has always hinted at what he is more so than the image he shoves on everyone so that they believe he's the good senator's grandson.

There's nothing good here.

His gaze zeroes in on me. It's only for a fraction of a second, but he pierces me down as if I'm the game he's intent on conquering tonight.

His lips curl at the side and I swear I see what resembles a wolfish smirk before his eyes tactfully slip from mine.

I resist the urge to look behind me in case he was having that eye contact voodoo with someone else. But somewhere deep down, I know, I just know it was directed at me.

What the hell?

We go back to the sidelines to cheer during the game. And while I usually hate this part, tonight's game is actually intense. The Knights aren't letting up and our team barely keeps a lead.

The fans goes wild when Owen scores. Prescott throws both Reina, then Brianna in the air as a form of celebration.

We stay on our toes, cheering and doing our halftime routine.

It's exhausting, but the adrenaline runs wild among us. The energy wafting off the field in waves is both intoxicating and addictive.

Near the end of the game, we're down, but there's a chance to turn the tables and win.

Sebastian passes the ball to Owen, who tosses it back once the quarterback is clear. Then the Devils' captain runs in a blur of motion as if he's weightless. The cheers grow louder and louder and I find myself clenching my fists in the stupid pom-poms.

One of the Knights' players tries to tackle Sebastian to the ground and he loses his footing with a collective *Ohhh* coming from the crowd.

But before the others pile up on him, he slips from under the player and sprints at full speed until he scores.

The crowd and the cheerleaders go crazy, and even our mascot dances in the face of the other one. The coach shouts at the top of his lungs as the players bury Sebastian underneath them.

It's a myriad of celebration and dancing and loud music. My heart thumps and I barely keep up with the routine.

Soon after, the time runs out and the referees signal the end of the game.

The Devils carry Sebastian on their shoulders and several media outlets try to land an exclusive interview with the star of the night.

That's when I realize there are tears in my eyes. I got so excited that I didn't notice I was that invested in the stupid game. I wipe them with the back of my hand, because if anyone accuses me of crying, I'll throat-stab them.

And I'm totally not going to ogle the quarterback tonight.

A reporter is asking Sebastian about the reason behind his energy as we pass behind them, heading to our locker room.

It happens so fast, I don't even see it coming.

One moment, I'm walking, and the next, Sebastian turns around, grabs me by the waist, and tugs me against him.

"The reason is her," he says, and then his lips meet mine.

FIVE

Naomi

SEBASTIAN IS KISSING ME.

As in, his lips are on mine.

His mouth is mashed to my agape one.

It feels different than what I've imagined. I thought his lips would be harsh, maybe made of granite like the rest of him, but they're surprisingly soft—tender, even.

At least, at first.

I'm so caught off guard that I do the one thing I haven't done since I was a little girl and blood flowed all around me.

I remain still.

If anything, I go limp against him as he nibbles on my bottom lip, demanding access into my mouth. And it's a flat-out demand, as if he has the right to kiss me and has for an eternity.

The hotness of his body pressed to mine and the strong scent of his cologne are dizzying.

And not in a good way.

But in more of an 'I'm losing control and slipping through a loophole' kind of way.

When I keep my mouth clamped shut, he bites down on the sensitive flesh of my lip. The sharp movement nearly rips the skin and draw my blood so he can suck on it.

Feast on it.

Assault it.

I open with a start, in equal measure due to his actions and my reaction. Sebastian doesn't slow down, doesn't take a breather, and he uses the chance to plunge his tongue inside.

If I thought his lips were tender, I take it all back. They're as merciless as the rest of him. He kisses like he plays, razing through my defenses, seizing the opportunity and scoring, over and over.

He doesn't only kiss, he's out to devour me. To paint black stars in the midst of the bright white lights. His tongue ravages my tender one until no air is allowed into my burning lungs. Until I'm wheezing, silently begging and imploring.

For what, I have no clue.

In just a fraction of a second, his hold on my waist is the only thing keeping me standing.

It's like a foreign entity has possessed my body and I'm caught in a trance. Partly because I want to end it and partly because I don't ever want this to be over.

The two facets clash and claw at each other, creating a suffocating tension in the confines of my shriveling heart.

I've never been touched like this, as if I could be swallowed whole any second. As if his large strong hands could hold my face—and other parts of me—hostage. As if his body could easily overpower mine and force me to submit.

And the scariest part isn't the confusion that accompanies those thoughts. It's the sharp tingles between my legs. It's the dipping of my stomach that matches his maddening rhythm.

It feels like hours have passed when he releases my lips, a small trail of saliva sticking between us as he pulls back. A strange sound echoes in the air and I realize it's mine.

His tropical eyes cage me for the second time tonight, only this time, the mask he always wears doesn't hide the fire in them.

Like fireworks.

Or maybe a volcano.

Either way, it's at the point of eruption and I don't want to be there when it happens. I don't want to witness the moment when the perfect star actually shows to the world that he's not so perfect after all.

And yet, I'm held prisoner by the power of his presence, entranced by the smallest details. Like the way sweat trickles down the side of his face, giving him the aura of a warrior. The way the black line shadows the color of his eyes. Or how his spicy scent mixes with sweat in a masculine kind of way.

Even the imperfection of his damp hair that haphazardly falls across his forehead looks flawless.

Sebastian swiftly shifts his attention to the side and that's when I'm struck by the fact that he just kissed me on television.

Fuck.

The reporter is saying something, but it filters through my buzzing ears. Not only because embarrassment is whirling through me, but more due to the fact that I'm caught off guard. That I didn't see the situation coming and couldn't act accordingly.

Sebastian doesn't let me go and I don't struggle. One, I'm still in some sort of a haze. Two, it'd draw more unwanted attention to myself. Three, it's fruitless to compare his strength to mine.

As I wait for the reporter to go away, I can't help inhaling his scent into my starved lungs. There's a high note of bergamot, pepper, and amber. Mixed with sweat from the game, he smells like a fighter. I can't help imagining him crushing someone in his path.

Or me.

My core clenches at the thought and I quickly shove it back to where it came from. But it doesn't completely go away. It remains there, lingering, biding its time, and taunting me with endless options.

And now, I think I'm in serious trouble because this scent? Yeah, I don't think I'll be able to erase it from my memories anytime soon.

The reporter finally leaves with a knowing smirk in our direction, but Sebastian's grip around my waist doesn't ease. If anything, he tightens it further until I wince.

"What the hell do you think you're doing?" I hiss, finally snapping out of whatever spell his scent just cast on me.

His eyes twinkle under the lights as if he's finding pleasure in whatever show he's putting on. "Which part? Kissing you? Or doing it publicly?"

"Both!"

"Why? You'd rather I did it in private?" His thumb strokes the bare skin above my skirt, grazing the line of my belly. A tender sensation blossoms at the bottom of my stomach with each caress. "I can take care of that."

"I don't want you to take care of anything except for leaving me the hell alone." I slam both hands on his chest to push him away, but he might as well be a buffalo. A dangerous one with boundary issues, because he takes that as an invitation to step further into my space.

His chest creates friction against my breasts that I want to hate, but I can't help the increasing tightness in my stomach. We're separated by his football gear and my sports bra and top and yet, it's like his naked skin is rubbing against my nipples, stimulating them, peaking them, and crossing the line of no return.

"But I don't want to." The words leave his sinfully proportioned lips with a seductive tilt.

"What do you mean you don't want to?"

"I don't want to let you go, Naomi. I rather like it here. Just like this."

"Well, I don't."

"Is lying a defense mechanism of yours?"

"Leave me alone before you meet my actual defense mechanism."

"And what is that?"

"I'd rather show you." I lift my knee to hit him in the balls, but his reflex is faster than mine. His large palm nearly engulfs my thigh and he loops it around his and positions it in a way that seems as if I'm humping him in public.

If my attempted attack fazes him, he doesn't show it as he smiles in that fake-ass way. Like some fancy politician in front of cameras. "Now, Naomi. If we're going to have a healthy relationship, there shouldn't be any violence present. Unless…it's the type of violence we both agree on."

A shudder grips me at the sinister undertone of his words, and although I don't really understand what they mean, an unfamiliar part of me rises to the surface with a force that startles the shit out of me.

It takes me a few seconds to get my bearings. "Who said I want any relationship with you?"

"You should. I recommend it."

I scoff, trying to squirm, to no avail again. "Of course, you would."

"I'm rich, handsome, and a star. Oh, I also come from a prestigious family. What's there not to like about me?"

"Everything you just mentioned. Oh, and your arrogance is the cherry on top. Sorry to crash it to the ground, but I don't do douchebags. Better luck next time."

He chuckles, the sound surprisingly carefree compared to his demeanor. "You are a funny one."

"No, I'm kinda bitchy. Ask your besties, Reina and Brianna, and they'll tell you the deets."

"I'd rather ask you. Dinner tomorrow?"

"In the funeral home before they cremate you?"

"Or just somewhere nice where we don't have to worry about dead people." He speaks calmly, a smirk tugging his lips, and appearing completely oblivious to my sense of sarcasm that usually works in shooing people away.

"I'm not sure if you got the memo, but I just insinuated that I'm not interested in you."

"No, you *insinuated* that I'm arrogant and that you hate all the qualities I mentioned about myself."

"Okay then, I'm telling you now that I'm not interested for the reasons mentioned above."

"So let's forget about them."

"What?"

"Forget about the background and who I am. Do you have any objections otherwise?"

"I can't just *forget* them."

"You can pretend to."

"Doesn't work that way. Your name and face and position in the college are what defines you."

His jaw clenches. "And what defines you, Naomi?"

"You tell me. Aren't you the one who forced a kiss on me, then wanted to take me out to dinner like some doting dick? We'd never properly spoken before you slammed me to the ground a few days ago, so I'm free to believe you're playing me."

"Or maybe I'm just interested in you."

"Oh, please. Name one thing you know about me."

He remains silent.

"You have nothing? Figured as much. Go play this game on someone else because I don't have the time—"

"You hate being a cheerleader and throw every tantrum under the sun to be kicked off the squad. However, the dean and the coach keep you on because of the checks your mommy writes to the college. You were raised by a single mother of Japanese origins and you have a tendency toward passive-aggressiveness and straight out aggressiveness when your race is brought up. You use sarcasm and self-deprecation as a defense mechanism, but you don't react well when those tactics are directed at you. You barely smile because you like being angry at the world and everyone in it and prefer to be an asocial weirdo instead of putting on a mask.

You sometimes wear black-framed glasses in class that make you look like an adorable nerd. Oh, and you listen to hard rock at a volume that will damage your ears in the future."

My lips part as I stare up at him. There's...no way he'd be able to know all of that about me. Not when we've barely had any contact.

Hell, I doubt he remembers the first time we met officially— or unofficially or whatever.

"So?" He grins. "How did I do?"

"Are you waiting for a score? If so, it's an F."

"Lying again, even though you're clearly impressed. Oh, and you're slightly trembling right now."

I go still against him, cursing my involuntary body reaction.

"Now I know what you truly are," he says.

"And what is that?"

"Tsundere."

"What?"

"It means someone who's hot and cold. Violent on the outside, despite being soft on the inside."

"I know what Tsundere means and I'm not a damn anime character."

"I'll confirm that during dinner tomorrow." He lifts my hand to his mouth and brushes his lips on my skin that instantly turns red.

I've always praised myself for being above having emotions, or at least, not showing them. But right now, it seems as if I'm an open book in front of Sebastian.

He finally releases me, his hard, warm body leaving mine as he turns around, then strides away.

"I won't be there!" I shout after him.

"See you tomorrow, Tsundere," he calls back without looking at me.

I'm left there, fuming and boiling with a thousand different emotions that I can't contain.

The most prominent of all—strange arousal.

The type that feels wrong and right at the same time.

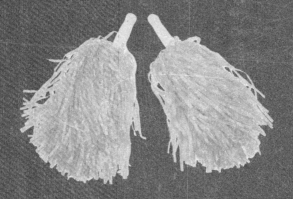

SIX

Naomi

MY FEET ARE WOBBLY AS I HEAD TO THE PARKING LOT.
The chaos and the endless sounds from the stadium buzz
at the back of my head with the continuity of a humming
earthquake.

I slouch against the door of my car, hand trembling as I open
it. Once I'm inside, I clutch the steering wheel in a white-knuckled
grip, my blank stare projected on the half-empty parking lot.

Did that…just happen? With Sebastian, no less?

Yeah, fine, so I kind of had some sort of an unhealthy fixation on him for as long as I've known him. I blame my younger,
immature teenage hormones.

But I've never acted on it, never looked at him—at least, not
when he was paying attention—flirted with him, or showed my
interest. Because unlike the idiot teenager I was, I now realize
someone like Sebastian Weaver isn't meant for me. It's not that
he's out of my league, but he's the shallow type—hello, quarterback and rich and comes from a line of politicians?

I'm shallow, too, for actually allowing him to prick my black heart once upon a time. It was a single prick, you know, like a needle that you barely feel, but just like a needle, it's already spread a chemical inside and now, I can't purge him out of my bloodstream.

Actually, I can.

I was waiting for the end of college so we could take different routes in life. He'll be the successor in a line of politicians or get drafted into the NFL, and I'll move to Japan to bug the hell out of Akira, then convince him to come here so we can plot chaos.

Point is, Sebastian was never supposed to notice me, not when he has countless girls—cheerleaders included—making voodoo dolls to gain a sliver of his attention.

But he didn't kiss them on TV. He didn't grab them and restrain them and imprison them against his weapon of a body.

I glide the pads of my fingers over the bruised plush of my lips and a sudden shiver jolts my spine.

Crashing images invade my mind. Images of his naked torso flattening against mine as his tongue claimed me and his strong hands drew me closer—

My phone buzzes in my bag and I release my lips with a start, then sigh when I find a text from my best friend.

Lucy: Want to hang out with us at Reina's?

Naomi: I'd rather worship at Satan's actual altar.

Lucy: Come on, Nao. Everyone will be there to celebrate the win.

Everyone including Sebastian?

I shake my head. Why does that matter?

Naomi: One more reason why I shouldn't be there.

Lucy: But it'll be fun.

Naomi: My idea of fun is ruining theirs, so I doubt they want me there. Go party and flirt with Prescott, Luce.

She sends back a Japanese crying emoji and I grin. Ever since I exposed my nerdy side and introduced her to them, they're all she uses now.

I'm about to hide my phone when it lights up with a call from an unknown number. My hand trembles even though I have a clue of who it could be.

Sucking in a deep breath, I answer, "Hello."

"Ms. Naomi Chester?"

"That's me."

"This is Private Investigator Collins. You called my assistant earlier today to schedule an appointment."

"Yes."

"Do you have time now?"

"Now?"

"If that's not possible, we can meet on Monday. But from what you told my assistant, it's urgent."

"It is." I look at my watch, then sigh. "Let's meet now. I'd rather not go to your agency." *And leave a trail that Mom can follow.*

"I understand. Do you know the diner called Tracy's that's located opposite the gas station?"

"Yes. I'll be there in half an hour."

"See you then, Ms. Chester."

The line goes dead, but it takes me a few seconds to lower my hand.

Reaching into my bag, I pull out an oversized hoodie, then put it on so that it covers my cheer uniform. It still has the Black Devils' logo on the front, but it's better than going out to meet a PI, dressed like a high school girl with a crush on the most popular guy.

With a sigh, I blast Rammstein from my car stereo and start driving to the intended location. Several vehicles honk and college students dance around campus in celebration of the win. So I opt to take a different route. One that's more deserted.

That's when I notice something's wrong.

I've taken this road several times before, mainly when there are busy events at campus like tonight. But this is the first time that it's been almost completely dark, except for a few lights scattered far apart. I'm mainly relying on my headlights as I drive down the road parallel to Blackwood's famous forest.

One where mobsters meet and bodies are found. They're mostly rumors, but I believe the shit out of them in this pitch-blackness that resembles a scene from one of my favorite true crime shows.

A faint light catches my attention in the rearview mirror and I squint. It's not as strong as my headlights and the driver of what looks like a dark-colored van isn't attempting to change lanes, even though I'm driving slow and there's an empty lane on my left.

It could be the darkness or the forest surrounding me from both sides, but my level of paranoia shoots up like a vengeful bitch.

I step on the gas to speed up and the van behind me matches my pace.

Holy Jesus and all the angels.

They're following me.

This isn't me actually losing my mind and being overdramatic. There's a dark van with dim headlights matching my speed and not changing lanes.

I reason with my mind that it could be an older person who's not familiar with Blackwood's roads. But in what world do old people drive black vans that are made for sinister purposes?

My head fills with images of kidnapped girls and sex trafficking and, holy shit, I think I'm going to throw up.

The high volume of the music drums in my head in sync with my beating heart and I put it on pause. I really don't want my beloved metal associated with the moment of my kidnapping.

I hit the gas, propelling the car to a maddening speed, not caring that my vision is restricted and I could slam into anything. I swerve the car to the other lane, and sure enough, the van follows.

Okay, kidnapper dudes. I'm not one to be messed with.

If they knew me even a little, they wouldn't dare to come near me. I'd fight to the death.

Or at least, that's the pep talk I give myself. The actual reality, though? I might not be able to get a chance to fight.

I keep stealing a look at the van every now and then, my heart thundering and my hands sweaty. My legs shake and I force them to remain still or I'll cause my own demise.

It doesn't take me long to arrive at the gas station, across from which there's an old diner. The car is still on my tail, and now that there's more light, I notice that it's all black. Even its windows are tinted, blocking my view of who's inside.

They're really kidnappers.

My gaze strays to my surroundings, trying to find anyone to ask for help. The police station is far from here and if I drive there, I have a feeling they'll make their move before I can reach it.

In my frantic search, my eyes lock on a man exiting his car in front of the diner.

The PI.

I signal at him with my lights and he turns around. Though I can't make out his features, he's tall, sporting a black shirt and slacks to perfection.

He nods at me and I rev the vehicle toward him in my hasty attempt to reach him. I pull my car to a screeching halt behind his and stare at the rearview mirror, my lips parting.

There's no one.

The van that followed me through the forest road to here isn't there.

I blink a few times, and sure enough, it's really not there and has vanished as if it never existed.

A knock sounds on my window and I flinch before recognizing the PI's build.

With a deep breath, I pull myself together, gather my bag with a shaking hand, and step out of the car.

I get my first good look at the PI and he's nothing like I

expected. First of all, he's Asian like me and has strong, charismatic features. His eyes are black and piercing and his double eyelids, a quality rare to those of us of Western Asian heritage, add a drooping quality to his stare.

His face is harsh and cut with a nose that's as naturally high as his cheekbones. Not only that, but he has long, thick hair the color of ink. It's currently tied in a low ponytail, but if it were loose, it'd reach his shoulders.

He sounded young on the phone, but I never thought he'd be this young. I expected someone in his forties or fifties, but he barely looks thirty.

"Ms. Chester?" he asks with a flawless American accent as he offers his hand.

I shake it firmly. "Uh…yeah."

Stop ogling the man, Nao.

It must be the chase from earlier that messed with my mind.

He motions at the diner's door. "Are you coming in?"

"Sure." I breathe deeply before I follow him inside.

Tracy's barely has any patrons, despite it being a Friday night. Partly because this town's football crazies celebrate at The Grill and partly because this restaurant barely functions.

Its decor is reminiscent of the nineties pictures I've seen in Mom's albums, and the black leather of the booths is chapped in places. The tables have some doodling like what's found on high school desks and the lighting is hardly there.

The waitress, a middle-aged woman with killer eyebrows, leads us to a booth at the back.

The PI orders omurice without checking the menu. Ha. They have that here? That dish reminds me of my childhood when Mom used to cook it for us all the time.

"Just soda for me," I tell the waitress.

"Right away, hon," she hums, the sound echoing in the distance as she walks away.

"I see why you were reluctant about meeting tonight," the PI says, and at my bemused expression, he motions at my hoodie. "Black Devils."

"No, believe me. I don't care about those douchefaces. I just wear their hoodies because we get them for free on campus." *You sure as hell cared when Sebastian scored tonight.*

Get out of my head!

I take a sip of my water and smile at the PI. "Should I call you Mr. Collins?"

"That would make me feel like an old man. Kai is fine."

Jeez. Beautiful people's names are as mesmerizing as they are. "Nice to meet you, Kai. Is that Japanese?"

"Yes."

"Wow. What a coincidence. I'm of Japanese heritage, too. At least, from my mom's side. How do you write Kai in Kanji?"

"The character of ocean."

"That's so cool. Mine is written with the characters of honest and beautiful."

His onyx eyes soften with a smile. "So what did you want to talk about, Ms. Chester?"

"Just Naomi." *Ms. Chester is Mom in my head.*

"What's your request for me, Naomi?"

I interlink my fingers, then release them and swallow more water, letting the cool liquid soothe my throat. Talking to a complete stranger about this is harder than I thought.

"I…uh…I want to find my father," I blurt the last part.

"When was the last time you saw him?"

"I've never seen him." My voice is barely above a whisper. "I was born to a single mother and never met my father."

The confession hangs between us in the thick air. But before Kai can say anything, the waitress returns with our orders. I clear my throat to release the knot that's formed there. I always feel like the rejected little girl on Father's Day at school whenever I talk or think about my father.

Stupidly, I know he could be way worse than what I painted

him to be in my girlhood dreams, but the need to find him has never lessened. In fact, it kept growing over the years until I could no longer ignore it.

The waitress disappears with another smile.

Kai cuts his omurice in half and starts eating with leisurely finesse. The way he picks portions and chews is so refined and elegant that I feel a strange satisfaction just watching him swallow his food. "What do you know about your father?"

"Mom refuses to tell me anything except that we're better off without him."

"I assume you disagree?"

"Of course, I do. Or else I wouldn't be here."

He swallows another bite and meets my gaze. He never speaks with food in his mouth and I appreciate that. "Wouldn't it be easier to ask your mother about his whereabouts instead of wasting your money on me?"

"If that were an option, I would've done it. Are you going to help me or should I search for someone else to give my money to?"

"Very well." He places his utensils on the table and wipes his mouth, and that's when I notice he's finished his entire meal. "I need something to start with. Was he married to your mother?"

"No."

"Is he American? Japanese?"

"I don't know. But I think American."

"Why?"

"Because Mom insisted on giving birth to me here."

"She could have left him behind in Japan."

I rummage through my bag and retrieve a picture I stole from Mom's secret drawer. The only picture she has of my father. My fingers are unsteady as I slide it across the table.

Kai's inquisitive eyes study it carefully. The date on the back is a few years before I was born. It's one of the few times I've seen Mom laughing with so much freedom, her head tipped back as she holds on to a man's arm.

Her hair was longer at the time, and her pink dress with provocative lace at the top.

The man is in a striped suit and has his arm around her waist, but his most important feature, his face, has been burned with a cigarette, leaving a hole in the picture.

After I found this frozen memento a few weeks ago, I had to do something about it. There's no way I can keep entertaining the fantasy of finding my father without taking action.

Kai's attention slides from the picture to me. "Why do you believe this person to be your father?"

"Mom kept all her pictures of her old friends, whether male or female, intact except for this one. She also hid it in a secret box that she shoved in the attic."

"What makes you think he's American?"

I tap the background of the picture. They're leaning against a bar, but behind them, through the hazy window, there's a Las Vegas sign and a blurred license plate. "That."

"You're merely speculating."

"No, I'm not. Mom wouldn't have come to the States or kept his picture for no reason."

"*Burned* picture."

"It still counts. The fact that she burned it means it has value, even if it's negative."

"I'll see what I can find."

I perk up, shoulders straightening. "You can find him?"

"If there's anyone who can do that, it's me."

A trembling smile curves my lips. Does this mean I can finally meet the mystery man who contributed to my existence?

SEVEN

Sebastian

HOW DOES SOMEONE GET USED TO DEPRAVITY? Does it help if it has flowed in our blood since the beginning of time or that every generation had done its best to deepen its impact?

The answer is no, it doesn't.

No, it shouldn't.

But who am I to start anarchy against the same system that made me? The system that saved me from the claws of death and hasn't shoved me back in its path like it did my parents?

Dad tried to escape the system, to start anew without the shadow of the Weaver name. But look where that led him.

On the steps of hell.

Don't get me wrong. I'm pretty sure each leader of the Weaver clan has made a deal with the devil sometime in their lives. So there's no doubt that we'll all end up in some sort of hellhole, but as Grandpa says, 'Our sins don't catch up to us today.'

Speaking of which, we're having a family dinner tonight. One I need to escape from early for my date with Naomi.

The thought of her ignites me with a hot, fiery spark. It shouldn't, not with everything I have planned, but fuck me if my dick understands logic. All that sucker has been thinking about since her warm stomach rubbed against him is ways to find himself in her mouth or between her legs.

Or shoved deep in her ass.

The kiss shouldn't have happened yesterday. It was supposed to be a peck, a pretense, but then my mouth found hers and a completely different need emerged out of nowhere. My tongue was only interested in feasting on her warm heat and engraving myself in it with a roughness she'd forever remember.

Soon enough, we were speaking an identical language only the two of us could recognize. She can deny it all she likes, but there was something between us last night. Something beyond the crowd and football and cheering.

Something beyond normal.

I saw it in her inquisitive eyes and I know she felt it in my touch.

Why did I let her feel it?

Fuck if I know. Could be because I enjoyed seeing her defenses crumble one by one, or witnessing the flutter in her thick lashes and the tremble in her lips.

Or sucking her fucking taste that I can't chase away.

All I know is that I'm in the mood for more.

I can't remember the last time I was in the mood for anything except keeping the cycle going.

In order to break it, I need to escape the Weaver curse, and I guess that's not going to happen anytime soon. Which is why I'm here.

My grandparents' extravagant mansion is located in the fanciest upper-class neighborhood in Blackwood. In fact, only the mayor and a few high-profile politicians live in the same area and it's resident-only.

Not only does it take up more space than it should, but it's also three stories high with tall white fences and lights shining in the night that can be seen from a mile away.

I park my Tesla in the area near the garage and spy for the Mercedes that belongs to my only ally in the family. However, I find nothing.

One of the staff smiles as she opens the door and I grin back before I kiss her cheek. "Lisa, how are you? How is Pedro?"

"Excellent, sir." Her smile widens as she speaks with a slight Spanish accent. "He's grown and has been looking up to you. He didn't sleep until he watched the game last night."

Poor kid, looking up to a fraud. My smile, however, remains in place as I reach in my back pocket and produce two tickets. "Give him these and tell him I'll get him my shirt next game."

"Oh, sir." Her eyes water. "Thank you so much. This will make his week."

At least that's one of us.

"My old folks inside?"

"Yes," she whispers. "You're late, sir, and so is Mr. Nathaniel."

I don't blame him.

If I didn't want to intentionally piss my grandparents off, I would've used the same tactic myself.

The bell rings again and I beat Lisa to it.

My uncle, Nathaniel Weaver, stands at the door in his sharp suit and with his clean-cut look that he uses to intimidate the hell out of anyone in or outside of the courtroom.

"Nephew!" He opens his arms, apparently not worried about the bottle of wine in his left hand.

"Nate!"

We clasp each other in a bro hug and he pulls back to offer me one of his rare smiles. "Congrats on the win yesterday. I watched it with my colleagues and now they're bugging me about autographs."

"No, sorry. That comes with a price, Uncle."

"Don't call me that. Makes me feel ancient."

"You *are* ancient. What are you? Thirty-five?"

"Thirty-one, Rascal." He gives me the middle finger behind Lisa's back as we step inside. "Ready for battle?"

"Always am."

The interior of the Weaver mansion is as extravagant as the exterior, if not more. Due to my grandparents' expensive tastes, it's full of rare finds, auctioned paintings, and exotic rugs.

The heads of a few dead animals hang in the entrance area as a showcase of Grandpa's love for hunting.

When I was younger, I believed they were spirits that would come for us one day. In a different world, that might have been true, but now, it's just another reminder of what a heartless bunch we are.

As soon as Nate and I step into the dining room, it's like we're in the midst of a chess game. The king is the man sitting at the head of the table.

Brian Weaver.

Being in his early-sixties doesn't take anything from his composed demeanor and sharp, piercing eyes that aren't only befitting of a politician but also of a Weaver.

The queen is the woman sitting on his right, wearing a soft smile. Debra Weaver is the definition of the saying 'behind every great man is a great woman.' She didn't only fight tooth and nail for his political career, but she was also as ruthless about it as he was. At least, behind closed doors.

On the outside, people can only see a soft woman with golden blonde hair and a queen-like posture and wardrobe.

Uncle kisses her cheek first and I follow suit before we nod at Grandpa, then take our seats on his right. Soon after, the cook brings in some sort of ham casserole that I don't recognize.

Grandpa is all about meat, although his doctor says it's not good for his health in the long-term.

"You're late," Grandma chastises, but it sounds

loveable—worried, even—when she's, in fact, mentally checking a strike against us.

"Only because I was looking for your favorite wine, Mom." Nate motions at the bottle he placed at her side.

She gives him a look before directing her hawk-like stare at me. "What's your excuse?"

"I have none. I just woke up late because of the game last night." I grin. "We won, Grandpa."

"As you should have. It's a given, unlike the show you put on camera." His stern expression doesn't change as he chews on his ham.

"Brian." Grandma reaches her hand out and he taps it reassuringly, then she offers me her pressed smile. "Who was she, darling?"

I swallow down my mouthful of food, letting the slightly greasy taste settle in my stomach. I've been raised by these people since I was six. Fifteen years later, and I still feel like I'm a subject of scrutinization.

However, Nate taught me the best way to win over my grandparents—tell them what they want to hear.

"She's no one." I take a sip of wine, even though I dislike the stuff. "Just a ruse of a moment."

Grandpa halts eating. "You want me to believe that you'd do such a thing?"

"He's at college and a star quarterback," Nate speaks while cutting his steak. "Kids his age do such things all the time."

Thank you, Nate.

"Not my grandson." Grandpa's voice hardens as his entire focus zeroes in on me. "You're a Weaver and you'll act as such. The family's future relies on you now that your uncle didn't choose politics."

"Slick, Dad. But in case you haven't noticed, not everyone likes politics. Ever thought about asking Sebastian what he *wants* to do?"

"You took away his right to decide that when you chose to work for strangers instead of following in my footsteps."

"If you mean screwing people over to get to the top, then no thanks. I have no intention of following in your blood-stained footsteps."

"Those blood-stained footsteps put a roof over your head and gave you the name you don't deserve, you ungrateful brat."

Nate opens his mouth to retort, but Grandma clinks her fork on the plate loud enough that everyone's attention slides to her. "Now, this is supposed to be a peaceful family dinner, not a place for throwing jabs."

Nate grunts as he goes back to eating, but Grandpa ignores his beloved meat and fixes me with his furious stare. "No such stunts are allowed in the future. Got it?"

"Yes," I say the only thing I'm allowed to under the circumstances.

Grandpa is right. By choosing law over politics, Nate took away my right to live my life. Now, everything needs to go per Brian and Debra Weaver's plan. After all, they didn't raise the offspring of the son they disowned for the prettiness of my eyes.

I'm here because I serve a role in the line of this family. The NFL? In my dreams. And if I had an actual dream? They'd turn that into a nightmare if they caught whiff of it.

That's why I have to keep up pretenses and wear a constant mask. If I like something, they should never, under no circumstances, find out about it. If I covet anything, I need to do my hardest to keep it hidden. Otherwise, they'll smash it to pieces just to keep me under their influence.

Sometimes, I resent Nate for escaping this fate and intentionally—or unintentionally—shoving me in it, but at the same time, I'm well aware I would've done the same if I were in his shoes.

Survival of the fittest is a motto in this family. One that Dad lost.

"Is she from class?" Grandma picks back up the conversation nonchalantly, almost as if she's talking about the weather when she's, in fact, fishing for any change in my demeanor.

"No." I pour myself a glass of water.

"She looked like a cheerleader."

"She is."

"What do her parents do?"

"Mom," Nate mutters, shaking his head.

"What? I'm just asking."

"Her mother owns an haute couture house," I say because it's better to answer Grandma's questions. She'll find out anyway, so I'd rather gain brownie points than hide facts from her.

She beams at my answer, but I recognize her fake smiles. After all, I learned from the best. "What about her father?"

"She doesn't have one."

"Doesn't have one?" She places a hand on her chest. "Poor thing."

Give me a break.

I'm out.

Retrieving my phone, I furrow my brow and pretend I'm checking something important.

"No phones at the table, darling," Grandma says.

"It's the coach. He needs us for an urgent meeting."

"Go ahead then," Grandpa says.

Nate leans into my side and whispers, "You're leaving me alone behind enemy lines?"

"I'll make it up to you next time," I whisper back.

"Worst wingman of the year award."

I stand and go to kiss Grandma's cheek. She pats my hand and smiles. "I'm glad you're doing well, darling, and that she was nothing. A seamstress's daughter isn't suitable for you."

I want to correct her, but I don't bother as I nod at Grandpa and leave. I couldn't escape this house faster if I wanted to.

It doesn't take me long to drive to The Grill. I slip through the back entrance to avoid any celebratory rounds Chad is planning tonight.

One of the staff tells me that our usual booth is empty, so I sit there and bring out my phone.

I wait and wait, but there's no sign of Naomi.

I text her at the number Reina gave me.

Sebastian: I'm here. You're not.

The reply is immediate.

Naomi: Never said I would be. Better luck next time.

A predatory smirk curls my lips as I stand up. She wants a game? I'll show her what playing is really like.

EIGHT

Naomi

I'VE BEEN BUZZING WITH EXCITEMENT EVER SINCE I MET the PI last night.

While my logical side argues that I'm merely chasing a pipe dream, every other side is on board with the idea of finding my father. I haven't been able to entertain any other thoughts since.

And yes, that includes forgetting about the van that almost kidnapped me or the out-of-body experience I had on national TV.

All I can think about is the possibility of meeting my dad. And yeah, okay, the national TV incident won't really leave my head either, no matter how much I chase it away.

The text he sent earlier didn't help. Is he still waiting at The Grill?

I shake my head. I don't care. At all.

Now I just need to stop thinking about it.

And being alone doesn't help. On a Saturday night, Luce and I usually hang out together, but she's busy with her new witch coven. I tried to distract myself by studying, but I really suck at preparing for exams in advance. I only excel when I study the day of.

Netflix also wasn't much help, but hey, true crime shows are better than overthinking everything.

So I put on shorts and my comfy hoodie and lay my fuzzy blanket on the sofa, then go to the kitchen for my ammunition. Soda, chips, nuts, and everything that would cause Brianna and her minions to have a stroke if they saw me consuming it.

The scent of smoke is my only warning of Mom's presence as she steps through the kitchen's sliding doors with a phone at her ear and a half-burnt cigarette in her fingers.

She must've not noticed I'm here, because she doesn't raise her head as she speaks in Japanese. And while I'm not the best at writing it, I understand and speak it perfectly. "I told you not to call me anymore."

There's silence before she continues, "That was a long time ago. When are you going to stop accusing me of that?"

More silence, then Mom takes a long drag, the burn visible on the cigarette. The longer she listens, the harder her limbs physically shake as she shouts, "I said, no!"

And with that, she hangs up, bringing the cigarette to her trembling lips. She seems weaker lately and she's lost weight. Her job is definitely sucking her life away at this point.

"A clingy ex?" I joke.

Mom's head rears up and she coughs, her breath catching. "Nao. How long have you been there?"

"Since the beginning." I finger the items on the tray to keep my hands busy. "Who was it?"

She throws up a dismissive hand. "No one you should worry about."

"Just like I shouldn't worry about my father or my family?"

"You don't have a father. As for your family, they kicked me out when I was pregnant with you, so I'm the only family you have."

"You're just saying that to guilt-trip me."

"I'm saying that so you'll stop having naive dreams. We only have each other."

"I also have a father somewhere. You just refuse to tell me where he is."

She steps closer, stubbing her cigarette on the edge of the sink as her eyes glisten with moisture. "I'm the one who faced social discrimination and did my best to give you a comfortable life. I'm the one who works day in and day out so no one looks down on you. What did your father do in all of that?"

"I wouldn't know, because you won't tell me."

"I'm protecting you."

"Just like you protected me from your boyfriend when I was nine years old? If Dad were here, that would've never happened!"

She raises her palm and strikes me across the face so hard, I reel from the shock of it. Mom doesn't hit me. Ever. And the surprise on her face matches my own as burning tears roll down my cheeks.

Her violet-painted lips shake. "I'm sorry. I didn't mean that."

"Forget it."

"I...told you to never bring that up again. It's all behind us now. I stopped dating and cut off my social life to take care of you."

"I never asked you to! All I ever wanted was my father and you never gave me that."

"And I never will." She sniffles, her expression hardening. "Stop being a baby and grow up."

I want to tell her that I've been a grownup since that night twelve years ago. That I figuratively lost my innocence and she wasn't there for me.

I want to scream that I hate everything she's done since then.

That I hate *her* sometimes. But that will only make me an emotional mess and I don't know how to deal with that.

My relationship with Mom has been on and off for twelve years now and I don't think it'll ever get better. I should've moved out when I graduated high school, but one drunken night, she begged me not to go, said she couldn't imagine her life without me, so I caved in and stayed.

And for what?

Nothing changed. If anything, she's gotten busier with each passing year.

I'm definitely moving out after college ends. I'll go to Japan and put some distance between us. Maybe that's what we needed all along. A break from each other.

The doorbell rings and Mom wipes her eyes and goes to answer it.

Using the sleeve of my hoodie, I rub at my eyes to make the evidence of my weakness disappear. We're the same in that way, Mom and I. We hate showing our emotions to the outside world and actively close down whenever there's a chance.

Grabbing my tray of goodies, I head to the living room but freeze when I hear a very familiar rumbling voice.

I must be imagining things.

Soon after, though, Mom walks back inside, accompanied by none other than the Black Devils' captain and quarterback.

The tray nearly falls to the floor and my legs struggle to keep me upright.

Sebastian is here. In my house.

What the…?

I blink twice to make sure he's actually here. Yup, there he is, dressed in designer jeans that hang low on his sinful hips. A gray T-shirt stretches across his hard abs that his denim jacket is unable to hide.

His hair is styled back and his star smile is on complete

display. So what if I can sense the hollowness behind it? Everyone else only sees the accomplishments and the quarterback image.

Everyone else is only interested in what's on the surface.

All this time, I thought I was, too, but something changed last night.

Or maybe it's been there all along and is only now making itself known.

"Your friend came to see you, Nao," Mom announces ever so casually, as if I actually have any friends aside from Lucy.

I finally find my voice, but it still comes out low, "He's not my friend, Mom."

"She's right." Sebastian offers her his million-dollar-all-American-boy smile. "I'm actually trying to court her."

She raises a brow, her gaze flitting between the two of us before she mutters, "Good luck with that."

And then she ascends the stairs, slowly disappearing from view.

Leaving me alone.

Or with Sebastian—which is way worse.

Ignoring him—and my general state of flustering panic—I try to walk at a steady pace. I miraculously place the tray on the coffee table and sit on the sofa without knocking anything over.

My voice, however, is a little strangled when I speak, "You can leave. The door is right there."

A heavy weight flops beside me, causing a dip in the sofa. The pungent scent of bergamot and pepper assaults my nostrils and overwhelms my senses.

My space is filled with his nefarious presence. I've never been this close to Sebastian before and now that it's happened two days in a row, I can feel a part of me disintegrating, almost as if I'm going through some sort of an internal crisis.

His face inches impossibly closer to mine as he coos seductively, "I didn't come here so I could leave, Tsundere."

"Stop calling me that."

"Why? Does it hit too close to home?"

I huff, ripping a bag of chips open and hitting Play on Netflix. "It'll get gory. You better go."

"I like gory."

"No, you don't, Mr. Prim and Proper."

"Just because I'm prim and proper doesn't mean I don't enjoy the exploration of the dark side." He steals a chip from my bag, his fingers brushing against mine for a second too long.

I hold my breath until he retracts his hand.

Swallowing the saliva that's gathered at the back of my throat, I steal a peek at him. At how illegally perfect he is, like a Roman god with all his sharp angles.

"What are you doing here, Sebastian?" I ask in a barely audible voice.

"Watching the life of some serial killer because you stood me up."

"Ever think that I stood you up because I'm not interested in you?"

"Or you stood me up because you are interested in me and scared of acting on it."

"You're delusional."

He breaks eye contact with the TV and focuses on me. "Want to make a bet?"

"What type of bet?"

"The type where if you win, I'll leave you alone. If you don't, you'll give me something I want."

I don't like the sound of that, but at the same time, I know this is probably the only way he'll end whatever sick fixation he has on me.

"Fine. What's the bet?"

"When I kissed you yesterday, you didn't moan."

My temperature rises a notch at the reminder of last night. I don't know why I thought he'd pretend it didn't happen like I've been trying to. Of course, Sebastian is the type of person who'd hit me over the head with it if for nothing else than to rattle me.

I clear my throat. "S-so?"

"That's the bet. I'll kiss you again. If you moan, I win. If you don't, you win."

I open my mouth to protest, but it ends on a gasp when his lips claim mine.

NINE

Naomi

ANY OBJECTION I COULD'VE MADE CRASHES AND DIES against the liquid heat of Sebastian's tongue.

There's no gentleness behind his kiss. If anything, it's deeper than yesterday's with a sinister meaning lurking in its depths. For a second, I feel hunted, followed, just like last night on the forest road.

Only, this time…he caught me.

My heart hammers, but instead of stiffening, my body opens to his wicked ministrations. His palms cup my cheeks, his thumbs pressing hard to keep me immobile as he explores my mouth.

Or more like, seizes it with simmering brutality.

The strokes of his relentless tongue and the nibbles of his teeth against the cushion of my lips is nothing short of a conquest.

Savage.

Merciless.

And with no end in sight.

He's consuming me in his rough viciousness, feeding off my

energy and confiscating it for his own. If I let him, if I allow this, I have a feeling he'll never stop.

Not that he appears to plan to anytime soon.

I jam a fist between us, pushing at his chest, but that only prompts him forward. Sebastian swallows me into his warm presence and feasts on me with the urgency of a doomed man.

The hum coming from our surroundings and the TV in the background gradually vanishes. Even the sofa we're sitting on feels ethereal, like we're suspended in midair.

Why?

Just why does he have this effect on me as if I'm still that teenager who met him for the first time?

The thought of those stolen moments coupled with his savage, unapologetic touch get to me in places that sure as shit shouldn't be affected.

I argue with my head that I shouldn't give in to this, shouldn't allow him to play with me, but my logical side seems to be closed for business with the fiery stimulation taking over my body.

A moan ripples in the air and I gasp in his mouth as I recognize my voice.

I lost.

Or more accurately, I never stood a chance to begin with.

Even with the bells of his win echoing in the air, Sebastian doesn't pull away. Doesn't stop. Doesn't gloat about making me so hormonal that I couldn't control my damn reaction.

If anything, he becomes more brazen, reaching a hand between us and cupping my breast through my hoodie. I'm braless, so his touch goes straight to my sensitive flesh.

Another needy sound tears from my throat as his thumb presses down on my aching nipple. He then twists it between two callous fingers causing me to whimper and shake.

His back and forth against my breast doesn't end there, though, and shoots between my legs, metaphorically prying them open.

Sebastian's mouth leaves mine with an agonizing slowness that catches my breathing and makes my lips tingle.

I stare at him from beneath my lashes and that's when I realize my eyelids have been drooping as if I'm caught in a trance.

My fractured breaths and his harsh ones fill the air as we stare at each other in ominous silence. One that says in blood letters that something is wrong.

Or maybe it's too right, but it can still go wrong.

Or maybe it's equally right *and* wrong.

His fingers circle my nipple through the hoodie and I suck in a sharp breath through my nostrils.

I've never had someone toy with me this expertly, promising both pleasure and discomfort in equal measure.

It's a free fall.

Torture.

Plain sadism.

"Were you ready for me, Tsundere?" he rasps near my ear, still tugging on my nipple, twirling, stimulating.

"Ready for you?" My voice is too breathy and strangled, as if I'm relearning how to articulate properly.

"You left these tits uncovered because you wanted me to feel them."

"That's…not true."

He swipes his thumb over the peak, back and forth, controlling my shattered breathing until it matches the rhythm of his. "But they're ready for me. Can't you see how much they want my mouth on them?"

Sebastian releases my face and starts to lift my hoodie. My insides burn red hot and my stomach quivers when his knuckles brush against the burning skin.

The thought of him seeing my breasts, actually touching them without a barrier, sends me into a spectrum of chaotic emotions. The swells of my breasts peek from underneath the material, my sickly pale skin contrasting against the black of the hoodie.

Sebastian strokes an index finger over the bottom swell, causing my thighs to clench. The view of his masculine finger and the tone of his skin against the paleness of mine steals my focus.

"Look at how creamy and big your tits are, Naomi. The cheer uniform doesn't do them justice."

His words trigger pressure against my most intimate part and I can feel myself letting go, allowing him to do whatever he likes with me and my body.

No.

This will blow away every wall I've spent years building.

Every barrier and layer I've carefully wrapped around myself since that red night.

I don't know how I do it, but I grab his wrist and push it away, then jerk up so I'm not caught under his spell anymore.

That doesn't stop the manic rise and fall of my chest or how my nipples still burn to be touched.

It doesn't stop my illogical need for more or how my skin twitches for it like an addict going through withdrawal.

Sebastian remains on the sofa, legs wide, appearing a bit too comfortable. Strands of his sandy hair fall in a beautiful mess over his forehead and darkened aqua eyes.

"In case you forgot, I won, Tsundere, and with a KO at that since you moaned three times."

I suck in an unsteady breath, praying that my skin isn't reddening. "That still doesn't give you the right to grope me."

His tongue peeks out, moistening the edge of his upper lip. I find myself imitating the gesture, recalling how that same tongue felt curling around mine, sucking and dominating.

"You liked it."

I snap my attention back to his, internally shaking myself. "Or maybe you think I did to satisfy your dick-shaped ego."

"I didn't know you thought about my dick's shape, Naomi."

"I don't."

"You just proved you do."

"It's a figure of speech, asshole."

"My asshole, too. No wonder they say the quiet ones are the wildest."

"I'm anything but quiet. I just don't like to talk when it's not needed—which is most of the time."

"You're talking now."

"That's because you're being infuriating."

"Oh, baby. Do I get on your nerves? Do you hate how you melt against me even though you think you hate me?"

My stomach dips at the way he calls me that. Baby. I always thought I hated that endearment, that it felt clichéd, but apparently, that was before Sebastian fucking Weaver used it.

Just how much more of me is he going to confiscate?

Clearing my throat, I place a hand on my hip. "I don't *think* I hate you. I actually do."

"Now, that's where you start lying. Your defense mechanism is cute."

"Don't call me cute."

"Why? Offended?"

"No. I just don't want to catch anything from your elusive vocabulary."

"You don't know me, Naomi, so you're projecting right now and not in a good way."

"You don't know me either!"

"But I want to know you."

His words hang between us like a silent prayer, prying and reaching for more.

A body tremor takes hold of me and it has little to do with how worked up I was a couple of minutes ago.

"Why?" I murmur before I can stop myself.

"Why what?"

"Why would you want to get to know me?"

"Why not?"

"Don't play with me."

"I haven't even started playing with you. When I do, you'll definitely feel it. For now, I'm merely telling you the truth, but if your low self-esteem forbids you from recognizing it, that's on you."

Did the bastard come here all prepared with this type of speech so he could get in my head? If that's the case, then surprisingly, he's succeeding.

He stands up and it takes everything in me not to flinch backward. His height is more appreciated up close. It's like his tall legs go on for miles and his broad shoulders eat up the space.

I'm like a tiny dwarf in comparison.

Not really, but sort of. And seriously, why the hell am I appreciating the height and body difference? Why am I thinking that he could overpower me in a flash?

I shouldn't.

I really, *really* shouldn't.

Inhaling deeply, I call for my inner feminist to kick out whatever black magic is holding my mind hostage right now.

"What are you doing?" I demand.

"Collecting my win."

I cross my arms over my chest to stop them from fidgeting. "First of all, I didn't agree with that bet."

"You still went along with it."

"It still doesn't count."

"Yes, it does." He stalks toward me with every word until he's towering over me. "Are you going to do it or should I stay here all night long?"

"You...can't do that."

"I hope you have room for me in your bed." He winks. "I can move a lot during the night."

I clench my molars to hold in whatever nonsense I was about to say, then I release a sigh. "What do you want?"

"Come with me."

"Where?"

"As the loser, you don't have the right to ask questions. You just follow along."

"I won't move from here until you tell me where we're going."

"Somewhere where your mother won't hear you moaning."

My attention instantly snaps to the stairs. *Holy Jesus.* When he was kissing and groping me earlier, I completely forgot that Mom could've walked in on us at any second. Hell, she could've had a front-row seat to the entire show and I wouldn't even have sensed her.

This bastard had me so completely hooked that I momentarily forgot where and who the hell I am.

I give him a dirty look that the jerk returns with a wink. Another thing I used to hate, but seems kind of charming on him.

Okay. More than kind of.

Now, he'll either stay and torment me or Mom will really walk in on us in the midst of something. Because I can still feel my body gravitating toward him.

He's luring me.

Trapping me.

And I'd be lying if I said my defenses weren't crumbling.

Sebastian extends his palm like some twisted version of a gentleman. "Shall we?"

I storm past him, heading outside. "Only half an hour and then I'm coming back home."

The night air causes the fine hairs on the back of my neck to stand on end. Or maybe the reason isn't the chill, but the heavy yet subtle footsteps following after me.

His long legs catch up to me in no time and before I can consider getting in my car, Sebastian places a hand at the small of my back and half-coaxes, half-shoves me into his Tesla.

I try ignoring how comfy the seat is. Someone could sleep in here.

No, Naomi. Nope. You're not thinking about sleeping while you're in the asshole's car.

I stare out the window as we travel the empty road. We don't talk and he doesn't play the radio, and that only adds to the itch at the back of my head.

If I were more social, I would find a way to break the stifling silence, but I'd just make it more awkward, so I hold my tongue. For someone who's treated like a god, Sebastian seems surprisingly comfortable with the silence.

Soon enough, we find ourselves on the forest road. The one I was followed on last night.

My fingers grab my seatbelt as I watch the trees that take on the shapes of monsters.

I hope that Sebastian is only using this as a shortcut as I usually do, but deep down, a murky feeling clouds my thoughts.

Something is wrong.

Completely and utterly wrong.

I shouldn't have come with him. I should've stayed in the comfort of my fuzzy blanket and watched true crime, not actually participated in it.

Maybe I'm just too paranoid.

After all, I watch more screwed-up shit than should be considered healthy.

My mind is being overly cautious and—

Sebastian draws the car to a halt on a gravelly road. Right in the middle of a dark, empty forest.

His voice gains a frightening edge as it penetrates my skin. "Get out."

TEN
Naomi

MY BLOOD ROARS IN MY EARS AS I STARE AT THE DARK forest and its trees that take the shape of the devil's horns.

Sebastian remains unperturbed behind the steering wheel, the sharp edges of his face shadowed by the lack of light.

The darkness makes everything sinister and haunting, clawing shivers from my skin.

"What do you mean by get out?" I hate the way my voice cracks, lowering to a trembling edge.

Instead of answering me, he steps out of the vehicle and rounds it to my side, then yanks the door open.

My heart jolts at the same time as he grabs my elbow, his warmth like a knife about to stab me.

Bleed me.

Leave me for dead.

My nails dig into the seatbelt and I shake my head. There's no way in hell I'm stepping one foot outside.

Oblivious to my reaction, Sebastian's head peeks inside and

I cease to breathe as the side of his body flattens against my chest while he undoes my seatbelt.

The razor-sharp edge of his touch slashes through me, figuratively cutting my clothes and sitting threateningly against my sensitive skin.

As soon as he releases me from the seatbelt, he pulls me out of the car. I stumble to my unsteady feet, hissing in a sharp breath as if I've been through a physical workout. He drags me toward the trees, even when I try to wiggle free from his hold.

The car is no longer visible, but its distant headlights cast a shadow on his face and the taut muscles of his body. That's when he finally stops.

"What is this?" I regain some strength in my voice and use it as armor.

The unfamiliarity of the situation is a disadvantage, though, and I feel like grasping for solutions I already missed.

Sebastian tips his chin at the forest surrounding us from every side, at the tall, gruesome trees and the pitch-darkness that's broken by the sliver of white light shining from the moon. But even that is interrupted by the height of the trees.

There's still the car's lights that cast a gruesome sheen on his face. Or maybe I'm only imagining that due to the way my pulse keeps skyrocketing.

This place is wrong. Utterly so.

He chose to stop in a deserted place I wouldn't recognize even in daylight. The road isn't visible from here, and only the distinctive sounds of owls and some hissing of night animals reverberate around us.

"Have you heard about Blackwood's forest, Naomi?"

I cross my arms over my chest and suck in a sharp intake of air. I'm pretending to be all composed when I'm, in fact, on the verge of freaking out. This looks like an episode of my true crime podcasts.

Maybe Sebastian is a serial killer.

Serial rapist.

Serial creep.

Maybe he uses his looks and charm to lure girls, do all sort of fuckery to them, then kill and bury them in the forest where no one will find them.

Or maybe you watch too much true crime.

Clearing my throat, I choose to hold on to my fake calm. "Of course, I have. I've lived in this town for four years."

"Then you must've heard about the numerous burial sites scattered around. They say our town doesn't have a high crime rate, but maybe that's because they were all hidden by influential people a long time ago. Maybe some of the disappearances reported to the police weren't runaway cases after all."

Okay. Now, I'm scared.

Scratch that. My survival mode kicks into full gear like when I was being followed by that van last night.

No one would talk about murder and crime in the middle of a dark forest unless violence is on their mind.

My knees knock against each other and my throat closes before I choke out, "Why are you bringing all of that up?"

"To put you in the mood."

"In the mood for what?"

He uses his grip on my elbow to draw me close. So close that I'm drowned by the sheer presence of him and how easily he could squash me.

Did I find the mass of body difference attractive at my house? How could I, knowing he could've used it to erase me?

The hot tenor of his voice vibrates with his breath on the shell of my ear. "To run, Tsundere."

"R-run?"

"Yes." He releases me. "I won the bet and I want you to run."

"Why?"

"Why do you think?" Despite the darkness taking refuge all around us, I can perceive the gleaming light in his tropical eyes.

They seem like a hunted island now, about to lure me to its shores and allow me no way out.

"So I can chase you."

A craggy sound catches at the back of my throat and something strange sparkles in my chest.

Something I don't want to know the name of.

I stare up at Sebastian and pause at how close he is, almost like he's intending on tasting my words and breathing in my air. That is, if he already isn't.

"I'm not playing." My voice is weak, barely audible in the deafening aftermath of his declaration.

"Who said you have a choice? Either you play or I leave you here. The road is about a twenty-minute walk, so you'll find your way…*eventually*."

I bang a fist against his chest. "You can't do that."

"Why not, when you're the one who's bowing out of a bet you lost?"

"But why? Why would you do this?"

"Because it's fun, and considering the way your breath hitched at the thought of being chased, I'm sure you'll enjoy it, too, baby."

God. Is he that attuned to my body language? Well, I guess I'm focused on his as well, but at the moment, his face is a blank slate. I can't get anything past the shadows scattered across it.

"Why didn't you choose someone else who's willing to play your sick games?"

Silence greets me and I can almost see the twist in his lips. "It has to be you."

"We don't know each other."

"I proved that I know you, Tsundere, and it even pissed you off."

"But…" I trail off when he raises a hand, indirectly shushing me.

"Time to run through the forest. If I catch you, I win another bet. If you manage to get back to the car first, you win. I'm going to give you a head start…ten, nine, eight…"

I step backward, my heart hammering at the intensifying gleam in his eyes. I have no doubt that he'll leave me in the middle of this godforsaken forest if I don't play along.

"Seven…six…"

I consider dashing past him and trying to find my way back to the car, but he's standing there like the Grim Reaper, the low light casting an ominous, terrifying shadow on his face.

My foot catches on a small rock as I turn around and do as he says.

I run.

The deep tenor of his voice echoes after me, "Five…four…"

If it's possible, my heart pounds faster as I disappear between the trees. I have no clue where the hell I'm going or if maybe he has some goons hiding up here, waiting to gang-rape me.

Wrong thought, Naomi. Super wrong.

I'm already terrified out of my mind. Adding those ominous scenarios doesn't help one bit.

Sebastian's voice fades, then disappears, which should mean I'm far enough away.

I hide behind a tree to catch my ragged breathing. If I return to the car, I'll be able to end this whole thing.

Problem is, I've gone too deep into the forest and took several turns so that I have no idea how to find my way back.

A hissing sound comes from behind me and I don't think as I break into another sprint. My hoodie sticks to my skin with sweat and my legs tremble, and I wish it was only due to exhaustion or fear. I really wish there wasn't this morbid feeling wrapping its tight knuckles around my shivering heart.

A feeling so close to…excitement.

I should be thinking about the possibility of other predators lurking in the forest—whether in human or beast form. I should be disgusted with how, deep down, something inside me seems to be unchained.

But none of those emotions rise to the surface. None of them is as potent as the bubbling in my veins.

I widen my stride but try to keep my steps as hushed as possible against the crunching leaves and pebbles.

It's as if a part of me has lost its shackles and I'm letting everything loose. A blinding wave of adrenaline tightens my muscles and I run so fast, the branches start to blur in my vision. Or maybe that's because of the sweat trickling down my forehead.

The feeling of being chased in a pitch-black place with no hope of finding an escape is…strange.

On one hand, it's exhilarating to have the power of running away.

On the other, the thought of being caught is completely terrifying but…takes my breath away, too.

Or maybe it's more than breathtaking, depending on what happens afterward.

I take a detour and pause when I see a white light. The car's headlights.

My pace picks up and I push through the branches with tightened fists. The light gets closer with each step until I'm smiling with triumph.

I can do this.

Only a short distance separates me from the Tesla. I can't wait to stand there with a huge grin while I wait for that loser, Sebastian.

I'll make him regret playing with me in the first place—

A shadow catches in my peripheral vision and I shriek as it charges toward me.

Sebastian.

I recognize his jacket, but I don't wait to look at him as I dart away from him and continue my run.

My lungs scream due to the lack of oxygen and my heart

rate picks up to an alarming level with every thud of his foot-steps behind me.

Thud.

Thud.

Thud.

The fact that he could catch me at any second, that he's get-ting closer, douses me with equal parts fear and bubbling energy.

I think I'm going to throw up from the force of it.

The trees clear in front of me and I'm finally in direct view of the car. I'm near the point of collapsing, but I carry on, push-ing my burning muscles to their limit.

Then a strong hand wraps around my hoodie and I squeal as I'm wrenched back. I lose my footing and fall down, my back hitting the solid ground.

I wince as my head bounces off the dirt, but my reaction soon freezes like the rest of me.

A dark shadow looms closer until Sebastian's body hovers over mine. A sinister smirk curves the corners of his sinful lips. "Got you."

I don't think as I thrash and wiggle against his wall-like chest. The physique I've admired for years could easily be my demise right now. The remnants of my adrenaline-induced energy roar to the surface with a final wave.

Slamming my hands against his chest, I claw, then try to kick him, but he grabs my wrists, easily overpowering me.

If anything, he seems to find it amusing that I'm even fight-ing, judging by the growing smile on his lips.

There's nothing fake about this one.

Nothing star-like.

Nothing for show.

Because right now? He's not even attempting to hide his true self behind it.

He let it loose, allowing me to see what type of deviant he actually is.

One who gets off on chasing.

On catching me.

On making me helpless and at his mercy.

My harsh breathing echoes in the air as I squirm and hit, as I wiggle and arch my back.

"That's it, Tsundere…keep fighting and clawing. It's such a fucking turn-on." As if to prove a point, he lowers himself so that a hard bulge presses against the soft flesh of my belly that's exposed due to the struggle.

My eyes widen, but it's not only from his reaction to the chase. It's also due to the knot that slowly formed at the base of my stomach when I was being chased and has continued to grow while I've fought him.

Am I defective?

How could I…be this attuned to this sickness?

Just when I'm contemplating whether I should keep fighting and feed off Sebastian's depraved side, he releases my wrists and eases off me.

For a second, I remain sprawled on the ground, bemused and shooing the remnants of disappointment scattered deep in my gut.

"Is it over?" My voice is choked, wrong.

"Nah. I won, remember?"

"So?"

"So you have to give me what I want."

"And what do you want?" At this point, I only wish for this to be done so I can go home, curl up in bed, and have a conversation with my screwed-up head.

Sebastian reaches for the fly of his jeans and slowly undoes the button. "Your mouth on my dick."

ELEVEN

Sebastian

THE DAY I DREADED IS HERE.

The day where I can't keep my mask in check.

The day where I can't control my sick, twisted cravings.

I've gone through a million defense mechanisms to bottle it all in. I played the social game and the diplomatic one. I excelled at maintaining a façade and painting a different image in other people's heads.

Not once have I let myself slip, despite the countless temptations. Despite the blinding urges and the compelling chances. Not even during my hot-blooded teenage years.

I've excelled at self-control. Having learned from my grandparents and Nate that the lack of it would only land me in trouble.

It'd make me end up like my parents. Disfigured in a foreign land.

For someone with a savage command over emotions, I can tell when I'm on the edge.

When my mask, that's almost become a part of who I am, can no longer remain intact.

Because here I am, standing over Naomi as she lies on the ground. The moonlight and the car's headlights cast a glow on her delicate features.

But there's nothing delicate about the stupefaction written all over her face.

She's on her back, her bare thighs locked in an awkward position, and her hoodie is twisted up at her sides, revealing her belly.

My attention is stolen by the erratic rise and fall of her chest—and her round tits that I felt the fullness of earlier and should've had in my mouth.

At the reminder, my dick hardens until it's fucking pulsing against the confinements of my jeans.

When Naomi stood me up tonight and I decided to ambush her at her house, I didn't count on it going this far. I only planned to tease her a little, to press her buttons and watch her adorable reaction to losing control.

But then I kissed her again. I touched her. I smelled her scent, some shit with lily and peaches that I wouldn't usually care about but I now want to take it to bed with me every night.

But most of all, I felt the moment a portion of her guard fell down and saw a hint of vulnerability.

I saw someone scared of the unknown, but curious about it at the same time.

And I had to explore that. I had to keep tonight going and take this to the next level.

One even I didn't realize I was capable of.

I've always fantasized about violence, but the chase? Fuck me, the chase nearly had me come in my pants from the thrill alone.

Watching Naomi sprint through the trees, scared but determined, stirred an ugly beast. One I've been keeping under wraps ever since I learned about its existence.

But now, I can't.

Now that I had a taste of Naomi's fear and tasted her subtle excitement on my tongue, I crave more.

And this need is different from that adrenaline-induced feeling during a game or the obligation to maintain control that's been engrained in me.

This thing that's blossomed inside me is primitively twisted and sickeningly raw.

And yet, I haven't put an end to it.

I won't.

She provoked this part of me and we'll both see it to the very end.

Naomi sits up, using her shaking hands as support. She takes a few moments to catch her breath and swallows audibly as she ogles my bulge. If there was ever a moment I was proud of my size, it's right now. I revel in the way her dark eyes widen and her upper lip twitches, but whether it's in awe or in fear, I have no idea.

When she speaks, her tone is quiet. "What if I don't want my mouth on your dick?"

"Is that why you won't stop staring at it?"

Her gaze flits to mine and even under the dim light, I can see how dilated her pupils are. Almost like they're turning black.

She lifts her chin and hardens her voice, but there's still a tremor in it. "Maybe I'm staring at it because I want to cut it."

"Or look at it."

"You have a wild imagination."

"Was it also my imagination when you trembled in anticipation? Or when your lips parted the moment my dick touched your stomach?"

"Y-yes."

"You don't sound very convincing, Tsundere." I pull down the zipper of my jeans and free my thick, erect dick with a low groan.

I honestly don't remember the last time I've been so hard, to the point of being on the verge of exploding with a mere touch of my hand.

Naomi's breath visibly hitches as she openly watches me, her face paling. Her beautiful mouth parts, accentuating the prominent teardrop on her upper lip that I sucked and nibbled on not too long ago.

"If I do it…" Her huge fuck-me eyes meet mine. "If I get you off, I win."

My lips curve in a smile. My little cheerleader catches on fast. I like that. It makes the game even more fun.

"But you can't make a bet when I'm collecting my win, baby."

"You made a bet when you were collecting your win earlier, why can't I?"

Clever fucking minx.

"What if you don't succeed?"

She lifts her shoulders. "Then you win."

I like that idea. In fact, I like it so much that I'm considering not coming and torturing my dick just so I can torment her further.

"Do we have a deal?" she implores.

I give a quick nod. "On your knees, Naomi."

She gulps, the sound echoing in the silent forest around us, as she moves into position. Her bare thighs are tucked together and strands of her jet-black hair stick to her face when she lifts her head and stares up at me.

The tang of anticipation and the tinge of fear on her face do strange things to me. Aside from making me want to fuck her face until it's smeared with her tears and my cum.

"You have to open your mouth for the whole process to start, Naomi."

She does so tentatively. Fuck. It's so small, I don't know how the hell she'll fit me inside her.

I release my dick and stifle a groan. "I need your hands on it first."

She hesitates for a second and I command her again, but with a jerk of my head instead of using my voice.

Surprisingly, she understands the unspoken order and

reaches her petite hands toward me. The moment they cautiously wrap around my length, almost like she doesn't know how to touch it, I briefly close my eyes. She strokes me softly, too softly. I focus on taking hard, guttural breaths so I won't come from the mere brush of her skin against mine.

When I reopen my eyes, Naomi is staring up at me and then looks at my dick while she strokes it, as if she's reading my reaction to her.

"Tighten your hold and do it faster," I grunt.

She picks up her pace, but it's not enough. She's still uncertain, treating me with kid gloves like I might break when it's the other way around.

The only one susceptible to breaking in this situation is her.

"Don't be scared of applying pressure. You won't hurt me."

Naomi tightens her tiny grip and moves it from the base of my dick to the tip. I hiss in a breath and she pauses, her movements unsure, before she resumes her task.

While I don't mind being fondled by her, this is neither the time nor the place.

"Take me in your mouth and stop the innocent virgin act."

She glares up at me, her gaze burning in the pitch-blackness, and I expect her to let her sarcastic side loose, as usual, but she slowly guides me inside her mouth.

Her technique is awkward at best as she tries to fit me in as much as possible. Is this a tactic so she can get away without sucking me off?

In her attempt to stuff me in, her teeth graze my dick and I grunt as I grab a handful of her hair and wrench her head back. "No fucking teeth."

Her eyes widen, but she nods as she closes her lips around my dick and sucks at a moderate pace.

"Are you sure you want to get me off? Because at this rate, I'll be falling asleep."

She frowns, and sucks harder, a challenge sparking in her eyes. But she's not dropping the act of pretending to be clueless.

Wait a fucking second.

Maybe it's not an act.

"Holy fuck. You've never put a dick between those pretty lips before, have you?"

It's barely visible, but a slight blush creeps up her cheeks as her gaze turns downcast. I tighten my hold on her hair and pull her attention back to me, her huge eyes imploring, almost begging me to tell her what to do.

Why is that such a turn-on?

I shouldn't help her win, but I couldn't give two fucks about that right now. The fact that she's on her knees for the first time ever, that she's so inexperienced in giving blowjobs that she's actually looking at me for pointers is a moment I want to tuck in a secret box and revisit later.

A weird sense of possessiveness grips me by the fucking ball. She's like this for me.

Only *me*.

"Use your tongue," I tell her firmly but not harshly.

She complies, unhurriedly at first, as if getting a feel for me, but then her rhythm picks up, matching my thudding heartbeat.

"Hollow your cheeks as you suck, baby," I growl.

Naomi is a fast learner. She doesn't even need me to tell her how to alternate between sucking and licking and figures it out on her own.

Her technique is still sloppy at best, but she makes up for it with the force of her determination. With the challenge shining in her dark gaze. With how her entire body is in tune with her strokes.

"Stop," I grit out from between clenched teeth.

She does, her brows drawing together.

"Open your mouth the widest possible and keep it that way."

When she does, I pull out to the tip, then thrust in, hitting the back of her throat over and over. I use her hair to keep her head steady and in the same position.

Moisture shines in her eyes and a shudder invades her.

She doesn't fight, though. Even as her gag reflex kicks in. Even when she drools, her face reddening, and the tears finally spill free.

They're curious ones, her tears, and there's this primal need pulsing inside me to see more of them. To smear them on her face with my fucking cum.

It's the first time I've ever thought about tears in such a way.

On her, they're a different way where I can dominate her until her submission rips free through them.

Naomi still doesn't attempt to push me away like any normal person who's having breathing problems would.

In fact, she tries her hardest to keep her mouth open for me.

Fucking fuck.

She's a lot more than I initially thought. The need for more shining in her teary eyes matches the raging urge inside me.

I don't hold back as I thrust to the back of her throat, claiming her wet heat over and over again.

My groans echo the sloppy sounds of my dick sliding in her mouth, rubbing against her tongue and slamming at the back of her throat. I choke her with it until her cheeks and neck turn a deep shade of red and her face is a map of drool, tears, and precum. I use her with a brutality that consumes me, and her, judging by how she gasps in air, then quickly opens her mouth.

She might be inexperienced, but the pleasure is nothing like any professional-level blowjob I've had before.

I want to last longer, to dominate her until nothing is left, but I can't.

The orgasm is so strong and sudden that it takes me a while to empty my cum down her pretty throat.

Then, before I'm done, I pull out and finish on her face, smearing her petite nose, her plump lips, and her soft cheeks. Even her eyelashes. I mark her in a way I've never felt the need to mark anyone before.

Fuck.

She won.

But it's not only about the bet. As I stare at her satisfied expression, even as cum and tears mar it, I feel like she won something else, too.

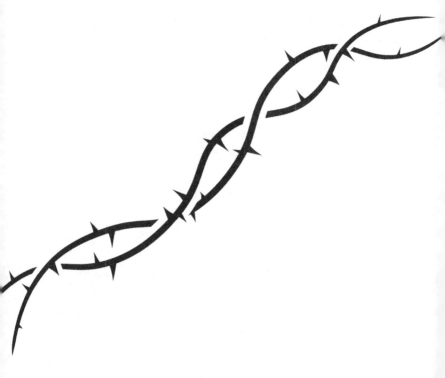

TWELVE

Naomi

IF GOING TO COLLEGE WAS HARD BEFORE, IT'S NOW CLOSE to impossible.

On Monday, I walk down the hall like a druggie experiencing symptoms of withdrawal. Not only are my fingers twitchy, but I keep watching my back as if expecting a sudden attack.

Okay, that's an exaggeration.

Or is it?

I honestly don't know anymore. I spent the whole weekend overthinking until my head nearly exploded. I didn't find the same level of joy in bingeing on my true crime shows and podcasts.

Instead, I kept replaying what happened two days ago in the haunting darkness of the forest.

The chase. The blowjob. How Sebastian came all over my face.

It should've been humiliating, right? But I found myself staring at the mirror, recalling how I looked after he drove me home.

I was a mess, but not in the negative sense—far from it. It's the most beautifully haunting mess I've ever had the chance to witness, to breathe in and feel up close.

Sebastian sent me a text that night. No clue how he got my phone number or even knew my address.

But then again, the Weaver surname could probably get him anything he wants. Including people's private information.

Sebastian: I'll dream of my cum on your face, Tsundere.

Then he sent two more on Sunday morning.

Sebastian: Do you want to meet in the forest for a morning run and other things? I miss your mouth already. If you want mine, just ask. *wink emoji*

A few hours later, he sent me a picture of himself, half-naked with droplets of water traveling down his cut abdomen.

He has two small tattoos—two lines of script at the top of his right pectoral muscle. One is in Arabic and the other is in Japanese.

I don't understand the first, but the second is a saying in Japanese that literally translates to 'The weak are meat; the strong eat.' As in, survival of the fittest.

I can't stop wondering about the reason he got it and if the Arabic words mean the same thing.

I totally didn't ogle him, though. Okay, that's a lie. I think I may have been staring at it since he sent it and that's such a bad idea. Not only is he distracting, but the view has triggered memories of the night at the forest that I haven't exactly been able to wipe from my head.

He also sent a text attached to the image.

Sebastian: You could be having a shower with me right now, but you're a coward.

I'm not a coward, I'm just selective about my battles.

And judging by the way he triggered parts of me I didn't even think existed, it's safe to say Sebastian isn't a battle I can take on right now.

Or ever.

Though I'm tempted to.

Really, *really* tempted and curious and confused.

But I didn't reply to his texts. I just couldn't.

So here's the thing, I've always noticed Sebastian, but he's shattered the image I had of him in my head. I thought he was like the rest of the football players but with some sort of baggage hidden behind his exotic eyes.

Turns out, the baggage is a perversion.

A sexual deviation.

Otherwise, why the hell would he get off on chasing me and coming all over my face afterward?

But instead of being disappointed in him and erasing him from my thinking, I've all but magnified him.

For reasons unknown, I'm interested in those parts of him.

In what made him the way he is.

In how he manages to hide it so well.

But most of all, I want to know why I reacted to it the way I did. Because when he took control of my mouth and smeared me with his cum? I burned to touch myself and relieve the ache that throbbed between my legs.

Something brushes against my arm and I jump, then release a breath when Lucy appears by my side. I remove my headphones, letting them hang around my neck. "Oh, it's you."

She studies her surroundings and the random students passing by. "Who did you think it would be?"

"No one."

"I don't think so. You're not usually jumpy."

"I stayed up late." *Which isn't a lie.* "So, traitor, where were you the entire weekend?"

"I told you Reina was having a sleepover at her apartment. Then I went with Mom and Dad to visit Grandma."

I roll my eyes. "Did Reina make you drink enchanted potions of black magic made of her pubic hair?"

"Ew, no." Lucy laughs. "It was cool. We talked boys and the squad."

"Wow. I'm glad I missed the fun."

"What did you do over the weekend? Besides worshipping serial killers?"

"Haha. Very funny. And that's exactly what I did."

She observes me closely as if it's been ages since she last saw me. "Nothing else?"

"Nope."

I wish I had the courage to tell her about Sebastian and the dubious things that happened in the forest.

Though we did talk on the phone about the kiss on TV. I called Sebastian a thousand names and cursed him to the darkest pits of hell. Poor Luce had to calm me down and bribe me by giving me her notes for the upcoming exam.

If I tell her that I met the asshole, sucked him off, and let him ejaculate all over my face, she might call me crazy.

Or perverted.

Or abnormal.

Truth is, I'm scared of admitting my feelings concerning everything that happened over the weekend. What if she thinks there's something wrong with me? In our fucked-up society, men get away with it, but women are always judged for the tiniest perversion, even by other women.

Lucy is generally open-minded, but I'm not sure to what extent when it comes to that small part of sexual fuckery.

And it is a small part. I saw the promise for more in his eyes when he dropped me off that night, and I'm not sure whether I'm excited or terrified.

Maybe both.

Lucy lifts her shoulder. "If you say so."

"I watched a weird indie movie, though."

"Oh! What type?"

"Eh, there was a woman who went on a sexual discovery mission."

She giggles. "Good for her. Maybe you should tag along."

"Me?"

She taps my arm. "I love you, Nao, but you're too uptight when it comes to sex."

"It's called being cautious."

"Too cautious maybe."

"Says the girl who only has sex with the lights off."

"That's not a prude thing. I just…don't want to look at their faces."

"Yeah, yeah, because you fantasize about Prescott fucking you, not whoever is there."

She slams her hands over my mouth and searches around us, probably to see if anyone heard. "Shut up. How the hell do you know that?"

I remove her hands, laughing. "Because I'm your best friend, dummy. I know you."

"I know you, too, and I can tell something has changed." She narrows her eyes on me. "What is it?"

"The weird movie. It's stuck with me and I can't chase it away."

"Do you have to? If you enjoyed something, it's allowed to stick with you."

"I didn't enjoy it." My voice is too defensive. "It stuck with me because of the graphic details."

"Nao, hon, you watch brutal retellings of serial killers' crimes and you don't bat an eye, but graphic sex is a trigger?"

Not when it concerns other people, but it might be when I'm the one on the receiving end.

I swiftly divert the conversation to Reina and the cheer squad, and Lucy gladly gets absorbed in the subject as we get to class. For the rest of the day, I avoid the Political Science Department—where the bastard Sebastian studies.

Thankfully, our department, Sociology and Psychological

Science, is far enough away that he and I could only run into each other in the cafeteria. So I suggest that Lucy and I have our lunch near a fountain behind the building, where I usually go to escape the witch hunt of the calorie police—aka Brianna and her fat-shaming squad.

But despite my tactical escape, I can't bail out of cheer practice.

Just when I'm contemplating skipping today, Reina catches me and nearly confiscates my damn headphones again.

When I get to the football field, my senses are assaulted with him. He's not even close, yet I can *feel* him.

Lucy is saying something, but I don't hear a word coming out of her mouth.

My eyes instantly find his light ones. He's talking to Owen, but his sharp attention is completely on me.

Sebastian is downright beautiful in everyday clothes, but he looks like a god in his football uniform with those two streaks of black underneath his eyes.

He winks and it's like I've been hit with a thunderbolt. I immediately cut off eye contact and hurry to the cheer squad.

Now he must think I'm into him or something.

Way to go, Nao.

I'm restless during the entire practice, waiting for it to end with bated breath so that I can retreat and rebuild my walls.

I barely manage to keep from looking at him, even though I feel his attention on me the entire time.

When Reina calls it a day, I practically flee from the field.

I spend more time than needed in the shower until almost everyone leaves.

When I come out, Reina and Prescott are talking to the coach in the office adjacent to the locker room. Their voices are clear, but not their words.

Hopefully, they'll leave before I'm done. I'm not in the mood for jabs today. Or any type of talk, actually.

My sense of self has taken a jab and I need to carefully nurture that part of me back to life.

I'm sliding my panties up my legs when the door opens.

Letting the towel fall, I speak without turning around. "Give me a minute. I'll be right out, Luce."

The voice that answers me is completely different from my friend's.

My spine jerks upright when it echoes around me. "Take all the minutes you need. I'll be right here."

THIRTEEN

Naomi

THERE ARE A FEW POSSIBLE REACTIONS I COULD HAVE TO seeing Sebastian in the locker room.

The most logical should be anger.

If not that, then maybe embarrassment.

Confusion, even.

But the thing that beats loudly in my chest is so similar to…relief.

What is that supposed to mean? Is there any logical explanation under the circumstances?

Sebastian's gaze darkens as he runs it over the length of me, his tongue darting out to lick his upper lip. "I knew those tits were beautiful."

That's when I realize I'm standing in front of him in nothing but my panties. I jerk backward, grabbing the towel and holding it against my naked chest.

He steps closer, the tenor of his voice low and chill-inducing. "I'll see you naked sooner or later, baby. Hiding won't serve any purpose."

"What makes you think I want you to see me?"

"Oh, you do." He jerks his chin in my direction. "You're trembling with excitement."

"Maybe I'm trembling with anger."

"Not with your pupils dilated and your cheeks blushing." He reaches a hand to my face and I flinch at the last second, so he only grabs air.

I have no clue how I'll react if he touches me and I'd rather not find out.

If it were up to me, I'd be running away from here, even in my half-naked state. But still, my legs won't move.

My heart won't stop thumping, grinding in remembrance of the last time I was trapped alone with him.

In the darkness.

On my knees.

I shoo those thoughts away as I keep out of his reach. But if I thought that would save me from his clutches, I thought wrong.

His hand shoots out in my direction and before I can think of what he's doing, he wraps it around my throat. His fingers press against my pulse point until my breath is nearly cut off.

"Stop fighting it, Naomi."

"Fighting what? You?" I try to hold on to my venom, even if his hold around my throat blasts a strange sensation through my limbs.

"No, you."

"*Me?*"

"It's not me you're fighting right now, Tsundere. You're going up against yourself, trying to erase the part that let go in the forest. You dislike succumbing to your carnal desires, even if a part of you is trembling for it right now. Even if your eyes are screaming at me to fuck you from behind like a dirty little slut while your coach is next door. And guess what? That part is the truest thing I've ever seen of you."

Something dark and sinister drops to the bottom of my

stomach along with his words, but the last thing I want is to get lost in them or the meaning behind my reaction, so I blurt, "I don't want you to fuck me."

"The fact that you focused on that part proves that you do. You just find it hard to let go. As it happens, I like that about you and I intend to bring you out and have you own that sexuality, baby."

"I'm not your baby."

"You are now. So how about you release that towel and let me see you?"

"No. And if you force me, I'll fight."

"I do like your fight, your squirming, and how you make me fucking hard, but it's not your reluctance I'm after. When I do see you, it'll be under both our terms." He strokes my pulse point, a hum ripping from his chest. "Do you hear your heartbeat? The excitement in it? That's what happened in the forest, you know. The chase and the wrestling made you hot and bothered, and being on your knees added fuel to your fire. Tell me, did you touch yourself as soon as you got home?"

"No…" My voice is too weak, too embarrassed.

"I did. One orgasm wasn't enough and I had to jerk myself off in the shower to the memory of your hot little mouth." He glides the pad of his finger over my bottom lip. "My dick misses your lips. I think it was love at first sight."

"Shut up."

"The only way for me to do that is if you get on your knees again."

"Never."

"Never say never, baby."

I slam both hands against his chest, exasperation getting the better of me, but my voice is still breathy, abnormal. "Why me?"

"Because it's you."

"That's not an answer."

"It's a perfectly adequate one."

"I just can't wrap my mind around the fact that you want all this depravity with me when you have the entire campus at your beck and call."

"The entire campus don't make me horny as fuck after a new-bie blowjob. You do. So how about you step down from your high and mighty tower and come down to my level?"

"So I can *service* you?"

"Among other things."

"In an alternative reality, maybe."

"You don't mean that."

"I totally do. Does hearing me say no bruise your super-star ego?"

"This isn't about my ego, it's about yours."

"Oh, give me a break."

"It's true."

"Are you telling me that if I say no, you'll leave me alone?"

"No."

"There. Your ego is bruised and you'll force me to bend to it."

"I told you, I find no pleasure in taking without consent. In fact, I'm more interested in fighting for it. Guess what? You just gave me a reason to fight, baby, and I won't leave you alone."

My chest swells at the meaning behind his words. It shouldn't. Yet a part of me can't stop the urge clawing at the walls of my heart.

The voices of the coach, Reina, and Prescott rise in volume from the adjoining room and that manages to shake me a little out of my stupor.

"Leave for now," I whisper.

"Remove the towel."

"If they find you here…"

"My family name will take care of me, and you, if you play it smart."

"This is coercion."

"Not if you don't want to. You can open those pretty lips and call for the coach, cause unnecessary drama, or you can give us what we both want and drop that fucking towel."

When his fingers slowly peel from around my throat and he steps back, a part of me feels as hollow as the deserted lockers.

For some reason, when he was clutching me by the neck, I was in a trance similar to when I was at the forest. One where I could let go and not have to worry about the consequences.

Now, it's gone and I want it back

At any price.

Sucking in a deep intake of air, I unclench my fingers from around the towel and let it fall down my body. My nipples peak at the slight contact with the cool air and I shudder.

Sebastian tilts his head to watch me and I keep my hands at my sides, even if every part of me screams at me to hide.

If I do, I'll seem insecure and weak. Two things I've been fighting my entire life.

His heated gaze travels from bottom to top, stopping at my breasts that physically ache under his gaze.

"Your body is made for fucking, baby."

"It's also made for kicking you in the crotch."

A chuckle rips from him. It's sudden and so carefree, I'm caught off guard, and in the worst way possible. Why does he look so beautiful when he laughs? Shouldn't there be some sort of a hazard warning for that?

"I love it when you act hot and cold, Tsundere." He steps closer, his laughter dying down, and he clutches me by the hand, slowly guiding me to hop onto a bench.

I'm now taller than him as he stands in front of me. "What are you doing?"

"Freeing you."

Before I can figure out what's going on, he lifts one of my legs and I squeal before I bite down on my lips to seal the sound.

My palm slaps on the wall behind me for balance as Sebastian rests my leg on his shoulder and dives straight between my legs.

His teeth nibble on my folds through the panties and I yelp, my heart jolting into overdrive.

His fingers dig into my other thigh as he licks and nibbles on my pussy with a savageness that leaves me breathless.

"Oh, God…"

"Shh…they'll hear you." The rumble of his voice against my aching core adds more pressure to the already building sensation.

My eyes widen as he adds a finger and rubs on my folds until an aroused sound echoes in the air.

"Feel that, baby? That's your wet cunt begging me for more."

"Shut up!"

"Are you embarrassed by how much you want this? How much you really love the debauchery of it?"

"No…"

He slides the panties away from my pussy and pounds two fingers inside in one go. "Your tight cunt disagrees."

My leg shakes so powerfully, I'm barely standing. I grip a handful of Sebastian's hair for balance as my body slackens against the wall.

His tongue licks my swollen clit, then nibbles on it with his teeth as his fingers power deep into places I didn't know existed.

It's rough and brutal. Absolutely savage in its nature so that all I can feel is him and all I can smell is his spicy scent.

There's nothing to save me from the moment, from the impact that I'm crashing onto.

A wave like I've never experienced before grabs hold of me and drags me under. My heart roars so loud, I'm scared it'll stop altogether.

Maybe I'll die in the throes of pleasure. Maybe this was always supposed to be the way to go.

The buildup is strong, but it's not as frightening as when the orgasm actually slams into me with blinding force.

My moans echo in the air and I release Sebastian's hair to slap a hand over my mouth.

I forgot that Coach and the others were right outside, that they could walk in on us at any second and see Sebastian eating me out and fingering me at the same time.

The image adds more intensity to my orgasm and my moans. I'm shaking so hard, my standing leg nearly buckles.

Sebastian peeks from between my legs and licks his lips suggestively. "Best meal in a while."

FOURTEEN

Naomi

SOMETHING IS OFF.

Me.

I'm off.

Ever since Sebastian had his tongue and fingers in and all over my most sensitive part, it's like I'm an entirely different person.

Because I want it to continue.

No. I actually want another scene like in the forest where I'll be on the receiving end this time. Or maybe it can start like in the forest and end like just now.

I still have that bet so I can ask for it…

I frantically shake my head. What the hell is wrong with me? Is there some loose screw in there?

Instead of finally leaving me alone, Sebastian exits the locker room first, saying he'll wait for me outside.

He leaves me panting and hornier than when he first walked in. It takes everything in me to put on jeans and throw on a shirt and my leather jacket before I go out.

The late afternoon chill assaults my sensitive skin as I head to the parking lot. Sure enough, Sebastian is waiting in front of his Tesla. With Lucy.

I hurry toward them, my cheeks about to catch fire.

Why is he talking to her? Is he telling her about how shameless her friend is and how I came all over his tongue while he ate me out…?

My thoughts trail off when I see them smiling and in a vibrant mood. Sebastian is generally very good to look at and admire, like those all-American boys who live the dream on behalf of most of the population. Not only that, but from my observations, he can be a great talker, a *charmer*—a trait he inherited from his senator granddaddy.

Everything about him is perfection. Like his sharp features, designer clothes, and sophisticated manner of speech that no one could ever pull off as naturally as he does.

And yet, there's the hidden side of him, the dirty-talking, perverted, and utterly destructive side that he showed me over the past couple of days. A side that I keep gravitating toward despite myself.

Lucy, just like everyone else, is in awe of the perfection he showcases to the world. The star image, the background, and the power his family holds. But I'm infuriatingly attracted to the other side of the coin. The dark, shadowed one.

And that's dangerous.

Because it might lure me in and never let go.

Why couldn't I be like Lucy and everyone else and just focus on his shallow existence?

More importantly, why couldn't he be shallow?

Because even his body language right now is relaxed, his arms at either side of him, his shoulders at ease, and his features welcoming. He's making my best friend feel comfortable more with his body than with his words.

Just what power does he have to make her fall for his charms like that?

And you. You forgot about yourself, Nao.

I shoo that tiny voice away as I slide to my best friend's side and grab her by the arm. "Hey, Luce. Sorry I made you wait."

"It's okay. Sebastian told me you have plans."

"No, we don't."

"Yes, we do." Sebastian winks at Lucy. "Does she always play hard to get?"

"Uh…yeah, sort of." My friend's eyes shine with joy at being included. He made her feel like her opinion matters. As if he already figured out that shyness is her weakness and he'd get brownie points by being friendly.

"Ah. I knew I'd have my hands full with this one." He nudges her shoulder with his. "Give me some pointers, would you?"

"She'll give you pointers on how to get the hell out of here." I jerk my head toward his car. "Leave."

"Not without you. I want a proper date."

"And I'm not giving it to you."

"Nao…" Lucy clutches me by the wrist and whispers, "You don't have to be so aggressive."

If she knew what happened over the weekend and just a few minutes ago when Reina, of all people, could've walked in on us, she wouldn't be saying that.

Sebastian lifts a shoulder. "If you don't come with me, I'll just stay here."

"Suit yourself. I hope you freeze to death."

"Cruel." He twists his lips into a pitiful look. "Lucy, can you help convince her? In return, I will tell you about when she lost her mask while her leg was over my—"

I slam my hand over his mouth, cutting off whatever nonsense he was about to say. God damn him. He'd really tell her about what just happened, wouldn't he?

This guy has absolutely no shame.

His larger hand engulfs mine and slowly removes it. "Does this mean you're coming?"

"Fine." *As if I have a choice.*

"Have fun, Nao." Lucy hugs me, skips ahead, then squeals behind Sebastian's back and mouths, "FaceTime later."

I roll my eyes as she disappears in the direction of her car.

"I like the way she calls you Nao. It's cute."

"Only Lucy and my mom are allowed to call me that."

"I'll add myself to the short list then, Nao."

My cheeks heat at the sound of my nickname coming out of his mouth. Since when did it make me hot? Clearing my throat, I blurt, "What if I find a nickname for you, too?"

"My family calls me by my full name. My uncle calls me Rascal. You can call me Bastian or Seb like everyone on campus."

"I prefer your uncle's version."

"Why am I not surprised, Tsundere?"

"Stop calling me that."

"But you are." He strokes the pads of his fingers over my cheek. "My own Tsundere."

I try to pull back, but he loops his hand around my nape, keeping me caged in place as he continues his ministrations on my face.

"How do you know that word, anyway?" I try to elbow him, but he anticipates it and twists his body out of the way, grinning.

"I used to watch a lot of anime."

"Otaku," I mutter.

"I know what that means, and since you do, too, then you're a geek as well. What's your favorite anime?"

"I...don't have one."

"Mine is *Hunter X Hunter.*"

"The manga is better."

"Aha. So you prefer manga. Noted. Let's buy you some and fuck on top of them."

It takes everything in me not to crack a smile at the tone of his voice. "Does everything need to be about sex with you?"

"Eighty percent of the time. I'm trying to free your dormant fantasies, after all."

"I…I don't have fantasies."

He lowers his head, surprising the hell out of me as he stares straight into my eyes with his imploring ones. "The stuttering just proved you do. I knew you were special."

With him being so close, the only thing I can breathe is his fragrance and hot breaths. His mouth is inches away from mine, his lips slightly parting—

Goddamn it. Stop ogling his lips.

Just when I'm about to pull away from him, an annoying voice filters in our direction. "If it isn't Naomi."

I push Sebastian away as Brianna, Reina, and a few others from their exclusive club saunter by us.

Damn it. Damn it.

The last thing I want is to be seen in Sebastian's company by this band of thieves. They'll never let me live it down and will make a whole big case about how he's out of my league and blah, blah, blah.

"Rei," Sebastian greets her with ease. But at least he's not trying to touch me.

She raises her brows at me. "You aim big."

"Don't you have some people to torture or make their lives miserable?"

She smiles. "Maybe."

"Yours included, Naomi," Brianna screeches.

"Go take a hike, Bee."

"It's Bree!"

Reina inches toward me and whispers so only I can hear her, "Careful what you get yourself into. You never know what happens in dark corners."

My breath hitches as she saunters away, followed by her clique.

Oh my God.

Did she see? No. It's not possible. It was only the two of us in the forest. But maybe I was so caught up in the role that I didn't notice what the hell was going on around me.

I stare at Sebastian. "Did you tell her?"

"Tell her what?"

"Never mind."

While they're somewhat close, Sebastian and Reina aren't so close that they'd sit around and tell each other their perverted fantasies.

My perverted fantasies.

"This is your idea of a date?" I stare at our surroundings.

It's the forest, *again*.

Sebastian drove us to a hidden big rock at a nook at the base of a hill. It's near the place where he chased me over the weekend.

The late afternoon sun casts rosy and orange hues all around us and in the distance.

I should be apprehensive, maybe even terrified, but being back here is once again filling me with that sense of relief I felt when he walked into the locker room earlier.

We grabbed some McDonald's on the way and we have the boxes between us on the rock as we eat.

Sebastian nearly finishes his double burger in a few bites while I take my time.

He lifts a shoulder. "I assume that if I took you to a restaurant, you wouldn't be comfortable."

"Your restaurant of choice is The Grill where everyone kisses your ass. Of course, I wouldn't be comfortable there."

He smiles. "If it were any other girl, they'd be fussing about how I don't want to be seen in public with them."

"I'm not other girls and I don't care about the public."

"You prefer being alone."

He didn't voice it as a question, as if he knows exactly what I'm thinking about. This part of him is scary, and I want to escape as far as I can from it, and yet, my feet won't take me anywhere.

I'm glued in place, muttering, "Sort of."

"To read manga?"

"I…don't do that."

"Do you hoard them?" The amusement in his tone pisses me off.

"Yeah, and masturbate with them. Happy now?"

"No. Now that you put the image in my head, I need the details. Or a demonstration. Both are acceptable."

"In your dreams. Besides, it's all digital now. No one buys physical manga anymore."

"The geeks do."

"I'm…not a geek."

"Oh, sorry. An *otaku*."

"Screw you."

"Believe me, there's nothing else I'd rather do. But we have to balance things out for that twenty percent non-sex part. Or maybe I should reduce it to ten percent. What do you think?"

"I think you have sex problems."

"I'm a healthy twenty-one-year-old male in his prime and that comes with a strong sex drive. And it's my mission to make you feel that it's all normal. Natural. Chemical."

"What if I don't want normal?"

He finishes his burger, eyes shining with mischief. "Then I can show you abnormal."

"That's…not what I meant, you pervert."

"I was thinking about different positions. Where did your head go, *pervert*?"

My cheeks flame and I stuff a few French fries in my mouth to stop from incriminating myself further.

Sebastian runs the tip of his fingers over my cheek. "You have a cute blush."

"I told you, I'm not cute!"

"Easy, Tsundere."

"So now what? We're just going to sit here while you annoy me?"

"I annoy you?"

"That's news…because?"

"You don't know me, Nao."

"I know you're a rich kid from a rich family with political shit going on. Oh, and you're the star quarterback nobody shuts up about and keeps shoving down everyone's throat—mine included, by the way. Does that sum it up?"

"Not even close. You just described the image I project, which is so similar to your metallic Goth, satanic follower image. Does it express who you are on the inside?"

"Of course not."

"Then why do you think mine does?"

Because I want it to. Because I'm still holding on to the hope that he'll indeed turn out to be shallow. Yet the more time I spend with him, the more I'm certain the opposite is true.

After chewing a bite of my burger, I choose my words carefully. "No, I don't. I believe everyone has layers they hide from the outside world."

"Precisely. Just like how we're both hiding how much we enjoyed that chase and everything that happened after."

"Sebastian…"

"It's a layer that you refuse to acknowledge because you're ashamed of it."

"You're…not?"

"No. It's who I am and there's nothing to change about it."

"But you're hiding it, too."

"Not because I'm ashamed."

"Then why?"

"To play the social game. But I don't have to with you, because we're compatible."

I snort. "How many girls have fallen for that?"

"None, because I've never found one compatible enough to say it to."

"Then keep searching."

"Why would I when you're right in front of me?"

"I'm not one of your toys, Sebastian."

"No, you're more. If it were anyone else, they would've screamed bloody murder the night I asked you to run, but you played along, fought and clawed."

"Anyone in my position would've done that."

"Not while having fuck-me eyes." He reaches a hand out and wraps it around my nape.

My breath hitches as I swallow the bite of food stuck in the back of my throat. My pulse speeds out of control and it's like I'm falling into a different state of mind from merely a gesture.

Not just any gesture.

His hand around my throat—tempting, hovering, threatening.

The thought that he could cut off my breathing in a fraction of a second keeps me on the edge in a frighteningly exciting way.

"And they certainly don't feel so fucking good when I attempt to choke them."

"What are you saying?"

"I'm saying we're similar, Nao, you and I. And I'll make you embrace it even if it's the last thing I do."

FIFTEEN

Sebastian

Coming to The Grill used to be normal. In here, I'm the center of attention and I also enjoy the mindlessness of it.

The feelings that reach me from everyone around me are a much-needed distraction from my ominous ones.

Coming from my background and being my grandparents' favorite charity case has forced me to turn off my ability to feel. Or rather, to stop relating to others and only watch them from a clinical view.

When I'm with my group of friends, I can decompress by observing them and letting their emotions wash over me.

Like Owen, for instance. He's loud, crude, and only thinks about getting his dick wet and being drafted into the NFL.

He's currently telling the girls his famous story of when he killed a bear with his dad.

And while I'd usually relisten to his ego-retelling and even encourage him to go on, I'm in no mood for anything.

Correction. I'm in the mood for kidnapping Naomi and chasing her.

Or fucking her against the hood of her car—or mine.

But that's not even the worst of it. If it were up to me, I'd do just that…and more. I've been holding on to my fatal thoughts so she won't run the next time she sees me.

There's so much more I've been plotting for her and those pouty lips that I need around my dick at least once a day.

But I've been playing it safe the past week, taking her to lunch or going to that rock in the forest just to talk.

I do kiss her sometimes and I went down on her again on the top of that rock, then fucked her mouth, but I didn't go any further.

Because one, she instantly pulls away the second I'm about to release my beast. It's like she senses when she's in danger and her survival instinct kicks into gear.

Which brings me to the second reason I've held back. She needs to feel safe first.

She needs to be able to let go on her own without any force on my part. Because while I'm certain we're compatible, while I'm almost sure she craves the depravity I hide, I want more proof.

Anything will do. A gesture, a word—or even a silent agreement would be enough. Without any of those, it's no different from grooming her and confiscating her will, and I have no interest in a shell.

I need her fight, her kicks and claws. I need her steel-like will to bend for me only because she wants it too.

But most of all, I want her genuine screams.

Her fear.

Her *everything*.

And in order for her to give me that, she needs to willingly open up.

Judging from how she talks about school and home, I say we're getting close to that phase.

How close, is the question now.

I used to take pride in my patient nature, but that characteristic is nonexistent when it comes to Naomi.

Devouring her lips and eating her sweet cunt for dinner aren't enough anymore. And neither is how submissive she gets when she's on her knees, letting me fuck her face.

I need more.

To own her whole.

To taste all of her.

I take a sip of my beer and relax against the booth. Maybe if I start telling a horror story, Owen will stop with his one-man show.

Or I can stop pretending that I like it here and just go to her.

That would sound like the best idea if I hadn't planned to make her miss me today. It's the weekend, so I haven't seen her since I dropped her off at her house after the game and kissed her senseless on the porch.

During the whole game, I was barely able to concentrate with her in my view. I couldn't stop staring at her tiny clothes and imagining her naked—or running.

In that moment, I fantasized about giving the game the middle finger, kidnapping her from the sidelines and getting the fuck out of there.

The thought itself was alarming, but no more than how much I've yearned to see her face every day. Or how I've looked forward to simple platonic meals with her where I've listened to her nerdy side talk about manga and anime and serial killers.

She loves the latter more than I'd like. And no, I'm not jealous of damn serial killers.

So after last night, I decided that she might be starting to take me for granted. Since I first got her in my sights, she's been reluctant about everything, acting as if she doesn't want me or what I'm offering, even while her cunt tightened around my fingers and tongue.

That's why I created the distance.

I didn't call or sext, as usual.

It's time she gets in contact first.

I scroll through my phone and find messages from Grandma telling me good morning and reminding me of her party schedule. Then there's a text from Nate and some others from random people on campus.

Nothing from Naomi, though.

It's been a whole day and there's still no news.

My lips twist. Is she really going to ignore me? Fuck her stubbornness.

"Do I smell defeat in the air?"

My gaze slides to my right where Reina has made a seat for herself. Placing one leg over the other, she watches me with what seems like nonchalance but actually hides her cunning nature.

She's a shark who's sniffing for blood. The moment she smells it, nothing will stop her from attacking.

While she thinks she's gotten a read on me, that's not entirely true. I've never shown what lurks inside until that night in the forest. And only with Naomi.

Everyone else's attention is on Owen, who's still obliviously talking about how he killed that bear.

I grin, casually sliding my phone into my Black Devils jacket. "Defeat isn't a word I believe in."

"It still exists." She tilts her chin in the direction of where I hid my phone. "She's a hard nut to crack, isn't she?"

"Not really."

"Then did you sleep with her?"

The fucking bet again. No idea why she's so insistent on something childish when I haven't even thought about the thing. It doesn't matter anymore. It probably never did.

"I take that as a no?" she asks. "What's taking you so long?"

"Ever heard of the edging concept, Rei? The prey tastes better after it's been chased and brought to its knees."

"And you think that's possible with Naomi?"

"If anyone can make it happen, it's me."

Reina raises a perfect brow, as if challenging me, but she doesn't press the issue.

"Make what happen?" Owen drops down on my left after he finishes his show.

Reina traces her red nails over the edge of her glass but doesn't drink. "Naomi."

"Dude!" My friend jabs his shoulder against mine. "You still didn't tap that Asian chick?"

Hot burning fire courses through my veins, threatening to douse the entire table, but nothing shows on the outside. Thank fuck, aka my upbringing, for that.

If I defend her or show any interest in her in front of them, it'll backfire. Reina will smell the blood she started this whole bet for and the rest of them will turn malicious.

They need to think this is merely a bet.

"She's such a bitch, I swear." Brianna stabs her fork in her salad. "I can't wait to see her fall to pieces."

"Bree," Prescott says in a semi-warning tone. "She's still a part of the squad."

"Not for long." She flips her bleached hair over her shoulder. "You think she'll quit after Sebastian destroys her?"

"She won't." Reina sighs.

"But isn't that the whole point, Rei?"

The cheer squad's captain stares at me. "Who knows?"

What the fuck is that supposed to mean?

"Come on, guys," Owen says. "She's pretty."

Brianna rolls her eyes. "You think anyone in a skirt is pretty."

"Not you."

"Is that why you keep begging me for a BJ?"

"There was begging, but not from me." He waves her off. "And you trying to divert the subject back to you is called narcissism, Bree. Don't be jealous because I said Naomi is pretty."

My teammate Josh licks his lips. "She reminds me of those Japanese porn actresses. Do you think she makes those erotic-as-fuck noises like them?"

In my mind, I'm jumping across the table, grabbing him by the neck, then bashing his head against the floor. Once, twice, until blood oozes from a crack in his forehead. Then I go on until he loses some of his teeth and starts wailing like a fucking bitch.

In reality, I remain still. I don't even reach for my drink. Any change in my body language will betray my thoughts. I've learned not only to conceal my emotions but also to never allow anyone to read them.

Thinking about inflicting violence, imagining the whole scene and its repercussions, is what helps me to cope.

Not now, though.

Josh's words still ring in my head. The fact that he's picturing Naomi in a porn scenario and fucking stereotyping about it burns hot in my veins. I need payback before I'll be able to get over it.

Most of those present at the table laugh as he goes on and on about Japanese porn and how he's an expert. If I change the subject, it'll be obvious, but there's no way in fuck I'll keep quiet for any longer.

The scenario where his head is bashed open on the ground is rushing faster to the surface, demanding to become a reality.

"Those sounds are fake," Prescott says.

"How do you know?" Josh points his beer at him. "Did you tap a Japanese girl's exotic ass?"

"No, but I know you're being a racist bigot right now, not to mention an asshole."

"Ohh, is the pretty boy feeling triggered?" our teammate taunts.

"Shut the fuck up, Josh. You're making a joke out of yourself." I stand and leave without another word.

If I'd stayed for one more second, I would've made my

fantasy come true, but murder isn't on the list of things I want my grandpa to get me out of.

I'd owe him for life—more than I already do.

Once I'm in front of my car, I take a moment to suck in a sharp breath.

I shouldn't be alone, not after I didn't act on another violent fantasy.

Maybe I should go bug Nate and sleep on his couch. He's the only person who understands my need to purge and doesn't judge me for it.

He's the one I go to when memories of that night become too much.

He knows. He listens.

One problem. Nate isn't the one I want to see right now.

I retrieve my phone in a last-ditch attempt and pause when I see a text from Naomi.

The pressure that's been constricting my chest all night long slowly lifts.

She texted first.

It's a picture. A sketch, to be more precise.

I've been taunting her to show me her sketchpad, but she always hid it. Of course, I saw it once when she went to the restroom. I was surprised by the images. She's a hidden gem, who has a natural talent at drawing.

Sure, her technique needs work, but the gift is definitely there.

Stealing peeks at her sketches behind her back is different from how she's willingly showing me one now.

The sketch is of a man wearing a dark hoodie and standing in the middle of a room—traditional Japanese, judging from the background texture. His face is shadowed and a bloodied knife dangles from his hand.

Naomi: Laugh at it and I will kill you.

I can't help the smile that lifts my lips. Her tough love

persona is so fucking alluring, I want to sink my teeth into her flesh and taste it up close and personal.

All these thoughts of violence that erupt at the thought of touching her are probably wrong, but I couldn't fight them even if I wanted to.

Whenever she invades my mind—uninvited—all I can imagine is throwing her to the ground, grabbing her by throat, and taking her roughly and without any boundaries.

Those scenarios have been reoccurring to the point that my conscious bled into my subconscious and I started having the wildest dreams about them.

To me, sex has always been associated with violence, but with Naomi, they're one and the same.

Sex is another word for violence.

Darkness is another word for freedom.

Leaning against my car, I type.

Sebastian: Tsundere.

Her text is immediate.

Naomi: Really? That's your only reply?

Sebastian: What do you want me to say?

Naomi: I don't know. Your opinion, maybe?

I can almost imagine the blush creeping up her delicate throat and to her cheeks.

And because I love keeping her on the edge, I wait for a full minute, watching the dots appearing and disappearing as if she's writing and erasing what I assume are curses.

Finally, she sends a text.

Naomi: You're a fucking asshole.

Sebastian: Because I'm keeping my opinion to myself?

Naomi: Because you always ask me to show you and when I do, you have nothing to say about it, you Machiavellian assholish jerk with the star image megalomania and rich boy issues.

I laugh out loud, rereading her choice words for me. Only Naomi would make me laugh by calling me names.

Sebastian: Nice to know what you think of me. You seem to have a lot on your chest, so let it all out.

Naomi: I also think you have narcissistic issues that your grandparents should find a shrink for. But hey, maybe it runs in the family and you inherited the right genes to be the next annoying politician.

Sebastian: Next annoying politician, huh? Not a bad idea since we get the best pussy.

Naomi: Have fucking fun. Peace.

Naomi: Actually, no peace for you.

Sebastian: You don't want to hear my opinion about the sketch?

Naomi: You can take that and shove it up your ass.

Sebastian: How about I shove it up YOUR ass?

Naomi: Maybe when you're the last dick available.

Sebastian: Last dick available to YOU? I can make that happen. And you won't only take me up the ass and cunt, but anywhere I want.

Naomi sees the message, but doesn't reply. That's what she does when she's speechless or embarrassed. She just retreats into her silent cocoon, which usually means she's aroused in one way or another.

All the talk about her ass and fucking has turned me painfully hard. My dick thickens against my jeans and I grunt as I readjust it.

If I don't do something about it, I'll spend the entire night in pure fucking torture.

I waited for the change, for her to reach out, and it happened. Maybe it's time to take this whole thing to the next level.

Though Naomi might not like the change of events.

SIXTEEN

Naomi

"I'll be fine, Mom." I balance the phone on my shoulder as I grab a soda with one hand and the remote with the other.

"Lock the balcony doors and make sure the alarm is activated."

"I will."

"The windows, too, Nao. You always forget about them."

"I won't forget."

Coughing comes from her end and it turns into a fit before she clears her throat. I want to tell her to stop smoking, that it's bad for her health, but I'm horrible at showing concern. It'd appear as if I were picking a fight and trying to get on her nerves. I guess I take after her in that department. Because while I love my mom, I don't tell her that. She doesn't say it either. Declarations of affection have been rare between us since that red night that turned my life into a tragedy waiting to happen.

I used to never sleep until she read me a story or watched

something on TV with me, and then we'd tell each other good-night in both Japanese and English.

After that night, I withdrew from her and stopped saying goodnight. Mom tried to get through to me in the first few years, inventing new activities to do together, but since I wasn't exactly cooperative, she stopped.

"I'll remind you later," she says once her fit subsides.

"Okay. Don't you have a show to prepare?"

"I do."

"Go on then."

She hesitates. "Nao…"

I straighten on the sofa and pause with the can halfway to my mouth. Dread locks my muscles and all sorts of scenarios ran rampant in my head.

Did she find out that I hired a PI?

Kai wouldn't have told her. We practically send emails back and forth daily and he tells me about where he's been and the leads he's following. So far, he's processed the picture and can make out the license plate of the car in the background. He found out that my father might have driven a car with New Jersey plates, so my theory about him being an American is most likely true.

Kai found those details after a lot of digging. I didn't know PI work took so long, but that makes sense with all the technical details and asking around he has to do.

Mom couldn't have possibly met with him or found out through my bank withdrawals since I only do those in small doses and I pay Kai in cash. It's just my paranoia talking.

"What?" The word scratches my throat on its way out.

"What do you think of California?"

"California?"

"It has great weather and you'll be able to leave the small town you hate so much."

"We're moving?"

"I'm just asking, Nao."

"More like, you already looked into a thousand houses and have signed with three real estate agencies so we can relocate."

"Not three. Just one."

"Mom! We're supposed to talk about this before you make a decision."

"It's better for both of us."

"I've been hearing that sentence since I was a kid when you relocated us from one state to the other and I'm so sick of it."

"You're angry. I get it. We'll talk when I get home tomorrow."

"Forget it. If you want to move, do it on your own. I'm no longer underage and I can live on my own. In fact, I should've moved out three years ago, but I stayed because someone begged me not to leave. Oh, let me think about who it was. *You!*"

"Nao-chan…"

I wipe at the tears trapped in the corner of my eye. "I have to study. Bye."

"Okay." She sounds defeated. "*Gambatte.*"

I slouch on the sofa, cradling my head with my hand as I finger my phone. I want to call Lucy, but she said she'd be out with her parents today.

I scroll through my last exchange with Sebastian about half an hour ago. When Mom said she wouldn't be coming home tonight, I made the mistake of having a glass of tequila. Being alone always puts me in a weird mood. It gets me to thinking about parts of my life I've been trying my hardest to keep buried. So I thought, *hey, a glass of tequila would make me feel better.* Apparently, it made me foolish, too, because I sketched something from a scary part of my subconscious and sent it to Sebastian.

I hadn't heard from him since he brought me home after the game last night. Something felt like it was missing all day long and I tried convincing myself it was because I've been conditioned to endure his constant bugging. That it felt peaceful now that he wasn't shadowing my every move. But after that drink, I succumbed to my impulse and messaged him.

I showed him a part of me, even indirectly, and his response to that was to be an asshole. A perverted one. My cheeks heat as I read his last lines. I contemplate replying, but just like earlier, I find no words. Just why does he have this type of effect on me?

If someone else told me that or spoke about me sexually, I'd poke their eyes out. No kidding, I once got an unsolicited dick pic and I sent him back a monologue about how the sight ruined my evening.

If Sebastian sends me a dick pic, however…

I shake my head. Why the hell am I thinking about Sebastian sending me a dick pic?

I raise the volume of my latest true crime show. The ominous events play out in front of me, and I gulp as one of the surviving victims describes the circumstances of the night of her abduction.

My mind turns foggy, and I don't know if I'm listening to her or actually replaying what happened. It was dark and no one else was there. I had to run until I couldn't feel my limbs.

I'm such a sick person.

I can't believe I'm replaying the thrill I felt that night in the forest when someone else suffered from something far more traumatizing in real life. When did I become like this? When did I turn into a glutton for something even I don't recognize? Is my childhood catching up to me after all? Is the monster from my nightmares real now?

I finger my phone before I swipe up the screen. I stare at the sketch I sent to Sebastian, at the invisible eyes and the anonymity of it. All this time, I've tried to bury that part of me and when it kept appearing in my moments alone and nightmares, I fought it. Then I denied it.

And yet, it's still alive.

In fact, it's been festering inside me all along.

I shake my head to focus back on the documentary. There's a blur of pictures before they move on to the retelling of events.

The shot is dark, shadowed, and the suspenseful music makes my toes curl.

A dark figure appears at the edge of the screen and then…

The lights go out.

Not just the TV. The lights are out in the entire house.

I freeze as my heartbeat skyrockets. I fumble for my phone to turn on the flashlight, but it clatters to the ground.

"Shit."

I fall to my knees on the floor and even that sound is haunting in the silent darkness.

My fingers are stiff and my pulse roars in my ears as dark images from the past shoot through my head. The smell of the newspaper, the weight of a body, and the blood.

Lots of hot blood.

My hand feels sticky, as if I'm touching it again, as if the motionless body is hovering over me about to tear through me.

I inhale a deep breath. *It's not real. It's over.*

Despite chanting those words in my head, I can't stop feeling the stickiness on my fingers, the liquid heat, and the sound of droplets of blood dripping into a pool.

Drip.

Drip.

Drip.

Then…there's a voice telling me it's all over now. That no one will hurt me anymore.

Or maybe, like the shrink said, I could've been hallucinating to make myself feel better. That's what victims do. They escape reality to feel better.

But not me. No.

My sweaty palm finally latches on to the phone and I nearly cry with joy as my stiff fingers swipe for the flashlight icon.

That's when I feel it.

Even before I turn around to see it, I sense a presence at my back, hovering, waiting, biding its time.

Maybe it's been there all along. Since I was fighting with my mind to let me go. Since I was a fumbling, trembling mess.

I open my mouth to shriek, but a strong hand wraps around my neck from behind, cutting off my breathing. "Shhh. Not a word. We're doing it my way tonight."

SEVENTEEN

Naomi

SEBASTIAN.

The one who's currently cutting off my air supply while looming from behind me is none other than Sebastian.

I'd intended to kick and claw, to yell at him so he'd let go, but not only is he confiscating most of my oxygen by grabbing my throat, he's also yanked both of my wrists behind my back and imprisoned them.

My phone has clattered to the ground and the flashlight outlines dark shadows.

Mine and his.

We're gigantic on the wall across from us, like some beasts coming out at night to let their instincts loose.

If it were anyone else, they would've panicked at being immobilized in the dark by someone who might as well be a stranger. And while that feeling bleeds into my bloodstream, it's not the only one.

It's not even the prominent one.

The temptation I've been escaping my entire life burns inside me, resurrecting and rising from the ashes like a phoenix.

"Se…bastian…" I manage through the small air opening he's allowing me.

And I know he is allowing it, because if he chose to, he could choke me to death in no time.

Hot breaths assault my sensitive ear as he whispers dark words, "Shh. Don't say my name. We're nobodies right now."

"W-what?"

"We've played house for long enough. Time to play chase."

"What do you mean by…chase?"

"I'll let you go and you'll run. If I catch you, I'm going to take you, use you, abuse you, and fill your cunt with my cum and make you choke on my dick until you're crying and begging me to stop." His voice lowers to a threatening range. "But I won't stop."

My stomach tightens with sensations I've never felt before and it extends to my core. I'm so stimulated by his words alone that I think I'm going insane. That I'm imagining things.

But I can't imagine it if he's here with me. If his thoughts are toying with mine, seducing them, trapping them in a chokehold.

Literally.

Figuratively.

The promise in his words is like my worst nightmare and my most coveted dream.

Right in wrong.

Wrong in right.

Yin and yang.

"W-what if I want to stop?" I don't recognize the neediness in my voice, and that's when it hits me.

Really hits me.

Maybe this is what I've needed all along.

Not the expensive therapists or the group meetings or hiding so my mom doesn't see what type of monster I am on the inside.

Maybe the solution has been to act on those urges I've felt since I was a teen.

Sebastian bites down on my earlobe and I whimper. "One word."

"What?"

"I'm giving you one word to stop it all. If you don't use it, everything is game."

"What is it?"

He glides his tongue up and bites down on the shell this time, making me wince as his voice drops. "Reality."

I shudder, my back going rigid against his hard chest. He's not even touching me, but my clit is throbbing and tingling in morbid anticipation.

Inhaling a deep breath, I whisper, "Do...I not get boundaries?"

"You only get that word. Use it wisely." He releases me, and I stumble forward as the rumble of his voice echoes in the darkness, "Now, run."

I hesitate for a second, contemplating whether or not I have the time to grab my phone. The shuffling of footsteps behind me erases that idea.

Not thinking twice, I bolt forward, metaphorically stabbing in the dark until I stumble over something. A table.

I grimace as the sting spreads through my feet, but I don't stop. I feel around, my adrenaline level spiking until it's pulsing in my limbs. My heart throbs as I squint, trying to make out anything in the darkness.

It's strange how the senses sharpen when our vision is gone. I can feel the air forming goosebumps on my skin and smell the sweat trickling between my brows. But most of all, I can hear the thudding of footsteps behind me, of someone coming after me.

Just like that night in the forest, a strange aura overwhelms me and my senses sharpen until it's scary.

I dash forward until I touch something. The railings. I grab on to them as I climb the stairs. Every now and then, I glance behind me and imagine a shadow on my tail.

Only it's not my imagination.

He is right behind me.

I shriek as I start taking them two at a time. His thudding footsteps follow right after. Hard. The sound reverberates through my ears and chest.

The rush of energy is so high that I'm physically dizzy. My legs scream with pain and I trip, falling to my knees with a thud. I lose my balance and I'm about to fall backward, but I catch myself last second.

I don't stand, though.

Or more like, I *can't*.

Sebastian grabs me by the hair and I scream as he pushes me face-first into the stairs. My jaw hits the hard flooring and my eyes sting with tears from the impact. I think I've broken something, but apparently not since all I can focus on is the large body covering me from behind.

Swallowing me.

Dwarfing me.

Dominating me.

His hard chest feels like lava against my back. Loud thumps penetrate my ears and I'm not sure if it's my heartbeat or his.

Or a mixture of both.

He grabs my shoulder blade hard. "Where do you think you're going, my filthy little slut?"

My breath hitches, it's in equal measure because of his words and the new depth in his voice. The raspiness in it as if he's indeed a different person.

A stranger.

This is happening.

"I'm going to ram my bare dick into that tight cunt of yours and rip you apart and you're going to take it like the dirty whore you are."

Holy fucking shit.

Is it possible to come by just his words and his hold on me? Because I think I'm getting there.

This is crazy.

He's crazy.

I'm crazy.

And yet, I buck against him, my ass nuzzling into the hardness of his cock.

It's so thick and big, I feel it through my shorts. I feel how much it'll hurt, how much I might not survive this.

But it's impossible to stop, not when I've gotten this far.

"Do you really think you can fight me, slut?"

I don't know what snaps me. If it's the name-calling or the condescension in it, but I squirm as a roar echoes through the empty darkness.

Mine.

I twist around, squealing as I hit and claw anywhere I can touch him. His arm, his face, his shoulder. I don't know, but I think I even rip his shirt.

My crazed movements are based on pure instinct, as if I've lost the rational, human side of me and I'm just an animal now.

Like him.

We're both pure fucking animals.

He grabs both of my wrists and slams them above my head on the stairs as the shadow of his abdomen flexes over me.

I try to kick him as I wiggle, releasing god-awful raspy pants filled with the need to survive.

"Let me go, you fucking asshole." I don't recognize my deep voice and the throatiness of it. I sound like I'm really in danger. And maybe I am.

The only problem is that I want it.

Deep in the darkness of my chest, I fucking need it.

Slap!

I gasp as the sting registers on my face. He just…slapped me and…I'm wet.

Holy fuck. I'm really insane.

"Run your mouth again and I'll fuck you raw in the ass." He grabs my chin with his calloused fingers and shakes me, and I swear I'm dripping into my shorts.

I stop fighting for a second and he uses the time to release my wrists, grab my hair, and ram me against the stairs. I yelp and my hands shoot for him in a mad act of defense, but it's too late. He's already ripping at my shorts.

I kick my legs in the air, fighting with everything I have. I fight like I've never fought before until I actually believe that I want out of this, that this isn't something I already agreed to by not saying that damn word.

Even in my madness, my strength doesn't match his. He yanks the shorts off and throws them away, then all but rips off my panties. I gasp when the gesture creates friction against my swollen clit.

He slaps me on the pussy and I squeal, my back arching. The stairs feel so rough against my back, but even they add a strange sense of stimulation.

"Look at your cunt weeping for me. Such a dirty slut."

"I'm not…not a slut…"

He smacks me on my most intimate part again and I whimper-squeal as he savagely thrusts two fingers inside me. It's so much rougher than when I handle myself, primal and filled with a blinding type of control.

"Do you feel how my fingers are stretching your channel? Soon, it'll be my dick and it's bigger and harder. Feel your juices coating me and inviting me in?" He rubs the heel of his palm against my clit at the same time as he pounds into me with his two merciless fingers and I'm a goner.

A fucking goner.

I don't even last a few seconds under his callous ministration as my mouth falls open and I scream.

The stimulation is the strongest I've ever experienced, and as a result, I come the hardest and strongest I ever have. The waves roll off me until I think I'm blacking out.

"Yes, strangle my fingers before you take my thick dick up this tight cunt."

His words add fuel to my orgasm and I don't think I fall down from it as the sound of his zipper reaches my ear.

He forces my thighs apart, not so gently. "Open them wide for me and keep them there."

I try to fight, but he pinches my clit, causing a sob to tear from me.

With his hand in my hair, he wraps the other around my throat and powers inside me in one brutal go.

My mouth remains open in a soundless cry and my eyes roll to the back of my head.

True, I'm wet. True, I was ready and stimulated from my orgasm, but nothing, *absolutely nothing*, could've prepared me for the violation of his huge cock. It's the literal definition of being torn apart and feeling every second of it.

"Mmm…a fucking virgin. Even fucking better." The satisfaction and pure sadism in his tone leave me gasping. "I can feel your blood coating my dick. The best lube I've ever had."

He pulls back almost all the way out and slams back in. Tears gather in my eyes from the sting of it.

God, it's painful.

It's painful like nothing I've felt before.

It's painful like I'm going to vomit my guts out and choke on them.

And the most screwed-up part is that I'm craving the degradation and the immorality of it all. My brain and body have morphed into addicts and this is my fix.

He drives into me with renewed energy, as if he's indeed trying to tear my flesh and leave me bleeding on the floor.

I'm gasping for air, spluttering and sobbing, and even that feels like too much to my battered state of mind.

"It hurts…oh, please, it hurts…" I don't know why I'm saying it. It's not like I want him to stop. In fact, I'm falling into the sting of pain more than I would ever admit.

But he doesn't slow down anyway. He takes it to the next level until my breathing is chopped off.

Until all I'm releasing are guttural sounds from deep in my soul.

I know it then.

He'll never stop.

Not unless I say the word to end it all.

But I don't want reality right now. Even with the pain, I'd rather stay in this alternative world.

"Mmm…yes, you're so fucking tight." His voice is deeper, darker, and laced with a frightening type of lust.

Animalistic, even.

He rolls his hips and then drives in again, making me see stars in the pitch-blackness. The stairs dig into my back and my air supply diminishes more by the second due to his hold on my neck and how dizzy I am.

The fact that I'm being fucked senseless by a shadow in the dark should be any sane person's nightmare. It should twist me up and drag me down. I should be crying because of the pain, and while I am, it's not only that.

It doesn't turn me off. It's the exact opposite.

I'm so wet that the audible in and out of his cock echoes in the air. The tangible smell of sex and sweat surround us until they're all I inhale.

And him.

There's always him, hovering over me, immobilizing me in place and powering into me over and over.

He goes on and on, ramming inside me like he's punishing me. Like I'm a hole he's using to get off. "Do you feel yourself strangling my dick? Such a whore, even while being a virgin."

I bang my palms against his chest, sobbing. "Stop...stop..."

"Ahhh...so fucking good." He tightens his hold on my throat until I think I'm choking or fainting or dying.

But something entirely different happens.

I come.

This orgasm is different from anything I've experienced. There's no buildup to alert me to the impact or those tingling sensations at my core whenever I'm about to reach a peak.

This one is so sudden, like slamming headfirst into a crashing wave. It steals my ability to breathe, think, or react. I go limp, unable to take it all in. I scream, but the sound is muffled by the lack of oxygen.

He picks up the speed of his thrusts, causing my back to slide up and down the stairs. It lasts through my orgasm, fueling it, heightening it, before he pulls out.

A groan escapes me when my pussy's nerves tingle, indicating how sore and battered it is. I blink in confusion, still caught in my orgasm-induced haze as I stare at him. Did he come already?

As if answering my question, he releases my throat but not my hair as he crawls up my body and settles on top of me so that his knees are on either side of my face.

Grabbing his hard cock in one hand, he slaps me with it across the lips and I taste the precum. "Open that mouth and take me like a good whore."

When I hesitate, he hits me three consecutive times on the lips. I open my mouth with a gasp and he thrusts inside, instantly hitting the back of my throat.

I choke and attempt to squirm, but his grip on my hair serves as a steering wheel while he powers in with a mad force. He uses my mouth in the most brutal way possible, making me gag on my drool and tears. He barely allows me any air before he drives back in and does it all over again.

And again.

My jaw is numb and my pussy aches, but the itch inside me is still there.

Waiting.

Probing.

Demanding more.

Just when I think he'll keep fucking my face all night long, he pulls out. "Open your mouth wide. Let me see your tongue."

I do as he tells me, wincing. His hold on my hair is so strong that I think some roots will rip.

Before I can mentally prepare myself, hot cum sprays all over my mouth and chin.

"Lick every fucking drop."

I try to, mindlessly running my tongue over the contours of my lips and tasting him…and me.

Holy shit. I'm tasting both of us right now.

He taps my mouth with his cock, not too hard now, but enough to get my attention. "Good slut."

And with that, his shadow disappears from over me.

I remain in place, sprawled all over the stairs with cum, drool, and tears streaking down my chin.

I have no idea how long I stay there, panting. A few moments later, the lights go on, but there's no trace of him.

My harsh breathing remains irregular as I lick the remnants of his cum from my lips. Disappointment tugs at the base of my stomach.

Reality is here.

EIGHTEEN

Naomi

"**N**ao?"

"W-what?" I stare at my best friend who has been talking for the past half an hour, but apparently, I haven't listened to anything.

Lucy bumps her shoulder against mine as we head to the lunch table. "What's wrong with you?"

"Nothing. I just didn't sleep much."

"Watching serial killers again?"

No. Contemplating whether or not I need help.

Ever since Sebastian left me on the steps of my house two days ago with blood coating my thighs and his cum on my face, I've been seriously thinking I have some loose screw that needs taking care of.

So no, I haven't slept. Instead, I've spent every moment obsessing over what happened, rethinking every touch and every brutal thrust.

Every hit and ever orgasm.

And…I got wet in the process. I might have touched myself to the memory, too.

That's not normal.

That's not how people react to being savagely fucked for the first time after being so paranoid about sex their entire life.

That's not how one's virginity is supposed to be taken.

But now that it happened, I don't think I'd want it any other way.

Something changed that night.

Sebastian and I passed the point of no return and now, it's just a huge clusterfuck.

It would've been different if he'd forced me. I would've reported him and started an uproar in our town. I would've gone against him and his political ties, even if it meant destroying myself in the process.

But that's not the case.

He gave me a choice and a way out. One I could've taken before he fucked me on those stairs. One where I could've ended the chase before it even started.

But I didn't.

I was too addicted to the thrill and like any addict, I burned for more.

For a redo.

For the next level.

I got what I asked for and more.

He didn't hold back, didn't take it easy, and I found myself slammed into a brutal alternate reality.

One I've been thinking about since it ended.

One I've dreamt about every time I've closed my eyes.

I thought he'd disappear and ignore me now that he got what he wanted, but he texted me yesterday.

Sebastian: You sure you don't want my opinion on the sketch?

I stared at my phone for a solid five minutes, trying to figure out what the hell was he getting at. He couldn't possibly be picking up where we left off in our conversation before he broke into my house and fucked me like I'm a whore.

His whore.

But I confirmed that's exactly what he was doing when the second text came.

Sebastian: Heads-up. I'm your number one fan, so don't forget about me if you become a manga artist.

My blood ran cold at how he was blatantly not addressing what happened.

How could he?

How was he able to move past it so easily?

I'm nowhere near that stage, considering how much I've been obsessing about it.

And Sebastian is the one I wanted to talk to the most. I couldn't actually tell Mom or call Lucy and say, "Umm…hi. I got raped and I liked it." *Or sort of raped or whatever.*

Either way, he's the only person I could broach the subject with. And yet, he acted as if nothing happened. So I bit the bloodied bullet and replied with the same tone I used in that exchange.

Naomi: Who told you I want you as a fan?

Sebastian: Too bad you don't get to choose who your fans are. One day, you'll be having a signing and I'll show up with a copy of your work and kiss you in front of all your other fans. They'll probably cause a ruckus and I'll tell them it's the perks of being your number one.

Naomi: As if I'll let you kiss me.

Sebastian: You won't have a choice.

Naomi: I'll ban you and ask security to escort you out.

Sebastian: That won't stop me, baby. I'll always find a way back in.

My heart still skips a beat whenever I think about his words. The fact that I don't have a choice. That he'll always find a way back in. Was he playing a sick mind game with me? Either that or I'm really losing it.

Maybe none of what happened over the weekend is real. Maybe I watch too much violent stuff.

But I can still feel the soreness between my legs. I've had it for days, despite the baths and reading online tutorials about how to relieve it.

That first night, I had to literally crawl and then wash away the blood from between my legs, so that couldn't have been a hallucination or a visceral dream.

I've felt the loss of what I considered my...secret.

Yes. I was a twenty-one-year-old virgin with trust issues, because I would rather have died than let a man be as physically close to me as that scum was eleven years ago.

But it was different with Sebastian.

Maybe because I had the choice, but not really. Maybe because he tore through me and took what he wanted while giving me what I needed.

Or maybe, just maybe, it's because my busy brain didn't get to function.

Because even if I said no, he didn't stop. When I begged, he fucked me harder. When I cried, he took more.

The only way to end it was if I brought us back to reality.

But I didn't.

Reality sucks.

"Hey, Nao."

I force myself to focus on Lucy again as we pass chattering students scattering through in the cafeteria. "Yeah?"

She bites her lower lip, her teeth digging into the flesh. "I want to tell you something, but I don't have proof."

"Something about what?"

She casts a glance sideways, her freckles darkening with the reddening of her cheeks. "It's about..."

"Lucy!"

I internally cringe at Brianna's screeching voice. She snaps her fingers at my friend from her position across the room and beckons her over.

There's nothing I want more than to go to her and break her wrist for calling my friend as if she's her dog.

Lucy, however, smiles and grabs my arm, dragging me to the queen bee's table. I'm about to twist myself free and leave as I usually do to avoid their brand of fat-shaming and veiled racist remarks, but something stops me.

Or rather, someone.

The cheerleaders are sitting with the football team. Meaning, Sebastian and his teammates.

Only his broad back is visible from this distance, but it's enough to make my throat dry and my limbs jittery.

It's enough to push me back in time until my presence is filled with him.

This shouldn't be a surprise since the football team often sits with Reina and her favorite cheerleaders. Apparently, it's a habit they've kept from their high school days since Reina's fiancé used to play with them.

Of course, I often avoided this setting like the plague. Not only because of the cheerleaders' venomous tongues, but also because I wanted to keep some distance between me and the football team.

It failed, anyway. And now, this situation is reaching heights I didn't think were possible.

I let Lucy drag me to the table. My breathing quickens, deepening and hollowing as I catch a glimpse of Sebastian. He's throwing French fries in his mouth as he listens to Owen talking animatedly about a bear.

He's just eating fries. The act is so simple, yet I can't stop staring at the scene. His Black Devils jacket stretches over his broad shoulders and developed chest and arms. His lean fingers close around the fries before he brings them to his mouth.

I gulp, recalling those same fingers inside me as that sensual mouth uttered the most degrading yet arousing things I've ever heard.

Since I first met Sebastian, I always found him beautiful with his dark blond hair, his sharp features, and eyes that resemble the most exotic sea to ever exist. But I didn't realize how dangerous that beauty was until I couldn't see him.

I didn't realize how damning it could be until he took from me over and over again.

There are degrees in beauty that move beyond the physical and he now holds a new peak.

Because I don't see his muscles as just eye candy. Now, it's a weapon. His entire body is, from his mouth to his big hands to his huge cock.

Sebastian slowly lifts his head and I freeze as his eyes meet mine, trapping me in their depths and the pause in his movements. Then he smiles and winks like he's been doing over the past couple of weeks.

"Come here, Lucy." Brianna makes a room for my friend on her left and Lucy gives me an apologetic look as she inches over to her designated place.

Brianna takes a slurp of her Diet Coke. "As you can see, there's no place for you, Naomi. Shoo."

Snickers erupt from some at the table. Sebastian, however, isn't one of them.

Thank God.

Reina remains calm, too, as she silently chews her salad before she addresses me. "It's not like you want to join us, anyway, is it?"

"No, thanks. My bitch battery is full for the day." Now that I've had my fill of him and made sure that this is reality, I can head to the garden and eat in peace.

I turn to leave when a strong hand wraps around my wrist and brings me to a screeching halt.

My lips part as I stare back at Sebastian and then his hold on me. He's grabbing me like when we're alone, savagely, without giving me any room…

My thoughts trail off when his assertive voice echoes in the air, "But I want you to stay, baby."

Silence falls over the table.

It takes everything in me not to die of embarrassment then and there. No matter how much I think myself above the social game, even I can't handle being doted on and called 'baby' in front of all his entitled friends.

Most of them hate me.

Lucy squirms in her seat, then her eyes meet mine and it's like they're begging me to do something. What, I don't know.

"She doesn't have a place to sit," Brianna snaps, twisting her pink lips in obvious disapproval.

"Yes, she does." He tugs on my wrist until I drop onto his lap. I gasp as I land straight against a warm bulge.

He's…hard.

Oh, God. At what point during the conversation did he become this hard?

Sebastian's arms loop around my waist so he's spooning me from behind. I shift, entirely unfamiliar with the position, but he casually tightens his hold around me. If I'd planned to leave, there's no way I'd be able to do that now.

Brianna is grumbling about something and Owen is changing the subject, but I can't for the life of me decipher what they're saying.

All I'm tuned to is his warmth at my back, the rise and fall of his chest, and his cock that's throbbing against my ass cheeks.

Or maybe it's my core that's pulsing.

I think I'm going insane, because all I can imagine right now is him inside me.

All over me.

Taking me with no mercy.

Sebastian slides his plate in front of me. "Eat."

"I'd rather we talk," I whisper, staring back at him.

He brushes his nose against my cheek and I shudder. "Then talk."

"Not here. Somewhere private."

He pauses, and I'm not sure if he's reading the desperation in my gaze or not, but then he murmurs in a dark tone, "The forest. At seven."

I gulp as images from that weekend assault me all over again. It takes all of my will to ask, "Why at seven?"

He strokes my cheek with his nose, making me shiver. "Because it's night and you become my whore at night."

NINETEEN

Sebastian

IT'S NOT SUPPOSED TO BE LIKE THIS.

When I went to Naomi's house that day and saw through the balcony door that she was alone, I planned to scare her a little, to play a prank by cutting off her lights and then jumping in front of her.

But the moment I grabbed her from behind, I knew, I just *knew*, that the child's play wasn't enough. The throb of her pulse beneath my fingers and the hitching of her breath was nothing like I've felt before.

Fear.

Raw fear that doesn't even exist in horror films.

Deep fear that I fed from like a fucking junkie in need of more.

So I took it.

Even when she screamed.

Especially when she screamed.

Her pussy tightened with each of her sobs and wails. I

believed the trembling of her limbs and the shaking of her legs as I tore through her cunt.

But I didn't stop.

Not when she was at her limit and not when she sobbed or when she begged me to stop.

And definitely not when I realized she was a virgin.

Fuck me. I never cared much about that, and I ultimately preferred experienced girls, but when her blood coated my dick, a shot of ecstasy burst through me.

I'm her fucking first.

No clue why she waited this long, but I couldn't give a fuck when she let my dick be the first inside her.

And now, I'm so tempted to make it the last.

Those thoughts intensified my fucked-up lust. I took and took until I became the beast I didn't think I was capable of embracing.

Turns out, even I could reach new levels. Because I have a new surprise for her tonight.

After I went home that night, I told myself it would be a one-time thing, that we would both forget about how we fed off each other's darkness and bury the experience in the past.

And yet, the thought of repeating it has been pulsing through me non-stop. It's occupied my every waking moment. Right after I got to my apartment, I stood in the shower and jacked off to the sight of her blood on my dick and came faster than a pubescent teen with stamina issues.

But I fought going back to her house and climbing up to her window. Attempted to, anyway.

It was half-assed, but I picked up our text conversation right where I left off as if nothing had happened.

I intended to keep it that way.

But then I saw her today on campus.

Just the sight of her in her short black skirt and white top made me think about smearing her with my cum all over again.

My thought process only consisted of holding her down as she kicked and clawed while I fucked her senseless.

And just like that, any attempt of forgetting about what happened that night withered into thin air. Because the truth is, I can't get enough.

I don't think that's possible in the near future.

Not when my heart thunders at the promise of a chase. Of grabbing her by the hair and forcing my dick into her tight cunt as she screams in both fear and pain.

Does that make me fucked up? Probably.

Do I care? Fuck no.

I've screwed more girls than I could count and yet, it's always felt as if something was missing. I've done it rough and demented. I've fucked them until they couldn't move, but while that got me off, it wasn't special. It doesn't even compare to the demented pleasure I felt when I tore through Naomi's hymen, breaking her figuratively and literally.

In a way, it feels as if I've been waiting for someone like her. For someone who enjoys the twisted shit as much as I do. Someone who screams, cries, and claws, even when, deep down, they love every second of it.

Someone who begs me to stop but doesn't use the word that would end it all.

Someone who comes by being roughed up.

I stand in front of my dimly-lit doorway mirror as I zip up my hoodie. A shadow covers my features. I have a face that I get praised for more often than I prefer. I'm called hot, sculpted, a beautiful creation.

A modern Adonis.

But no one knows the type of monster hidden beneath the physical perfection.

No one except for my Tsundere.

The Weaver clan excels at being pretty but barbarous. Powerful but corrupted.

I guess I take after them more than I thought.

Usually, I dislike being put in the same box as my ancestors, but I couldn't give a fuck about it right now.

The only need pulsing in my veins is to pick up where I left off with Naomi and maybe take it to newer heights.

I look at my watch and it's seven-fifteen. I'm late on purpose so that my pretty little toy stays on her toes.

After tying my shoelaces, I step out of my apartment. It's located in one of the buildings owned by a friend of Grandpa's. Because he and Grandma need to keep an eye on me at all times, even after I moved out of their house.

The elevator opens and I pause as my uncle steps out, carrying a takeout bag.

Nathaniel Weaver is another example of how well we hide behind the beautiful façade. His fancy suits and groomed looks gave him the title of 'most sought-after lawyer' in a magazine once.

They said, and I quote, because Grandma was proud and sent it over a thousand times, "Senator Brian Weaver's son, Nathaniel Weaver, is the heartthrob of Brooklyn, the dream of every socialite, and the hardest fruit to reach. He has the looks of a Greek god, but he's just as cold."

And it's true.

Nate might have tried to fill the gap the absence of my parents left behind, but he doesn't play nice with outsiders—or his own parents—at all. He's emotionless and aloof, calm and calculated.

And he has this foreign ability to read minds. Which is why meeting him right now is the worst-case scenario.

Can he see the nefarious lust shining in my eyes? Or perhaps he can decrypt my need to inflict pain over and over again?

His dark gaze measures me up and down. He does that a lot, intimidating his opponents with silent observation until they crack on their own.

"Where are you going, Rascal?"

I twist my neck and stretch my arm behind my back. "A jog."

"Now?"

"Yeah. I run better after people have gone home."

"You can also hide a crime better when no one is looking."

I grin. "That, too."

"What are you up to? Do I need to be your lawyer?"

"Nah."

"But you're up to something."

"It's legal, but it could be...a little immoral." *A lot.* But getting Nate's parenting parameter up isn't something I'd play with.

"Just because it's legal, doesn't mean it's right."

"Aren't you the one who told me legal and illegal don't matter, because justice is circumstantial?"

"And yet, here you are, twisting circumstantial beliefs in your favor."

"Isn't that why you said it?"

"I said it so you'd have no misconceptions about the world you live in."

"You also mentioned that the concept of truth is an outdated righteous belief that no longer applies to modern society. Truth is the mold we shove ourselves into in order to escape the world's harsh reality. So, in a sense, we all have misconceptions we try to escape in our own way."

"That's a reach."

"Then are you implying that you didn't say those words for me to learn from them? Or did you perhaps think I would accept them, blindly trusting your senior judgment?"

He smiles, the lines easing from around his usually rigid eyes. "Argumentative."

I grin back. "I learned from the best."

"You should ditch politics and join me. We'd have so much fun."

"Being destroyed by Mr. and Mrs. Weaver, you mean?"

"They can't destroy us when we're on the same team."

"I'd rather play smart."

"Which is another word for safe. I didn't peg you for someone who refuses challenges, Rascal."

"I love challenges, but not when they ruin me." I pat his shoulder. "Talk to you later, Nate."

He grabs my shoulder in return, his humor disappearing. "Don't do anything stupid."

"That was purged out of my dictionary by Mrs. Weaver." That's what we call Grandma behind her back, sort of like putting distance between us.

"Apparently, she left remains. I recognize impulsive foolishness when I see it, and your eyes are shining with it right now."

"Don't worry. It's all under control."

"That's what your father said and we both know how he ended up."

My jaw clenches. "I'm *not* him."

"Good. Because Mr. and Mrs. Weaver aren't the forgiving type. They weren't with your father and they won't be with you."

I wink. "Everything is game as long as I don't get caught."

He shakes his head once.

"What? Isn't that what you teach your clients?"

"No. If you don't see what's wrong with your statement, I won't spell it out for you."

And with that, we both leave my apartment building. I wait until Nate gets into his car before I head to mine.

I had planned to run to the forest, but his unexpected visit made me lose time I don't have.

Fifteen minutes later, I park down the road and hike the rest of the way. The sun has finished its descent past the horizon, leaving a small line of violet in the distance.

The color black is slowly staking its claim on the tall trees and the dirt path. My muscles tighten with exertion as I run the distance upward, keeping my steps as quiet as possible.

It's not hard. If anything, it doesn't take much effort to be a shadow.

It's been in me since the moment I had to disappear so I wouldn't meet my parents' fate.

The moment I became a shadow and watched their vacant eyes stare at nowhere as blood marred them.

Logically, that's when my need for violence started.

I recognized it when I was a boy and had to do something about it after I beat up one of my classmates in elementary school. My grandparents got me into coping therapy and I had a shit-ton after that.

But the only way I could slowly get past the need to hurt was when I embraced sports. Nate used to play catch with me and then wrestle me to the ground, making me kick and scream.

So I chose football.

A violent enough game to wean down my constant need for violence. I wanted to go with boxing when I was a kid, but Grandma clutched her pearls, which was an indirect no.

I've managed to survive all this time.

Until her.

Naomi.

I can no longer control my violent urges when it comes to her. They blossomed the first time I chased her through this forest. Then they peaked when I took her like an animal on the stairs.

And now, they can only go up.

My feet come to a halt behind a tree when I make out her silhouette in the darkness. She's standing by the rock, grabbing one of her arms as she stares sideways.

I'm more than a half hour late, yet she didn't leave.

She waited like a good prey.

I don't have to see her face to recognize the darkness. I can feel it even all the way to here. I can taste it in the air, and if I touch her, it'll break through me and yank out the beast inside me.

My breathing deepens and I slowly let the metaphorical shackles drop around me.

I don't have to put a mask on right now or pretend that the twisted feeling lurking under my skin isn't there.

I get to let go, to feed on another human's screams and fights.

By the time I'm finished, she'll realize that not ending the fantasy was a big fucking mistake.

One we'll both pay for.

TWENTY

Naomi

TONIGHT, I'M PREY.

Again.

My feet curl into my flat sneakers as my vision help-lessly searches for a hint of a shadow.

The glow of my smartwatch in the darkness indicates he's thirty-seven minutes late.

I should've given up and gone home by now. I should've grabbed some chips and curled up in front of the TV and lis-tened to Mom talk about her latest show with her assistants.

But I didn't.

My feet have gone numb from standing and pacing, but when I attempted to sit down, I couldn't stay still for more than a few seconds.

The buzz of energy that's been confiscating my breathing is too powerful to simply ignore.

But he's not here.

Maybe I read what he said in the cafeteria wrong and he

didn't mean for us to meet here and pick up from where we left off.

Maybe I was only projecting my own fucked-up wishes.

God. I need to talk about this to someone. Other than Akira. Because I'm a coward, even to a pen pal I've had for years. I simply asked if he thought it was crazy if I had weird fantasies that no one would find politically correct like being chased and caught or something.

I'm still contemplating whether or not I should go to the post office and beg to get that letter back. Maybe Akira will think I'm a weirdo and I'll lose one of the only two friends I have—

A rustle comes from behind me and I freeze for a fraction of a second before I dash behind the rock. I don't even know what I'm doing as I crouch. My stiff, unsteady fingers grip the edge and I slowly peer over it.

There's no one.

Maybe I'm imagining things and letting the wait time get to my head. Maybe it's just one of the night creatures...

My busy thoughts trail off when I sense a presence at my back right before a strong hand grabs me tightly by the hair.

I shriek, but the sound is cut off when a palm slams against my mouth. It smells familiar yet foreign at the same time. Bergamot and amber is Sebastian's signature scent, but right now, that's not the only thing that penetrates my nostrils. I'm also breathing in a tangible muskiness, an animalistic masculinity that's accentuated by the way he's grabbing me.

It's not only his smell that's different from his normal football star image that I'm familiar with. There's also the way he breathes, how his chest rises and falls. It's harsh and violent but also calm and collected.

Calculated.

He's not a mindless beast who's out for the kill. No, he's a manipulative one out to toy with his prey.

Me.

He uses his hold on my hair and yanks my head back so his face is peering down on mine. I can't see much aside from the hoodie covering his head, but I can almost make out the spark in his eyes. The sadism in there is so deep and it translates in how tightly he grips me by the hair.

It's different from how he touched me today in the cafeteria. How he stroked my stomach and gently ran his fingers over my lip as he fed me. The contrast between then and now is so high that I get some sort of whiplash. It's like he has a split personality or something.

His lips find my ear as he whispers, "Have you been waiting like a good little slut?"

"No!" I elbow him in the chest and squirm to free my hair, but that only makes him grip it harder until I'm screaming. For real.

It hurts. It hurts so bad.

And any fighting I do only causes him to tug on the roots, tilting my head back farther, until all I can think about is the pain.

His free palm slides across my breasts before he grips one of them so savagely, I whimper. His fingers dig into the soft skin, and even though it's through the clothes, I feel the brutality of it to my bones.

"Stop it!" I wiggle, but he doesn't give me room to do anything.

"Look at how these tits are begging to be hurt, to be used and abused like the rest of you, my filthy little toy."

"No, stop it—ahhh!" I scream when he pinches one of my nipples through my bra and tugs on it.

Just when I'm focused on that, he yanks my top, ripping it down the middle and releases my breasts from the bra.

I gasp as he flattens his large palm against my aching nipples and rubs them together so roughly, I nearly come then and there. The friction is so damn tantalizing that it burns in my pussy. It's like constantly being on the verge of twisted mayhem and sick pleasure.

"Hmm. Your huge tits are made for fucking. You'll take my dick in there, won't you?"

"No…"

He slaps my aching nipples and I squeal. "What did you just say, slut?"

"No!" I sob.

His lips brush against my ear as he whispers, "And you think I care? The more you say no, the harder my dick gets to fuck the word out of you. The more you beg, *no, please*, the harder I'll tear through that cunt until there's nothing left."

This is sick. This is so sick, but I do it.

I provoke him.

Rearing my head back, I butt him in the chin with a roar. At first, I mean it as a form of egging him on, but it gets too real too soon.

My adrenaline level hits the roof as I release myself from his hold and slap and claw at him. My screams and shrieks mount and echo in the air like a fucked-up dark symphony.

I'm not even sure where I'm smacking as I let my adrenaline-induced side take over.

But my blows are short-lived.

He grabs me forcefully by the arm and twists me around as he shoves me against the rock. Breath knocks out of my lungs as my face and chest land against the solid surface and then his hand wraps around my neck as he fumbles with my skirt.

I kick my legs in the air. "No, no, no…"

"It's time you learn your fucking place." His voice is hoarse and aroused as he jams two of his fingers against my lips from behind, forcing their way between my teeth. "Bite and I will fuck you raw in the ass. I bet it's virgin, too, waiting for my thick cock to tear it."

"No, please, stop it…don't hurt me…don't hurt me…"

"Shut the fuck up and take my dick like the slut you are." And then he's thrusting his cock inside my pussy and his fingers in my mouth at the same time.

I gasp, wailing a "please," but it barely comes out as a mumble.

He spreads my legs as his cock forces its way inside me, tearing me with its entry until I'm sobbing and blubbering. I'm begging for his mercy, for him not to hurt me, but it's only a mumble of sounds and sobs.

They're as useless as the meaning behind them.

My pelvis hits the solid edge of the rock with each of his thrusts and I can feel the bruises forming. I attempt to squirm, but he pins me down by jamming his elbow on the small of my back.

My nipples feel as if they're being cut by the rock's harsh surface. I'm completely exposed to him as he rams into me with a roughness that leaves me breathless.

The safe word is on my tongue, waiting, biding its time for me to end this madness. It hurts like hell and the pain increases with each passing second.

My screams and shrieks seem to fall on deaf ears, or more accurately, the louder I scream and bawl, the rougher his pace gets. The more I wet his hand with my tears and drool, the faster he rams into my aching pussy.

I'm still sore from the first time, but now, he's taking it up a notch, making pain the only companion I have in the darkness.

In my attempts to speak, to beg for him to not hurt me, I bite his fingers.

I freeze.

Oh, God. No. I can't possibly take his size in the ass.

"I'm sorry, I'm so sorry!" I speak against his fingers. "I didn't mean to!"

The groan that comes from deep within his throat is animalistic in nature. His hand comes down on my ass and I shriek. "I said no fucking teeth."

Slap. Slap. Slap.

Fire burns from his handprints on my ass. My voice turns hoarse with my broken cries and pleas for help, for him to stop this.

He spanks me another time and I come. Just like that, the pain has turned into blinding pleasure.

My thighs and legs tremble, my heart nearly spilling out on the rock as he picks up his pace.

The madness continues as I shake around him. He doesn't slow down. I'm beginning to learn he never does. Not when he's on a mission to break every part of me.

He rams faster, harder, like he's intent on tearing me apart, and for some reason, that triggers another orgasm.

"That's it, my slut. Choke my dick like you never want it out of this tight cunt."

I clench around him, riding my orgasm even as I sniffle through the pain. His low growl echoes in the dark forest as he yanks his cock out. The first spurt of his cum paints my ass, followed by the second and the third as he curses in a low voice.

The hot liquid stings against the hot welt caused by his hand. A sigh mixed with broken cries comes out of my lips as he pulls his fingers from them.

I want them inside me again.

I really need him to anchor me at this moment so I won't be able to think about anything past him and our darkness.

His and mine.

Because I have no doubt about it now.

We're compatible like he said.

Sick.

"Please…" I beg. "Stop." *Don't stop.*

Please. Let me be alive.

He grabs my assaulted ass cheeks and I gasp, but before I can focus on the pain, he's thrusting inside my pussy again.

And he's hard.

Holy shit.

How can he be so ready right after he came all over me?

"No, no, please…"

His palm holds my back as he mounts me so that he's half-covering me from behind while he rams inside me with savageness that steals my air.

"Please…I'll do anything…just stop…"

"You'll take my dick like you were always supposed to, like the toy you are. That's what you'll do."

"No…no…please…God…it hurts. It hurts so much."

"And it'll hurt even worse from now on. Because I haven't even gotten started yet, my slut."

TWENTY-ONE

Naomi

IT'S A BLUR OF MOTIONS.

After the third orgasm, I lost count of what actually happened.

I lost count of how many times he pushed me down against the dirt and spread my legs so he could fuck me deeper.

Or how long he slammed me against the tree and choked me with a hand around my throat as he drove into me like a madman.

Or how many times he slapped my breasts and pulled me up by my nipples, then forced me to take his cock to the back of my throat and choked me with it.

The more I begged, "Please, no," the more ruthless he became. The harder I cried, the more merciless his touch turned.

I was dealing with a beast, one with no Off buttons and nothing to stop him.

Except for a measly safe word that I stubbornly refused to use.

Because if I do, this whole thing will vanish into thin air. I'll no longer be chased and fucked savagely.

I'll no longer feel alive.

And I do feel alive during the entire act. With every thrust and every slap. Every dirty word and every degradation.

No invisible shackles prison my ankles and no hidden fear paralyzes me. The pain is my aphrodisiac and the roughness is my fix.

And I simply get to let go.

By the time Sebastian finishes, I'm curled into a fetal position on the rock with his cum trickling between my thighs, running down my ass cheeks, and clinging to the tips of my breasts.

I think he orgasmed three times and ejaculated twice. I have no clue how the hell he managed to pick up right after he finished, but apparently, it's possible. His stamina is the craziest thing I've ever come across.

I might have been a virgin, but I watch porn, and he was on a whole different level than that. I'm perversely into the hardcore stuff, but even the intensity in those doesn't compare to whatever the hell happened tonight or what he's capable of.

My inability to move is no joke. I'm panting, gasping, and still weeping softly as my core pulses.

And the most perverted part is that I would do it all over again. Hell, I wouldn't even mind if he hadn't stopped.

That would kill me, though. For real. Not like in some fantasy.

The rustle of clothes sounds from the side and I tilt my head slightly in its direction. He pulls his sweatshirt up and from his silhouette in the dark, I can tell there's no underwear. Commando. He came prepared to ruin me beyond repair.

Why do I love that so much?

He lowers his hood until it's covering his head and shadows his eyes, and then he turns.

To leave.

To erase everything that happened.

I barely survived last time, but I can't do this anymore. I…

don't think I'll be able to live with myself if I just take his abuse and pretend nothing happened afterward.

My mouth opens, but only a wince comes out as I attempt to sit up. It takes me several deep breaths until I can speak. "Wait…"

He stops, his back shadowed by the silver of the half moon, but he doesn't turn around.

"I…" The words get lost. What do I want? To have a conversation? To hear him say anything aside from how I'm a good, filthy slut and toy?

God. I'm starting to sound victimized and I hate that feeling. I don't want to be victimized.

"Can we…talk?" I finally mutter.

"One word," he says with a calm he never uses when he whispers dirty words in my ear. "You only have the right to that."

"But…"

"Fight harder next time, and I might let you enjoy it."

And with that, he disappears between the trees.

I gulp, the bitter aftertaste stuck at the back of my throat. I want to follow after him, but my inability to move keeps me pinned in place.

For a few minutes, I just lie there. My gaze gets lost in the darkness of the forest and the dusty blanket of stars above. A gust of wind blows through my damp hair and forms goosebumps on my bare skin.

I slowly crawl to a sitting position, whimpering softly due to the soreness between my legs, on my nipples, my ass, my throat, my jaw. *Everywhere.*

It takes me effort I don't have to stand up and put myself together. Well, as much as possible, considering my torn short and panties.

I bend down to fetch my phone that I hid by the side of the rock when I got here. I foolishly arrived at six forty-five because I was overly excited.

And that sense of thrill had bled into my everyday life.

Today, I noticed the people when I never have before. I noticed the way they walked and talked, the way they laughed and scowled. I even stopped to admire the beauty of Blackwood's forest and its tall trees.

And it's due to feeling alive after years of just…existing.

It's the exhilaration after desperation.

I used to only breathe air before; now, I breathe life. The same life that I went to countless therapists to be able to get back but never managed to.

Turns out that consenting to a fucked-up fantasy might have been the answer all along.

And the thought that more is still in store for me fills me with morbid anticipation. But there's also a bitter taste that hasn't disappeared since he left me.

For the second time.

I pause with my phone in my hand when I find a few missed calls. One from Mom, one from Lucy, and one from Kai.

My heart skips a beat as I click on the Call button while I slowly make my way down the path to where I left my car.

I clear my throat a few times, afraid of how my voice sounds after all the screams and sobbing that transpired not too long ago.

The PI answers after a few rings. "Kai speaking."

"It's me, Naomi. You called me?"

"Yes."

A gust of wind hits me in the bones as I cautiously ask, "Is there anything new?"

"There's progress, yes."

"Why do you sound so…serious?"

"I'm always serious."

"I know that, but it's more than usual. You're scaring me."

"There's no other way to deliver the news, Ms. Chester, so here it goes. I found the owner of the car we managed to process from that picture, but he's dead."

I physically reel back, a savage pulse pounding in my throat.

I always thought about finding my dad, but I never actually considered the idea that he might be dead.

Maybe because, all this time, with the way my mother made it her mission to hide any information concerning him, I thought he just lived elsewhere. That he wanted to find me as much as I want to find him, but Mom got in the way.

"He...can't be dead." My voice is brittle. "Look again."

"The owner of that car died due to a traffic accident twenty years ago."

One year after I was born.

Does that mean I met him when I was a baby and then he just died?

I internally shake my head, refusing to believe my father is dead. If that were the case, Mom would've mentioned it, right?

"Look again, please."

"I'll check to see if I missed anything, but I wouldn't be optimistic."

After Kai hangs up, two fat tears slide down my cheeks. They're so different from the tears of pleasure that never dried from my face.

I crouch in front of my car and quietly cry into my unsteady palms. My chest racks and the haunting noises I make reverberate around me.

There's always been a hole in my chest that couldn't be filled, no matter what I tried. One I thought only my dad would occupy, but apparently, that's not possible anymore.

That hole was supposed to stay hollow, because like Mom has always said, my father doesn't exist.

"Nao."

My head jerks up and I stare at the eyes that were malicious not even fifteen minutes ago.

He has a flashlight on and his hoodie is open, revealing a white tee. His shiny dark blond hair is slicked back and his jaw is set.

Sebastian.

He's back to being the star quarterback, not the beast from my fantasies who called me a slut and made me come with it.

"What is it, baby? Why are you crying?" His voice is calm, soothing almost.

I don't know if it's the stress from knowing about my father or the bitterness I felt earlier, but they all climb to the surface, ripping at the last screw that's been holding me together.

Jumping to my feet, I storm over to stand in front of him, but he doesn't even flinch, almost as if he was expecting the attack.

"Am I supposed to pretend nothing happened just now, Sebastian? Again?"

His expression remains the same. "I thought that was what you wanted."

"Maybe that's what *you* want."

His eyes roam over me in deliberate slowness. "We want the same thing."

"I don't want to brush over everything that's happened as if it's…it's…"

"A fantasy? Taboo?"

"As if it's nothing," I breathe out on a sniffle.

"It's definitely *not* nothing."

"Then act like it. *Talk* about it. Don't leave me wondering if I've lost my mind or if I should check myself into a mental institute."

His jaw hardens and I think he'll say that's exactly what I should do, but the lines around his eyes ease. "You don't need a shrink just because you're different."

"Then what else do I need in this madness?"

"Someone who understands your needs and fulfills them."

"But…what we're doing is fucked up."

"The best things are."

"Don't you have second thoughts about it? Any form of hesitation?"

"I'm assertive enough to accept that I'm an anomaly to what society expects from us, and I'm fine with that. I'd rather be abnormal than fit into a mold that's not designed for me."

"Even if it means raping someone?"

"Not someone. *You.*"

"It could be someone else tomorrow."

He shakes his head. "We're not that common, Tsundere. I wouldn't be able to find someone whose crazy matches mine."

"So you would leave if you were to stumble upon such a person?"

"Never."

My breath hitches and an involuntary hiccup leaves me. "How can you be so sure?"

"It's who I am. I don't lie to myself, so when I say I only want you. I mean it."

"So you're stuck with me?"

"No. *You're* stuck with *me*, baby."

A slow sigh mixed with a whimper heaves out of me. "But it's…abnormal. I recognize sexual deviant behavior. It's what makes serial killers who they are, and that's sick and twisted and…"

"Sick and twisted are only labels they try to contain us with. We're not serial killers just because we enjoy consensual non-consensual sexual activities. We're grown adults who recognize our fantasies, and unlike the cowards who only dream about it, we actually make it happen."

"But what if it's more than that? What if this is only the beginning of divergent behavior?"

"Why is that a problem?"

"You can hurt people."

"I'm not interested in hurting people. I'm only interested in hurting *you.*"

My heart hammers and everything inside me seems to melt

under the impact. God. There's nothing I want to do other than let him hurt me all over again.

"Maybe you already have."

He frowns. "You…didn't use the word, so I thought you could still take it."

"I don't mean that." I clear my throat. "You fucked me without a condom."

"So?"

"Hello, pregnancy?"

"Oh, that."

"Yes, that. What would you have done if you'd shot your spawn inside me?"

"Take care of it when it comes."

"What makes you think I want children this young?"

"It's not planned, so if it happens, it happens."

"Are you serious?"

"Very."

"But there'd be another life we'd have to be responsible for."

"So be it. Why do you have to make it into a fucking event?"

"I don't know, oh, let me think, maybe because it would be? We're college kids, Sebastian, and we're not even in a relationship."

"We are. You just refuse to admit it and what great parents we'd make, Tsundere."

"This isn't the time to joke around! A child out of wedlock would cause a political scandal in your family."

"I couldn't give two fucks about that."

"Why wouldn't you?"

"That's the difference between us, Naomi. My focus is solely on you and me, but your attention is scattered elsewhere."

"You…really wouldn't care if I conceived." It's not a question, because I see his answer loud and clear in his relaxed features.

"I wouldn't make it a fucking issue like you're doing, but now that you've put it in my head, I'm curious to see you…"

"Don't even think about it. I'm on birth control shots."

His face turns blank, as if he's disappointed. "Then what was the whole drama for?"

"Condoms!"

"Yeah, no. I don't like them with you."

"You could've given me something, considering all the girls you've fucked."

"I've never fucked anyone without protection."

I swallow. "No one?"

"No one but you, and I'm keeping it that way," he says it as if it's an established fact he doesn't want to argue. "As for my medical record, I'll send you the one from the physical I had before school started. It says I'm healthy and in my prime."

"Fucked up, too," I mutter.

"That makes two of us, baby. I like hurting you and you love being hurt."

"Why?" I murmur.

"Why what?"

"Why do you like hurting me?"

"Because when I do, you fight, and subduing you alleviates my need for violence."

"Even when I tell you no and beg you to stop?"

"Especially then." His voice doesn't change, but it's like his words are stroking a dark corner of my chest.

Maybe talking about it wasn't the best idea after all. At the moment, I don't have the stamina to bare myself or to entertain the buried memories that are attempting to puncture the surface.

"What about you?" he asks.

"What about me?"

"You like it when I'm rough. You come harder and your pussy feels scared and in need of more."

My cheeks burn. "Stop it."

"You wanted to talk. We're talking."

"I take it back." I turn to my car. "I'm tired."

He grabs me by the wrist. "Not so fast, Tsundere. You don't get to run away."

"From what?"

"From facing the reason you're like this."

"Who told you there's a reason?"

"I wasn't sure before, but the way your pulse quickened beneath my fingers just now proves I'm right."

I pull my hand free. The manipulative jerk. "I…don't want to talk about it."

"*Yet.*"

"*Ever.*"

"You will eventually tell me."

"Why would I do that?"

"Because, in return, I'll tell you my reasons." He leans in and wraps a hand around my throat, slowly stroking the pulse point. "Until you're ready to go down that road, you're mine to destroy."

TWENTY-TWO

Akira

Dear Yuki-Onna.

What you're doing is completely fine. There's a thing called rape fantasy and it's completely healthy.

I searched it and the psychology reports say it's the woman's way to gain control and surrender. It's also related to masochism, wide imagination, and a broad range of BDSM.

It can also be something someone with sexual trauma is interested in because it gives them control over a situation similar to one from their past where they couldn't.

So it's completely healthy. You should do what makes you happy.

Is that what you hoped I'd write back? Is that what you had in mind when you sat down and wrote me your version of a twisted sob story?

I don't even know what you were trying to accomplish when you said that. Just what on earth are you thinking? You and whoever is indulging in this sick arrangement are perverted.

And spare me the bullshit of how this isn't about you or that this is a hypothetical situation. I've known you for three years and you can't lie for shit.

I've been meaning to confront you about your issues for a while, but I might as well do it now. It's long overdue.

When you said you have friends, I call bullshit. It's simple really and doesn't take a lot of mental work to figure it out. If you had any friends, you wouldn't be talking to some random stranger from the other side of the globe. You're lonely and it's not even cute or quirky. It's your choice, so stick with it and stop bleeding my ears (or more accurately, my eyes) with nonsense about how people don't understand you.

Do you even understand people? Yeah, you don't. Because you don't care enough about anyone other than yourself.

Here are some facts, Naomi. You're selfish. I don't know what happened to make you that way or if it just runs in your genes, but you have issues.

Every time you write to me, all you do is talk about yourself and think you're funny because you're naturally sarcastic about everything—yourself included.

When you say you hate men, I want to reach my eyeballs and gouge them out. You don't hate men. If you did, you would've veered in the other direction or in no direction at all, but you watch porn.

Straight porn.

Hardcore straight porn.

And don't even try to deny it, because I don't believe asking for recommendations of my favorite sites every other month is a coincidence.

So, no, you don't hate men. You just hate your inferiority complex. You hate that you can't muster the courage to start a conversation or to lose the resting bitch face long enough for someone to approach you.

You've taken the word introvert to a whole different level and turned it into a hostile situation that you can't escape anymore.

Your love for true crime and serial killers don't make you edgy or smart, it just makes you cynical about every life situation.

So basically, even your hobbies are a method to veer you away from society and make you suspicious about everything in your surroundings.

Including your own mother. The woman you said immigrated, gave birth, and raised you all on her own.

You say your mother is always absent and doesn't have time for you. But what do you do when she makes a dent in her schedule for your sake? You're too uncomfortable to spend time alone with her anymore because you still hold a grudge against her.

Now, you didn't tell me what type of grudge it is. Hell, you didn't even mention that word. But I'm not an idiot. I know there's bad blood between you two and you're just taking it out on her.

You say you hate the cheer squad and the cheerleaders, but you mirror their nasty behavior the entire time. And deep down, you admire your captain because she's everything you aren't. You curse her any chance you get, but you're in awe of how comfortable she is in her own skin.

Which can't be said about you.

Not only do you hate yourself, but you're also sometimes out to destroy yourself.

And your latest method for that is some sort of fetish about being chased and eventually caught, then raped. In what world would anyone consider that normal?

The fact that you want it in the first place should be a red alert.

Stop.

Go to a shrink and get some help.

Because you're just spiraling out of control at this point. And soon enough, you'll get bored of this fetish and destroy yourself by using another method.

What will it be next? Alcohol? Drugs? Prostitution?

Maybe you'll end up in one of those psyche wards eating your own shit.

Oh, I'm sorry. Did that hurt?

I don't care. I didn't start writing to you so I'd be the only audience for your pity parties or attempts to make yourself feel more grandiose than you really are.

This is me, true and unfiltered, and this is how I'm going to be from now on. I'm done playing nice and pretending that I approve of the shitty decisions you make.

From now on, you'll get a reality check from me.

If you hate it, I don't give a fuck. Don't write back.

But I'll continue writing. Don't read my letters if that bruises your fragile ego, but I'll keep them coming.

Go complain at customs.

Seriously. I have zero fucks to give at this point. Going forward, we'll do it my way.

P.S. This is my actual personality. All the previous letters were me playing it down and being nice. I've had a wake-up call lately and realized I was always a bastard, so it's pointless to pretend I'm someone I'm not.

Until next time, Yuki-Onna.
Love (but not really),
Akira

TWENTY-THREE

Naomi

I F I HAD A DOUBT ABOUT POSITIVELY LOSING MY MIND, it's gone.

I am insane.

It's been two weeks of pure madness. Of running in the woods and being chased around my dark house when Mom isn't home.

Two weeks of pretending my monster isn't the same football star everyone drools over on campus.

Two weeks of drifting.

And in these weeks, I've felt more alive than in my whole life.

Or more accurately, since it was snuffed out of me during that red night.

But even the feeling of being alive is shadowed by something else. Something eerily gloomy and haunting.

Something…bad.

I recognize it even though I try to hang on to the fantasy, to the addiction. To the fact that I'm not just a floating existence in the middle of a thousand others.

I'm special. I'm different. At least, to him.

Not Sebastian, but the beastly side of him.

The one who doesn't take no for an answer and gets off on having me cry and writhe as he chokes me with his dick, then breaks me with it.

The one who wants me so badly, he's blinded to everything but me.

The beast and I have a common ground. He gets off on the hunt and violence, and I can finally admit that I get off on being chased and degraded. On being used, roughed up, sensually ravished.

The beast and I meet in the dark, in the forest, and do our taboo ritual on that rock or against the filthy dirt.

The beast and I have an arrangement. I take his darkness and he swallows mine. I get off on his unapologetic dominance and he gets off on my unconditional submission.

The beast abandons me battered against the rock and doesn't look twice in my direction.

But soon after, the man appears.

Sebastian.

He carries me to his car, cleans me, and drives me home. He sometimes even buys me ointments from the pharmacy. But he never once looks at me with pity or guilt.

I don't think he's capable of those emotions and I'm thankful that I don't have to deal with that side of it all.

In that moment, after the beast in him and the fantasies in me are satiated, I swear there's some sort of a glow that surrounds us.

A high.

A warped sense of satisfaction.

We get to pretend whatever depravities that happened between us didn't actually happen. We get to pick back up as normal, functioning college kids.

But maybe I do need help, as Akira so bluntly put it.

Ever since I received his letter a week ago, I've been fuming. Not only because of his hurtful honesty and all the things he's bottled up for years but also because he waited all this time to say anything.

I've always wanted someone I could bare my soul to. Someone I could tell anything without them judging me. Lucy can't be that person, because deep down, she's pure. Normal. She wouldn't understand.

Besides, I see her every day and that could turn too awkward too quickly if we talk face-to-face.

Akira was the one person I could slowly open up to and even talk to about porn and stuff. He didn't see me and couldn't judge me.

Or so I thought.

Obviously, he could judge me well enough through a letter and be a major asshole, unlike what he said he wasn't in the first letter I got from him.

But for some reason, it didn't make me only mad, I was also…relieved. For a while now, it really felt as if I was the only one who was talking in our interactions. They felt stilled, almost…as if I was trying so hard to keep it alive.

Maybe that's why I pulled that move and told him about my screwed-up fantasy. I wanted to provoke a reaction out of him.

Well, I got it.

A very rude one at that. But it still counts.

I want to tell him to go fuck himself for kink-shaming others, but I haven't cooled down enough to articulate it in words.

Lucy and I head into class after lunch as she gushes about a party Owen is having soon and tries to convince me to go. If Sebastian will be there, maybe I will.

I don't know if it's only because of him, but I don't feel so asocial lately. Even if I do still need my small bubble.

The football team is having a meeting with their coach now, and that sucks because I didn't get a chance to see Sebastian today.

That could be part of my sour mood.

We usually sit together, whether with the football team and the cheer squad or alone—or more like, he sits me on his lap, oblivious to everyone whispering and throwing jabs at us. And I love that about him, the fact that he lets no one penetrate his armor.

Having meals and talking about politics, law, manga, and anime has become normal. Our time together is something I look forward to every day.

Sometimes, he suddenly appears in my house whenever Mom isn't there and either ravishes me or just sits down and watches serial killers with me.

He says it's entertaining, watching me engrossed in those shows.

Lucy changes the subject to a Spanish series she's bingeing on Netflix, but she lacks her usual energy. If I wasn't paranoid about the whole thing with Akira, I'd be sure she's also drifting away.

When we're just outside of our next class, Josh, a guy on the football team, slides in front of us, blocking our path.

He has a tall build, but it isn't buff. His features have this foxy look and when he grins, they become even foxier.

"What?" I go straight to the defensive. We may sit together at lunch, but we're not close by any means. In fact, he joins in on the snickering and snide remarks by Brianna and the others.

"Come on, Naomi. We're friends."

"What's my favorite color?"

"Black."

"It's navy blue. How can you be my friend if you don't even know my favorite color?"

"You act as if Captain knows, too." He scoffs, laughing at his own joke.

That might be true, but it's not like Sebastian and I have any sort of relationship or anything.

All I ever connect to is the beast inside him, really.

So no, I'm not actually hurt that Josh is right and Sebastian doesn't even know my favorite color.

I place a hand to my hip. "Do you have a point?"

"Save me a piece when he's done with you."

"Josh…" Lucy trails off on a reprimand, her gaze flitting between the two of us.

"Come on, we all know it's all a lie." He sizes me up in a sleazy kind of way that makes my skin crawl.

My best friend's face contorts and she looks like when she used to have her intense periods that left her feeling crippled.

Or when she saw Prescott making out with a sophomore the other day.

I place a hand on my hips. "What is that supposed to mean?"

"You're so stupid, you don't even realize it." Josh shakes his head slowly. "Or maybe you're blinded."

"Off you go, Josh."

Our attention turns to Reina, who waltzes to the middle of our small group with her imaginary queen bee crown on top of her head.

She's wearing a stunning pink leather skirt and a peachy-colored top with lace sleeves. Her knee-high boots give her a sophisticated edge only she can pull off.

Josh throws his hands in the air with a surrendering gesture. "I'm just counting the hours."

"Go," she repeats, adding a subtle motion with her chin.

He shrugs and wets his lips. "I want to be next."

And with that, he heads down the hall.

Lucy releases an audible breath while she stares at Reina as if searching for her holy approval.

Our captain's attention is on me as she says, "Go first, Lucy. I need a word with Naomi."

"No, thanks." I flip my hair back. "We're not exactly besties and last time I checked, we don't have alone time."

My friend, however, smiles. "Just cool down, Nao. I'll be inside."

She's my bestie and I love her, but she needs to drop the pacifying manner where everyone needs to come out as the winner.

Once it's only Reina and me, it's like the walls are slowly closing in on me. Still, I summon my bravado. "What now? Are you going to threaten to kick me off the team?"

"Why Sebastian?"

Her question takes me completely by surprise. The way she speaks is detached, cool-headed, which is what I've always loathed about her. Or *maybe admired, as Akira eloquently put it.*

I'm so surprised that it takes me some time to answer. "What type of question is that?"

"One that's simple enough. You always put yourself one step ahead of everyone, so how come you're falling for Sebastian?"

"I'm not falling for him!"

"I might believe that if I hadn't seen the way you look at him. It's like you've waited your entire life for him."

Shit. Shit. "That's not true."

"And now, you're just denying it and it's pissing me off."

"Oh, I'm pissing you off? Good. So how about you take the hint and leave me alone?"

"You can easily get rid of me if you tell me, why him?"

"I didn't really have a choice. He pestered me."

"So you wouldn't have agreed under different circumstances?"

"Of course not. He's a shallow quarterback with nothing behind his physical appearance. He's not my type."

She smiles as her gaze breaks from mine and flits behind me. "Hear that, Bastian? You're not the lady's type."

I swallow as his scent invades my nostrils. Reina gives me a condescending stare before she steps past me into class.

Wincing, I turn around to face him. His features are a makeshift mix of emotions I'm unable to peer through.

In my attempt to shove Reina off my back, I spoke against the thoughts I hold in my very core.

"What are you doing here?" I whisper. He doesn't usually come to our department.

He reaches into his pocket and gets out a bottle of apple juice, my favorite, and throws it in my direction. I catch it between clammy fingers as his detached voice wraps a noose around my throat. "I thought I'd come see you since we didn't have lunch together. I was in for a surprise, apparently."

"About what you heard…"

"Oh, you mean the fact that I'm a shallow quarterback, who's not your type?"

"That's not what I meant."

"Do you always say what you don't mean?"

Yes, and that's why he calls me Tsundere. But there's nothing playful about him right now. If anything, he seems to have taken it personally.

And I hate that, somehow.

I especially hate the monotone way he's speaking to me. As the beast, he's all growly, rough, and demanding. As the man, he's witty and playful. An asshole sometimes, but never this closed off.

When I don't say anything, he turns around and leaves.

"Wait…" I stumble over my words but can't find the right ones.

His broad frame slowly disappears down the hall and my jittery insides catch fire. It's like a part of me is disappearing with him.

Or maybe it's a part of us.

I barely chance a glance at the classroom and the decision to ditch it comes so easily. I'm half-jogging in my attempts to catch up to Sebastian.

Thankfully, I know where he parks his car and I catch up to him right as he starts the engine. I don't think twice as I hop in the passenger seat, panting.

He stares at me. "What are you doing?"

"Going with you."

"Where do you think I'm going?"

"I don't care."

"It could be a dangerous place."

I scoff. "I think I'm used to that already."

"You have no idea how dangerous some addictions can become, Naomi."

"Is that what we have? An addiction?"

"An addiction. An obsession. A madness. Take your pick. Oh, or maybe it's shallow, too."

I release a shaky breath. "I was agitated by Reina and I just didn't want her to know…"

"Know what?"

How deep it really goes for us. Or at least, for me.

But I don't say that or it'll become a reality I'll have to face.

"What we have," I say quietly.

"So we have something. And here I thought I wasn't your type."

"You don't have to be sarcastic."

"Because that's your thing?"

"Stop it."

His eyes darken. "You know I love that word."

The base of my stomach shrivels as blood pumps to my face and neck. Ever since the night he asked me to open up about what happened to me in return for him opening up about himself, Sebastian keeps his monster-self separated from who he is.

This is the first time he's actually alluded to what we do in the dark while being the star quarterback.

Is this progress or just…dangerous?

Clearing my throat, I ask, "Have you ever thought about hurting others?"

"Of course, I have. All the time."

"Why don't you act on it?"

"Because it'll give me a label and a bad reputation."

"And that's so bad?"

"When you come attached with my family name, it is. I need to have a good reputation so no one suspects me."

"Wow." I relax into my seat, fingering the bottle of apple juice as he pulls out of the parking lot. "Since when did you come to that conclusion?"

"Since a boy in elementary school was called a bully for giving me a bloody nose. When the fact was, I broke his toy. No one believed him after he beat me up because in the world's eyes, he had a bad reputation and I was the victim."

"You weren't."

He lifts a shoulder. "They believed it. That's what matters."

"Does that mean everything you do is make-believe?"

"To an extent."

"So…your true self is the beast?"

He smiles, a predatory one. "Is that what you call me in your head?"

"Just answer the question," I blurt, embarrassed to my bones.

"I wouldn't say I'm him entirely. Just like not every part of you is the prey."

"That's what you call me?"

"That or toy."

For some reason, that doesn't feel odd or degrading. I get off on the name-calling during sex, but this feels different. Almost like our secret language.

I stare at Sebastian. Like really stare at him and his sculpted beauty that's fit for models. Why would a person like him get off on that depravity? What turned the boy who was beaten up at school into the beast?

"Do you keep those two facets of you entirely separated?" I ask.

"Maybe."

"It's a yes or no question."

"The answer depends on your answer."

"My answer to what?"

"What happened to you?"

My fingers tremble and I jam the straw into the bottle of juice, then take a long swig. "I was born without a father and… it fucked me up. When I was younger, I looked at other kids and hated my mom for not letting me have a father. Then I thought maybe she had me from one of those fertilization clinics and I was supposed to be fatherless. You might say that's not a big deal. I thought so as well until I realized I wouldn't be the same if I'd had a father. Or maybe I'm just trying to make an excuse and be…normal. Because normal families don't have bad shit happen to them."

"They do." His voice is quiet. "My parents were normal people without much ambition. They were so normal and righteous, they left my grandparents' sides to live a bland life, but they died in an accident, anyway. Striving for normal didn't save them. It may have made their deaths more imminent."

"I'm…sorry."

"Why?"

"Huh?"

"Why are you sorry?"

"Isn't that what people say in these circumstances?"

"I don't get the sentiment behind it. They were my parents and I don't even think of them anymore. Why would you be sorry for their deaths when you didn't know them and didn't have anything to do with it?"

Oh, God. I suspected it before, but I'm almost sure now. "Do you maybe…lack empathy?"

"The ability to understand and share the feelings of someone else."

"I don't want the definition. Do you feel it?"

"I suppose not."

"That's…a form of antisocial characteristics."

"So I've been told."

"By whom?"

"My gazillion therapists and my uncle. They don't want me to be that way, so I managed to make them think I do feel empathy."

"But you don't."

"Your point is? Do you want me to pretend in front of you as well?"

"No. Don't do that."

"Good. I wasn't planning to, baby." He smiles, but I don't return it.

My mind is filled with a thousand theories about him. He's completely different from the Sebastian Weaver I'd painted in my head, and for some reason, I prefer this version a lot more than the fantasy.

Even the imperfections add more to his alluring personality.

He's different, but he's unapologetic about it.

He's different, but he's not fake.

Not like me.

TWENTY-FOUR

Sebastian

SINCE WE DITCHED ANYWAY, I TAKE NAOMI TO MY DEVIL'S lair.

Kidding. Just my apartment.

While I love chasing the fuck out of her in the forest, I want to debauch her in all ways possible inside my home.

I watch her inquisitive gaze as she takes in the modern setting of my house. It's all in gray, black and white. Though, I only saw the world in the two extremes of those colors before her.

Her eyes widen the slightest bit when she watches all her surroundings as if making sure there's always an exit option. Her distrustful nature is cute, but she needs to get rid of it when around me.

I suppose that would happen with time.

I grab an apple bottle juice from the fridge and toss it to her. She catches it, then we sit together on the sofa across from the TV. I inhale her in, filling my lungs with lily and fucking peaches. It's become a fix now, a drug I need constant doses of but could still never get enough

"Why did you bring me here?"

"What type of question is that? To fuck the shit out of you, of course."

A delicate blush covers her cheeks. "Do you have to be crude?"

"Crude is what I do."

She slurps from her juice and lifts her chin. "I want to watch the newest true crime show first."

"Are you seriously picking true crime over fucking?"

"Everyone has different priorities," she teases, struggling to hide her smile, and failing.

"I'm going to have a talk with those serial killers and Netflix for producing them like candy."

"HBO Max, too. And Hulu."

"You think this is funny?"

She nods with a huge grin as she reaches to the remote and turns on Netflix. I steal it out of her hand. "We'll have a bet."

"You and your bets. What now?"

"Are you a scaredy cat?"

She tips her chin defensively. "No!"

"Then you'll win this rather easily."

"Win what?"

"Instead of true crime, we'll watch a horror movie. If you shriek, close eyes or hide, I win. And that means we'll go with my 'fucking the shit out of you' plan, which includes countless orgasms, by the way. If you do none of those, we'll watch true crime. One episode, though, then we'll go back to my plan."

She laughs, the sound is like fucking music to my ears. I love knowing that she's a closed off person on the outside but is a mushy girl with me.

Only *me*.

After she agrees to the bet, I put on The Conjuring. That shit apparently made a few of the cheerleaders cry with horror, as per Owen's retellings, so I trust it'd work.

I don't watch it, though. My entire attention stays on her.

She's still slurping from her juice, but as the time goes by, the straw is there, but she's gulping her own saliva instead of the juice.

Ominous music from the film fills the room which means there'll be a spooky scene soon. I slowly reach a hand behind her, keeping it on the sofa. When the jump is about to happen, I touch her shoulder.

Naomi shrieks, jumping up, then hiding her head in my lap as she throws the bottle of juice away. Her chest hits my thigh and I can sense her skyrocketing pulse.

I burst out laughing as I wrap my arm around her back. "You lose, baby."

"Screw you, okay?" She peeks up at me, making sure to not make eye contact with the screen. "That's cheating."

"I call it gaming the system."

"Asshole."

"You're such a scaredy cat for someone who worships at true crime's shrine."

"They're not the same." She motions at the TV, still hiding. "Can you turn it off?"

"Maybe I want to continue watching it."

"Sebastian!"

"Yes, baby?"

"Don't you want to…you know?"

"I don't know. Why don't you remind me?"

Naomi runs her hand over my dick and although it's through the material of my pants, it's like she stroking my bare skin. My erection jumps to life and she takes it as an encouragement to fasten her pace.

I groan, throwing my head against the sofa.

Her touch is still innocent like the first time, but it's more explorative now, curious. She's a fast learner, my Naomi.

"Turn it off," she coos in a breathy tone.

"Are you going to take me at the back of that pretty throat?"

She licks her lips. "If you want."

"You'll make me nice and wet for when I will fuck you?"

"No."

"No?"

"You'll make me." She bites her lower lip. "Please make me."

Fuck me.

Only she would ask me of these things and make it sound like a fucking erotic dream. Her crazy matches mine, after all, and I'm a lucky bastard to have stumbled upon it.

A low groan spills from me as I fumble for the remote. The moment I turn off the movie, a loud sound echoes in the air.

At first, I think it's a bomb or something. But it comes again. My fucking doorbell.

I dig my fingers into her hair. "Open your mouth."

"Shouldn't you see who is it?"

"Don't fucking care. They will go away."

She's unsure for a second, but I unbuckle my belt and free my cock. Naomi takes me to the back of her throat, just like she promised.

I grab her by the hair. "That's it. Make it nice and wet."

Her eyes meet mine as she sucks and licks, her cheeks hollowing. I'm two seconds away from pushing her on all fours and fucking her on the ground, animal style.

The distinctive sound of a 'Beep' echoes in the silence and I freeze.

Only one person knows the code to my apartment in case of an emergency.

And sure enough, he appears at the threshold of my living room, carrying his briefcase. His expression remains the same as he takes in the scene in front of him. "Am I interrupting something?"

"Fuck, Nate." I hide Naomi with my body so he doesn't see her flushed face or her lips around my dick. The last thing I want is for any man, Nate included, to witness her in this state.

She releases me and scrambles away, her face heated.

I tuck my painfully hard cock in and glare at my uncle aka the fucking cockblocker. "Ever heard of the word privacy?"

"You weren't answering the door or your phone so I thought there was an emergency." He runs his critical gaze over Naomi. "It's a different type of emergency, I see."

She winces, then stands up. "I'm…I'm going to go."

I grab her by the wrist and pull her back to my side. "If anyone needs to leave, it's him."

"Nonsense." Nate places his briefcase on the sofa. "Let's make dinner and talk."

"Or you can walk out of the door and leave us alone?" I suggest.

He ignores me and offers his hand to Naomi. "Nathaniel Weaver. I'm this rascal's uncle and guardian of sorts."

"I'm twenty-one. I don't need a guardian."

"Don't believe what he tells you. He does," Nate whispers to her with his charming smile.

Naomi smiles back, taking his hand. "Naomi Chester. Sebastian and I…study at the same campus."

"The girl from TV has a name," Nate says and she blushes again.

I jump up and break them apart. I don't like that he's using his rare kind persona, and I don't want her to ever think of him as someone charming.

He's my uncle and I hate him right now. Fucking sue me.

"The rascal doesn't bring his girlfriends home."

"We're not really…"

"We are," I say firmly, cutting her off.

Nate smirks and I flip him off. The bastard knows I'm acting out of character and he won't let me live this down.

"Let's have that dinner," he says and heads to the kitchen area.

"Sure." Naomi starts to follow, but I keep her at my side.

"Are you on my side or his?" I hiss in her ear.

"I want to meet your uncle. Besides, you're being rude," she murmurs back.

"He's the one being rude by barging in here," I say aloud.

"I heard that, Rascal."

"Good. Leave, then."

"No."

"Grandma said she wants to see you."

"Hearsay."

"I'll send her a picture that you're here as evidence."

"Circumstantial. Now, come make yourself useful."

Naomi chuckles softly and I poke her side. "What are you laughing at?"

"You and your uncle have a loveable relationship."

"I call it 'he's a pain in the ass' relationship."

"It's loveable, anyway. I like seeing you this way."

"What way?"

"Human, I guess. Real."

"You, however, are always real."

She leans in and kisses my cheek. "I'm more real with you."

Before I can grab her and use PDA to kick Nate out, she slips from between my fingers and goes to the kitchen.

I follow after, grumbling, and contemplating how to get rid of my uncle.

We end up having more fun making dinner, as my uncle and I banter and Naomi joins in the teasing. When we sit down to eat, it feels…like home.

The one I lost when I was six years old.

TWENTY-FIVE

Sebastian

I'M THE HEART OF ALMOST EVERY PARTY THAT'S THROWN on campus. My name is the one people use to invite everyone over.

That's what Owen did tonight.

He turned his parents' house into a club and even invited a trendy DJ that he paid a small fortune for.

That's the thing about Blackwood. If you have money, you're compelled to show it so you're considered part of the *IT crowd*.

It's common in our circle. My own grandmother tells me to throw parties just so she can brag about me in front of her friends. Her usual speech would be something along the lines of:

"Sebastian's grades are so promising. His are even better than Brian's when he was in school."

"Football? Oh, that's just a hobby he'll quit once he's out in the world. Sebastian...tell them how you got an *A* by just contradicting your professor."

A story Grandma likes to retell over and over because, in her mind, it's signed and sealed that I have the political genes that make a Weaver out of me.

So while everyone expects me to like parties, I loathe them.

The only reason I show up is to make an appearance before I disappear into a corner where no one can find me. Then my dark, twisted thoughts attack me and I usually force myself to participate in the mindless fun.

Not tonight, though.

Tonight, my blood is boiling and my fists are clenched around my phone as I search the crowd.

For her.

My toy.

I planned to make her run for it today. It's been a week since I last chased her, even though she's dropped hints in each of our conversations. She was asking me without words why I haven't grabbed her and held her down.

Why I haven't unleashed the beast on the prey.

She's a masochist, my Naomi. Only a few days without our twisted game and she came out of her shell to implore about it.

I brushed off her subtle advances and pretended to be clueless, when, in fact, I've been plotting for tonight.

It's not fun when the prey knows she's going to be chased. Since I sensed that she started to expect it, I had to change gears.

I kept her on her toes all week long, barely touching her beyond a kiss or a dirty fingering as she watched her true crime shows while her mom was in the kitchen.

I didn't always let her finish either.

She called me names and cursed me in both English and Japanese while I merely smirked.

I loved having her on the edge and seeing her flinch every time I got near. I loved her gasps when my fingers plunged inside her and the sound of her muffled moans as she tried her hardest not to orgasm.

But what I loved the most is the anticipation that's been building inside her to the point of overflowing.

It took so much edging to reach that level of torture. I was even tormented in the process, giving myself blue balls. I resorted to masturbating violently, imagining Naomi's cunt strangling me as I held her down. I fantasized about fisting her dark strands around my fingers, sucking on her dusty pink nipples, and clamping my hands on her hips as I fucked her against the ground.

I masturbated to the image of her sprawled out, fighting me as I ravished her tits until she sobbed and her cunt wept for me.

Or the image of her wide, dark eyes as she stared at me while gasping for her orgasm.

Or the image of her clawing and squirming beneath me as her cunt strangled my dick.

But that could only last for so long.

Tonight was supposed to belong to the beast and the toy. But I didn't count on her coming to Owen's party. Not when she's adamant about destroying every form of her social life.

It wasn't until I saw the selfie Lucy posted on social media that I nearly lost it.

I almost lose it again when I spot her in the crowd.

Naomi is wearing a red dress with a completely bare back. The material in the front hardly covers her tits and is bound at her stomach with a golden ring that reveals her belly button.

She looks hot and fucking sinful and I want to rip that dress off her and fuck her with it bunched in her mouth.

But those aren't the only thoughts running rampant in my head. My gaze is zeroed in on every bastard who looks in her direction or licks their lips as they pass her by.

I inhale a deep breath.

I'm not the type who lets their emotions get the better of them, not since I was trained to be cool-headed and never show my intentions in public.

Being an open book is a sure way to become a target. And I was only ever meant to be a predator.

So why the fuck am I fantasizing about pounding every last fucker to the ground?

Owen, Josh, Prescott, and a few others from the football team and the cheering squad surround her like sharks in infested water.

There's Lucy and Reina as well, but I'm blind to them. All I can see are dicks that need to be cut off for looking at my girl while she's dressed like that.

My girl.

I pause at that thought.

Since when did Naomi become my girl?

All this time, all I've ever thought about was the game we played and the jackpot I hit for finding someone compatible with my darkest side. I never considered it anything beyond that.

That's a lie.

I looked forward to spending time with her, to hearing her talk about stupid serial killers and the latest podcast she's obsessed with. Even her rock music is growing on me.

Sometimes, when she falls asleep on the couch, I watch how peaceful she is. She has this weird habit of balling herself into a fetal position with her head lying on her hand.

In the span of a few weeks, I've learned more about her than I have any other human. Like her love for apple juice, her unhealthy obsession with true crime, her passion for rock music, her justice-oriented side since she volunteers for children's organizations.

And most of all, how free she looks when she thinks no one is looking or when she sketches.

They say the more you know someone, the less you like them.

It's the exact opposite for me.

I'm fucking infatuated with this girl. And the twisted sex only plays a small part of it.

Because even without the sex, I feel something is missing if I don't see her for a few hours.

Maybe infatuated isn't the right word, because I'm on the verge of becoming a criminal to ward any unwanted attention off her.

I summon my mask as I stride toward the group. I make sure to creep up from Naomi's back because I like the sound of her small gasp when I startle her. It's similar to when I thrust my fingers inside her tight cunt.

"Are you sure you won't change your mind?" I hear Josh ask her when I'm near. "It should've been me instead of Captain, anyway."

Naomi's brows scrunch in that soft way that makes her tiny features even tinier and her pale complexion paler. She looks like a doll sometimes.

Maybe that's why I've been on a mission to break her.

And keep her.

"What do you mean, it should've been you?" she asks, and it takes all I have not to pummel Josh into the ground. Looks like the extra training I've made him do lately for payback hasn't been enough.

I need to up my game.

Josh darts out his tongue—that will be soon cut off—and licks his lips. "It should've been me."

"You say that as if you would've ever stood a chance." I slide to Naomi's side and subtly wrap an arm around the small of her back. Her pink lips slowly part and I revel in the shiver that takes over her body as I stroke her bare skin with my thumb.

But I don't look at her for long. If I did, I'd want to rip this thing off her here and now, and then I'd need to put that fucker Josh—and everyone who has a similar thought—in their fucking place.

So I fixate him with my neutral expression that makes people intimidated. "You think you're a match for me?"

He releases a nervous laugh that no one returns. "Look, Captain. I was just joking around, man."

"You weren't. I saw the glint in your eyes when you were licking your lips while you were ogling her cleavage. Do that again and I'll jam your teeth to the back of your skull, then use them to rip your balls off your dick."

A collective gasp echoes in the air and then a multitude of clearing throats follow.

They don't know me as the type who threatens. I didn't in the past because I didn't need to. I merely got things done in the background, whether by using forms of manipulation or secret violent incidences that I could get away with.

But I had to put the fucker Josh in his place so he doesn't look in her direction again.

Naomi stiffens by my side, but she remains silent. It's Owen who nudges me and whisper-hisses, "What the fuck was that for?"

I ignore him, still directing the full blow of my hostility at Josh. "Is that fucking clear or do I need to start acting on those threats?"

"Go act like a caveman someplace else," Naomi bites out and elbows me. It's hard and sudden enough that my hold loosens from behind her.

Her cheeks are red and her stomps are harsh and unmeasured as she shoves through the crowd.

I grab Josh by the collar of his shirt and his eyes widen as I whisper, "Next time you look at what's mine or run your loose mouth, it will be your last. Watch your fucking back."

I shove him away and ignore Owen's protests and Reina's coy smile as I follow the path Naomi took.

The crowd of people is so large that it's impossible to find her. Even when it must be hard to run in her skimpy clothes.

I make a whole round before my mind goes in the opposite direction.

I'll chase her, but not through a crowd.

Retrieving my phone, I type.

Sebastian: Go around the pool area and into the west wing.

The tick that indicates she read my message appears immediately. Her reply is back in a second and I can almost imagine her scathing tone if she were to say the words.

Naomi: You don't get to treat me like a piece of meat in front of everyone, you fucking asshole.

Sebastian: He was a problem and I had to take care of it.

Naomi: By being a caveman?

Sebastian: If need be.

Naomi: That's not how it's supposed to be.

Sebastian: None of this is how it's supposed to be, baby. Now, stop making this a fucking event and go where I told you. I'm going to tear through your ass until the whole campus hears your screams tonight.

Maybe that will douse the fire that's been burning inside me since I saw the way that fucker was looking at her.

The dots that indicate she's typing appear and disappear, then reappear again before her reply comes in.

Naomi: What if I don't want to?

Sebastian: You clearly do or you would've broken the spell.

Naomi: You're still an asshole.

Sebastian: Stop tempting me with yours. Now, go. Walk toward the west wing and keep going.

I'm heading there myself, my strides long and purposeful as my breathing deepens with the promise of the hunt.

Owen's parents' house is big enough that they have a few wings. The loud music slowly fades away as I step out of the populated area and stalk in the shadows of the vast garden. The small light coming from the few bulbs gives me a restricted view of the place.

This part of the property is rarely used by Owen's family and is only taken advantage of when they need to ride the horses in the stables.

But that's not why we're here.

The sound of neighing echoes in the air and soon after, I spot the red fabric of Naomi's dress.

She's walking slowly, her gaze shifty as she watches her surroundings. There's nothing I love more than that look of both fear and excitement etched on her beautiful features. The way her lips part and her eyes widen. Even her nostrils flare the slightest bit, but it's not visible in the semi-darkness.

The horses neigh again and Naomi flinches, slapping a hand to her chest.

My dick grows rock fucking hard as I stalk in a parallel line to her, remaining in the shadow of the stables so she doesn't see me.

It'll be fucking worth it when I finally jump her, then tackle her to the ground and take her like the caveman she described me to be.

The light of her phone casts a glow on her face as she types with stiff fingers, her gaze shifting at the slightest sounds.

Soon after, my phone vibrates.

Naomi: And then what?

Sebastian: And then you run.

TWENTY-SIX

Sebastian

I F I SAT DOWN IN FRONT OF ANY OF THE THERAPISTS WHO my grandparents made sign NDAs that basically said their souls would be sold on the black market if they divulged any of my secrets, they would have told me I need coping mechanisms.

Maintenance.

Cognitive behavioral therapy.

Group therapy.

All the good stuff therapists love to sing in different tunes to avoid spelling out the word insane.

You're different, they would say. *It's okay to be different.*

That's about the only thing I came out of therapy with.

Being different could be either a blessing or a curse, depending on how I treat it. If I act like a victim, that's all I'm ever going to be.

If I act like the assailant, however, things could diverge in another direction.

I found out early on that I couldn't be obvious about my purging. And that's when it became tricky. My bursts of violence could only be hidden for so long before my grandparents caught up to my activities.

So I bottled them inside until they began to fester and metaphorically attack my internal organs like cancer, with no cure.

Until her.

The girl who's running because I ordered her to.

Because she wants it as much as I do.

Because she has bursts of violence, too. Only, she's on the receiving end of it.

Her direction is neither methodical nor calculated as she lets her legs carry her across the vast grounds.

My blood pumps hot in my veins and the internal festering I've been experiencing for years disappears. My chest constricts, but my legs stretch and I sprint behind her.

My nostrils flare and my muscles turn rigid with the promise of the chase.

Naomi flinches when her foot catches on something on the ground, but my pretty little toy doesn't stop.

Doesn't pause.

And doesn't ever...*ever* look back.

Like a perfect prey whose only concern is to run away.

She's fast, even with the way her dress clings to her thighs with every move. Even with how her pace is frantic and disorganized at best.

I breathe in her fear that's permeating the air and listen to the sound of her shattered breaths that break the silence of the night. The music from the main house still reaches us, but I don't hear it over my controlled movements and her frantic ones.

Naomi gives it her all. It's never half-assed or a makeshift attempt at escape. She sprints at the highest speed her body allows.

Like she's running for her life.

Sometimes, I believe she's really scared, that deep down, this whole thing has taken on more weight than it should.

Sometimes, I believe it when she begs me to stop and tries to crawl away from me.

Sometimes, I think it's the wiser option to stop.

But I don't. *Ever.*

Because the thing that beats inside me, the beast as she called it, is unrestrained. She shouldn't have given him a taste, because now, all he wants is more.

Even if that ends up destroying both of us.

My pretty toy is fast, despite her short legs, but I'm faster.

She's determined to run, but I'm more hellbent on catching her.

It doesn't take me long to be right at her heels as the sound of my shoes echoes in the air. She squeaks, literally, and that fuels me with an unrestrained lust for violence.

And her.

It's a new urge I didn't know I had until I fucked her on the stairs of her house.

I don't only have the urge for violence now. I have the urge to fuck Naomi, own her, and make her scream.

I have the urge to drag my fingers through her hair, suck on her tits, and watch her fearful yet thrilled expression.

Her pace picks up and I let her believe she can get away from me. The prey tastes sweeter when she thinks there's a way out.

There isn't.

Not from me, anyway.

And definitely not for Naomi.

She darts around in a zigzag pattern, probably thinking she can lose me that way. I block her right, forcing her to change direction toward a cottage Owen and I visited not so long ago.

Her eyes widen when they land on the small building, probably not expecting to find it at the corner of the vast piece of land.

Her moment of hesitation is all it takes to bring her down.

My hand shoots forward and I grab a hold of her nape. The

scared squealing sound she releases is music to my ears. Even her scent of lily and peaches is mixed with the primitive smell of fear.

Her limbs flail around as she squirms and attempts to free herself from my hold, to no avail.

It's cute that she thinks she can fight me. Even after all this time of being effortlessly subdued by my strength, she's never gone down without a fight.

She likes it, she said once.

The fight. The wrestling. The clawing.

She likes toying with the beast and provoking him for more. But most of all, she likes leaving her mark on me as much as I leave it on her.

I clutch her wrists and yank them behind her back, then fist my other hand in her hair. "Not a fucking word."

"No...please..." Her lips are trembling more than usual. Her pulse beating even harder than the last time I fucked her against a tree in the forest.

For a normal person, that would've been a red flag, something to back out from, but my beast roars to the surface, taking control of me.

All I see is red.

On her skin.

On her cunt.

Everywhere around her.

"Please...*please*..." Her voice breaks and wetness shines on her lids.

"Shut your fucking mouth." I push her inside the cottage and she stumbles, her legs nearly failing her before she gets back up again.

I hit the light switch with my shoulder and I kick the door closed behind us. Interruptions are the last thing I want for what I'm planning for her.

Naomi freezes, her wild dark eyes studying our surroundings.

Her gaze flits around the space that's completely filled with mirrors. Owen's mother collects them or something.

My toy's dark, mesmerizing eyes are big and dilated as they meet mine through the mirror across from us. Her petite lips part and her chest rises and falls harshly as the realization of where I've brought her slowly registers.

My gaze holds hers hostage as I speak. "You will watch your face as I fuck you. You'll look at how fucking wanton you become when my dick fills that tight cunt of yours."

Her head shakes the slightest bit. I wouldn't have perceived it if it weren't for my hold on her hair.

"No…please…please…don't…" Her eyes beg me more than her words. The way they widen, filling with fresh unshed tears. The way they soften until she looks like the most breakable I've seen.

And that's all that my beast sees. The need to ruin her.

"You came here dressed like a slut. Is that what you want to be treated as? Do you want your cunt filled with my cum?"

"No…"

"How about your ass?"

"No…please…"

"Have you had anyone in that tight hole of yours, my filthy slut?"

"No…"

"So it's as virgin as your cunt was when I first took it?"

"Yes…"

"Will you bleed for me this time, too?"

"Please don't hurt me…please…stop…"

It's a game of ours. Her *please, no* means *yes, please* and her *stop* means *go on*.

I shove her down and she gasps as her knees hit the floor. Then I release her hair and lift her up so her ass is in the air. She tries to look back, but I smack her on her half-visible ass cheek. "Eyes ahead. Look at your flushed cheeks."

She's hesitant for half a second before complying. Soon after, her dark gaze meets mine through the mirror. Her wrists are in my hand at her back. Her shoulder blades and her cheek hit the floor as I feel up the round globes of her ass.

Every time she sucks in a breath or releases what resembles a mewling sound, my touch becomes rougher and more demanding.

I rip down her panties and inhale her sweet arousal. It smells different from when she's compliant or when I shove my fingers inside her cunt at her house.

It's more potent now, more enticing. More...terrified.

I hit her ass and she startles, then as if out of a trance, she fights.

Fuck how she fights.

Her tiny body jerks and her legs try to kick me in the balls, even when the elastic of her panties leave red lines around her thighs.

My dick is rock fucking hard against my jeans as I hold her tighter, showing her who's in charge.

I spank her again and she jolts, a sob tearing from her throat and bouncing off the walls. "Stop...please..."

My hand flattens against her firm globe of flesh and what resembles a moan mixes with her whimpers. "Please...please..."

"That's it. Beg me for it. Beg me to fill your cunt with my dick."

Her eyes widen as they lock on my lighter ones through the mirror.

I don't recognize the manic look in my eyes, the complete abandon and the fucking need for more.

More of her.

Of this.

My nails sink into the softness of her flesh hard until she gasps. "Do it. Beg."

"W-what?"

"You'll beg for it like a good slut tonight. Say, please fill my holes with your cum."

She shakes her head, but it's hesitant—lost, even. But one thing doesn't lie. The reddening of her cheeks as she fixates on me.

"Beg for it, Naomi."

Her lips part, probably because it's the first time I've used her name during our fucked-up fantasy.

We've had some sort of an unspoken rule that says we're different people during the chase. I'm the beast and she's the toy.

I'm the monster and she's the prey.

But I couldn't give a fuck about any of that tonight.

Maybe it's because of the way she looks in the sexy-as-sin dress or how her body feels hotter. Or maybe, somewhere in my brain, she's already evolved to more.

The fucked-up sex was once all the connection we had, but now, it goes hand in hand with everything we have.

Breaking the invisible rule might not be the wisest thing to do, but I couldn't care less.

Maybe she couldn't care less either, because her tongue darts out to lick her lips before she whispers, "Please…"

"Please what? Say the fucking words."

"Please fill me."

"With what?"

"Your cum… Please fill me with your cum."

I don't even know how the fuck I have the presence of mind to free my dick. All I can register is her whimper as I slam inside her wet heat. She's soaking, but her expression contorts as I go all the way in.

I like it when I hurt her. Her body naturally submits to mine and she releases these small noises that make me harder. Her expressions of both awe and pain that I can't get enough of.

Or her.

Because that's what this is all about.

Her.

It might have started with my twisted urges, but they soon mixed with her own fantasies, and now we're just two fucked-up souls feeding off each other's depravity.

We're two monsters who made peace with the darkness.

An animalistic groan spills from me as I pound into her. "Beg, Naomi. Beg me for more."

"Please…give it to me. Please…" She strains, moaning, and her breathy voice is the sexiest thing I've ever heard.

"Harder?"

"Yes…yes…yes…hurt me…fuck me…"

"Rougher?"

"Yes!"

"Like this?" I pull back almost all the way, then pound back in while my finger forces entry into her ass.

She shrieks her orgasm as her cunt strangles me. "Yes…yes… please…please…more!"

"Do you want me to tear into this tight hole as well, my dirty whore? Want me to stretch it so I'm the first one there?"

"Please!"

I didn't think I would ever enjoy hearing her say yes or beg for my rough, unapologetic side, but my dick thickens inside her. The mere sound of her voice is an aphrodisiac made for me.

Only me.

I coat another finger with her juices and ram it into her tight hole. She bucks off the floor, her back arching, but she's completely helpless as she rides out her orgasm.

Her back hole contracts around my fingers, the tight ring of nerves swallowing me in.

"I can't…please…" She sobs. "You're too big in my pussy… I can't fit you there…"

I release her wrists and she falls on her elbows, but instead of attempting to escape, she stumbles back into position.

My voice drops in volume and I feel the shiver in her when I speak. "You think I fucking care?"

As if possible, both her cunt and ass clench around me and I use the chance to thrust in a third finger, slower this time, lubing her with her own juices.

Naomi's shriek is one of both pleasure and pain as tears cascade down her cheeks.

"Do you feel me stretching you so you can take my dick?"

She lowers her head, but I grab her by the hair, fingers digging into her scalp as I pull my fingers and dick out of her. "Look at me own every fucking hole you have to offer."

Tears fill her eyes, but a look of complete ecstasy covers her features as I slam into her tight hole.

"Oh, fuck…" I bite my lower lip as my balls slap against her ass cheeks.

Naomi screams a piercing sound that nearly pops my eardrums. Her face is flushed red as her tears wash over her wretched expression.

I stop for a second as her stiff back muscles stretch around me.

"Don't…stop." She gasps, then blurts, "Don't stop. Please don't stop!"

"I wasn't planning to."

What seems like a relieved expression paints her face before she sobs. "Fuck me…fuck me harder, Sebastian."

She doesn't have to ask me twice.

I drive into her with a level of madness I haven't felt before. One where it's only me and her.

I don't give a fuck if it's the beast and the toy or the quarterback and the cheerleader.

All I need is her strangling me, crying, begging for more.

Then begging me to stop.

Then begging for more all over again.

My balls hit her firm ass with every thrust, making her cry out until her voice is hoarse.

My deep, guttural growl fills the air as I come inside her.

I don't even think about it as I ejaculate all the way in, filling her with my cum until she's mewling, whether in pleasure or pain, I have no clue.

One thing's for certain, though. We broke some sort of a glass wall between us tonight. It might have been invisible before, but it was always there, stopping us from going too deep.

Too raw.

Too hard.

Now, there's nothing to stop us.

Not even ourselves.

TWENTY-SEVEN

Naomi

THERE'S INTENSE AND THEN THERE'S WHATEVER THE hell just happened.

A few weeks ago, I wouldn't have dreamt something like this would be my reality. That I would reach the level of depravity I only watched in true crime shows.

But this is different.

What Sebastian and I have is more dangerous than some deviant sexual behavior serial killers possess.

We don't fantasize about hurting people; he fantasizes about hurting me, and I fantasize about being hurt by him and being the subject of his rough desires.

It's probably not that simple, though, is it?

Because no matter how twisted we become, we're still thirsty for more.

I know I am.

Fuck Akira and anyone who judges me for my fantasies that I'm not using to hurt anyone.

After our breathing levels out, I'm well prepared for

Sebastian to leave me on the floor and never turn back. It's his modus operandi, and using names won't change that.

At least, that's what I thought.

As I attempt to crawl into a standing position and beg Luce to drive me home, strong arms wrap around me, imprisoning me in place.

I startle, a small gasp falling from my lips as I grip Sebastian's strong shoulders for balance.

He brings me down so we're both lying on a small carpet that barely fits both of us. He pulls me closer so I'm lying on his chest and his steady heartbeat is right beneath my ear.

Even his pulse is as strong as him. Steady, powerful, and alluring.

The pads of his fingers stroke my shoulder blade in a steady rhythm. I catch a glimpse of us in the mirror across the room. The image is different from when he was taking my ass savagely and without holding back.

We're naked after he stripped us both earlier. Our scattered clothes form a mess on the floor. But that's the last thing I'm focused on when his strong body spoons around me. His leg is thrown over mine as if he's forbidding me from running.

Or maybe he seeks the closeness.

But that doesn't make sense. Why would he when our arrangement has been clear and direct since the beginning?

We're using each other and that's all, right?

He does pursue me afterward, but that's only after he's spent some time away. Be it half an hour or even a few minutes.

There always needs to be some distance put between us so the beast can morph into the man I know. The star quarterback with a fan page that worships at his feet and even knows his morning routine.

Not that I'm stalking him on social media or anything.

I'm not that desperate.

Oh, shut up, Naomi.

Anyhow, point is, this is the first time Sebastian has gotten close right after he's finished.

Maybe he's still the beast.

Maybe he's not done tormenting me.

Though the promise of another round causes my core to throb, I really don't think I'll be able to take it. I can already feel the soreness in my ass and even my pussy. I need to go home and rub some oil on it.

And yeah, I kind of have a collection of those ever since this crazy asshole started chasing me.

"What are you doing?" I murmur, staring at his reflection in the mirror.

Sebastian is entranced by the back and forth of his finger on my shoulder as if he's relearning something about his anatomy—or mine. "What type of question is that?"

"A simple one. You...shouldn't be here right now."

"Then where should I be?"

"I don't know...outside?"

"So you want a wham-bam-thank-you-ma'am kind of thing?"

"That's not what I meant."

His fingers crawl up my shoulder to my collarbone until he wraps them around my throat. The hold isn't tight, but the threat is there. Even the subtle drop in his voice is an indication of his mood. "Whether I leave or stay is only up to me to decide, so how about you get used to that, baby?"

He's calling me baby, so he can't be in his beast mode right now.

"How am I supposed to take it?" I taunt.

"Like a good girl."

"Don't call me that."

"Do you prefer being called a good slut?"

"Stop it." My cheeks burn. "I don't appreciate being called a slut outside of...you know."

"That, I do know." He loosens his grip but doesn't release me as he fingers the pulse point.

"How…do you know?"

"We've been together for long enough that I can read your body language. It's the first thing I notice about people."

"Why?"

"Hmm." His voice is absentminded, seeming deep in thought. "I think it's because I was taught to be mindful of what type of image I project onto the world."

"And that gave you the opportunity to learn about people's body language?"

"Yes."

"Just like that?"

"Just like that. You would be surprised how much people divulge about themselves with a simple gesture. A rub of the nose, sweaty hands, fidgeting, or even looking at a person for too long gives me a hint of their state of mind."

"Only a hint? Why not the whole picture?"

"Because it's never enough. Their clothes, posture, and way of talking are what completes it. Usually, one meeting is enough to determine whether the person is a friend or foe."

"What category was I in?" I tease.

Sebastian's expression, however, is blank. Only his furrowed brow is an indication of what I assume is confusion. Or maybe it's displeasure.

"Neither," he says quietly.

"I thought those were the only categories you have. Are there others I should know about?"

"Not yet."

"Come on, that's not fair."

"Never claimed to belong to that neurotypical category."

"Because you read people?"

"Because I tactfully avoid the bad kind."

"Aren't you bad yourself?"

"Depends on the circumstances."

"Such as?"

"Being threatened, for instance."

"Considering your selective skills, you'd be able to prevent danger. You should become a detective."

"Long hours for minimum wage? No, thanks."

"Greedy, too, I see."

"I'm not greedy. I just recognize my worth. It'd be an insult to my IQ to follow a career that won't lead me anywhere."

"So helping people get justice leads nowhere?"

"Depends on your definition of justice."

"There are more than one?"

"Of course. What do you think of when the word justice comes to mind?"

"That people should pay for what they've done."

"That's just simplistic."

I hit his shoulder. "And what's your non-simplistic view?"

"Justice is a system that's been put in place so the powerful can get away with their wrongdoings under the blanket of righteousness. They legalized their barbaric ways and made laws to protect themselves from naive fools who still think that good will always win. Like all systems, justice is daily tampered with so that truths are twisted and the innocent are wrongly accused for no other reason than being a convenient scapegoat for the people who call the shots."

"Wow. That's such a cynical view of the world."

He raises his brow, a small smile tugging on his lips. "You of all people ought to understand that since you're sarcastic about everything."

"Being sarcastic doesn't make me cynical."

"With your dark sense of humor, it does."

"I don't have a dark sense of humor."

He lifts his hand and shows it to me. "See that?"

I frown. "What?"

"The black covering my hands when I accidentally touch your humor."

"Not funny." I fight a smile as I run my fingers over the script of his tattoo. "What does this mean?"

"My mind is my only cage."

"That's beautiful, especially coupled with the Japanese one. Did someone translate them for you?"

"No."

"So you translated it yourself? That's impressive. Usually people get all sorts of wrong stuff tattooed on them. I can speak for Japanese, but I heard it happens for Arabic, too."

He raises a brow. "Is my Japanese correct?"

"Perfectly. When did you get them?"

"When I was eighteen."

"I wish I was brave enough to get one."

"We'll go together and get matching tattoos."

For some reason, that idea doesn't seem so crazy to me. I snuggle into him as a chill travels down my spine. He's so warm, and I don't only mean physically.

There's something about him that I'm slowly learning. He has a black and white view of the world but acts as if it's gray. In a way, he's emulating feelings he doesn't have and I find that utterly fascinating.

Is it a defense or a coping mechanism? Or maybe he really is antisocial.

At any rate, all I want is to learn more about him, because apparently, I've been fooled by his image all this time.

When I shiver again, he reaches for his jacket and throws it over my nakedness. "Though it's a pity to hide your tits."

"Are you a sex addict?" I joke.

"Maybe. Who knows?" He lifts a shoulder as if that's a normal occurrence. "Now, back to your beloved justice. Do you still believe in it?"

"I do. I believe in the concept that what goes around comes around."

"Isn't that karma?"

"Another form of how justice manifests."

"Why?"

"Why what?"

"Why do you believe in justice?"

I lick my lips and I can feel my walls slowly crumbling. Maybe it's the fact that our conversation is so easy or that I appreciate him holding me instead of leaving me a bit too much.

At any rate, the words leave me easier than I would've ever thought. "When I was in kindergarten, there were a bunch of white girls who bullied me. One of them said I was yellow like a banana and often called me names. She told me her mom said that it's because of yellow people like me coming here all the time that her dad can't find a job. Due to the constant jabs and bullying, I didn't want to go to school anymore, even though I loved my kindergarten teachers. I hid in my closet and refused to come out. But one day, Mom grabbed me by the elbow and yanked me out of there.

"'Did you do something wrong, Nao-chan?' she asked me and when I shook my head, she said, 'Then why are you hiding as if you did?' So I explained the situation with big ugly tears. I felt so wronged, so victimized, and it made me frustrated. I thought Mom would share my feelings, but her expression remained stern as she told me, 'Don't be scared of people who judge you because of the color of your skin or where you came from. Look them in the eyes and show them with action that you're here to stay.' And I did. I got back to school and didn't bow down. When they became vicious, I became just as vicious. Soon after, that girl and her friends lost interest and stopped bothering me."

Sebastian remains silent for a beat before he asks, "Is that why you believe in justice?"

"It's part of the reason. The other part is because I need it to be real."

"What for?"

"So those who hurt people weaker than them pay." My voice breaks at the end and it doesn't escape his notice.

He stares down at me and I lower my gaze as I swallow. "I was nine and he was Mom's boyfriend."

I feel the way he turns rigid, how his muscles become as hard as granite. When he speaks, his voice is tight and closed, "What did he do?"

"He came into my room when Mom stepped out to do some late-night work. She didn't usually leave me alone with him and he hadn't made a move on me before. But I knew, somehow, since I didn't feel comfortable around him. It was as if he was biding his time for the right moment.

"For that night. I remember…waking up startled as if I'd had a nightmare, but I couldn't remember it. I recall my hazy vision slowly getting used to the darkness, to the motifs of the sun on my curtains, the curves of them and the way they seemed like headless monsters in the darkness. I've never forgotten that sight, even twelve years later. I also remember the scent of alcohol, pungent and harsh to my nostrils. It's why I don't like drinking much, even now. It's strange how the brain remembers things like that, but I couldn't erase them if I tried.

"It took me a few disoriented seconds to realize there was a heavy weight perching over my small body and hands feeling up my chest and between my legs. I remember wanting to vomit as a coaxing voice told me to stay quiet, whispered it with his alcohol-scented breath near my ear. But then…I lost track of it all. It was dark, too dark, and there were screams. I think they were mine, at least at some point. I swear there was red, too. Like blood. It was sticky and all over my fingers and face, but I don't remember how it got there. I don't even remember how I fainted.

"The next time I woke up, I was tucked against my mom's

chest as she cried softly in my hair. It was the first and last time I've seen her cry. She's more powerful than the world itself, my mom. She's the strongest woman I know, but she was weeping like a child. I couldn't return those emotions because grief wasn't what I was feeling back then. It was anger. Blind, ugly anger. I was mad at her for leaving me with him. I think I've been mad at her since because justice didn't happen. She just cut off ties with that scum and he got to move on with his life as if he didn't ruin mine. She let him get away with it so he could find others to prey on."

Burning tears prick my eyes when I'm finished and the sting hurts just like the memories from that night. As foggy as they are, they're still there.

Haunting.

Taunting.

The red night made me who I am, whether I like to admit it or not.

It made me scared of people, of attachment, of allowing anyone close.

And most of all, it made me grow apart from the only family I have. My mom.

Sebastian remains quiet even as his finger strokes my throat.

I sniffle, waiting for long beats and getting nothing. Did I divulge too much? Should I somehow take it back?

"What's his name?" he finally asks.

"Why are you asking?"

"Answer the question."

"Sam."

"Sam what?"

"Miller. Sam Miller."

He nods as if satisfied, but he doesn't say anything, his gaze lost someplace else.

"Why do you want to know his name?"

"Just curious."

"That's all you have to say after what I just told you?"

He breathes deeply for a few beats. "I also understand why you enjoy being my prey."

"You think I'm depraved, don't you?"

"I think you're brave."

"How can someone who enjoys the repetition of their child-hood trauma be brave?"

"It's not the repetition you enjoy."

"I obviously do."

"No. You enjoy knowing that you can end it at any time. You're brave to recognize what you want while having control over the situation. So, in a way, you like having the power you weren't fortunate enough to possess back then."

My lips part. "Are you…using your people-reading technique on me?"

"I always have, Tsundere."

I clear my throat. "Let's pretend what you're saying is true…"

"There's no pretending. You and I know it is."

"Fine. Let's take it from that perspective. If I enjoy it for the control, why do you enjoy it?"

"For domination."

"But I can end it at any time."

"But you don't."

"I could."

"But you wouldn't."

"How do you know that?"

"You're addicted to this as much as I am. You love being fucked hard until your voice turns raw and you're sobbing through your tenth orgasm."

"That…still means I could use the words."

"You won't, because you know that will destroy the connection we have."

"And let me guess. You get off on that type of domination?"

"Besides the one where I throw you down and dick you into the nearest object, yes. But that's not all."

"Your need for violence?"

I Ie nods. "I've had it since I was the lone survivor of the accident that took away my parents."

"I'm sorry."

"I told you to stop apologizing for things you had no hand in."

"It's in my nature. We can't all be emotionless vaults like you, who only feel when violence is involved."

"That's the thing." He looks at me funny. "My urge for violence has become less important since you."

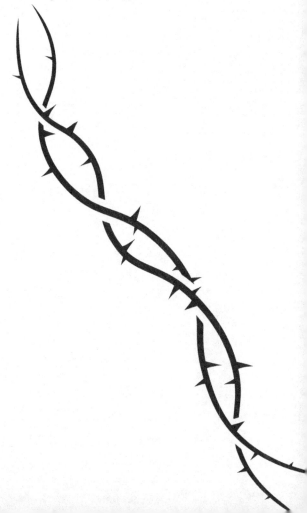

TWENTY-EIGHT

Naomi

YOU KNOW THAT FEELING WHEN YOU'RE SO EXCITED, YOU can't stay still?

When your fingers keep clenching and unclenching to do something and you feel like throwing up from the strength of those emotions?

That's me right now.

I skip over the steps as I go downstairs. I'm humming along with a tune from a rock song I was blasting first thing this morning while I got ready.

Today, I abandoned my headphones in my room and I even wore a short dress with pink and white stripes. Mom made me this one for my birthday two years ago and I never wore it. I was even mad that she'd think I'd appreciate something so cheerful.

Today, I'm in the mood for brightness. For…happiness, I guess.

After last night, there are no other words to describe what I feel right now. Not only did I have a heart-to-heart with

Sebastian, but I also ripped open the stitches and allowed a weight to lift off my chest for the first time since that red night.

The therapists don't count. They thought my negative emotions toward my mother were toxic. That I was destroying the mother-daughter relationship we could be having. They secretly judged me for it and I secretly saw my mom reflected on their faces.

Sebastian, however, didn't. He didn't call me a freak or irrational.

He understood.

Not only that, but he told me things about himself, too. Instead of going back to the party, we kept on talking. Me, about my dad and how I hired a PI to find him just so he could tell me that he's most likely dead. And Sebastian told me about his uncle and how they have a power struggle against his grandparents.

Nathanial Weaver intrigued me since I met him that time. Not only is he cool, collected, but he also seems to be the only person Sebastian respects enough to hold on a high pedestal.

I say respect because I don't think he's capable of caring. At least, not in the traditional sense of the word. But even that doesn't stop me from celebrating the fact that I feel more emotionally close to him than I have been with anyone else before.

Even Lucy doesn't know about how deep my mess goes. She's aware of my 'daddy issues' but not really my 'mommy' ones. She always looks up at Mom and says she's this strong, independent woman that she strives to become one day.

That makes one of us.

After I got home last night, I was in such a delighted mood that I sat down and wrote a letter, too. This time, I sent it.

Dear Akira,

I know you said you don't want to listen to me whine or talk about my problems, but you're going to. Deal with it or stop writing me.

But even if you do, that doesn't mean you'll get rid of me. In case you didn't notice, you're kind of stuck with me and my antics. Again, deal with it, you grumpy asshole.

You said I'm just someone who's pretending their life is hard and that I whine more than I take action. You might be right, but fuck you, Akira.

Fuck you for judging me and kink-shaming me because it makes you feel good about yourself. Are you the morality police? Or are you just scared about trying out your own kink? And don't tell me you have none, because you mentioned breath play porn once and that's too specific to not be a fetish. But instead of finding someone who gets off on the same thing, you probably only jerk off to staged porn.

Fuck you for implying that I'm pathetic and sick just because I went for what I want.

Fuck you for thinking anything two consenting adults do is wrong when you're the one who's screwed in the head.

Because you know what? I'm brave enough to stand up for what I want. Instead of running away, I barged in the middle of the scary storm and embraced it. What did you do?

Aside from hiding behind your pen and jabbing at me to enable your grandiose self-esteem.

Guess what? That self-esteem of yours is merely inflated, just like the thought that you actually have any type of moral compass.

And no, Akira, I don't have that compass when it comes to my needs. And the person you described as being as perverted as I am is the one man who didn't judge me.

Unlike you, asshole.

Go hang a talisman. You'll need it when Yuki-Onna storms through your window at night.

The very opposite of love,
Naomi

He'll probably send back a scathing reply, but I couldn't care less at this point. I'm not letting Akira or anyone else tell me that I'm doing something wrong. Not after what happened last night between me and Sebastian.

And it's not only about how I'm walking funny today, despite the number of oils I rubbed on myself or the hours I spent soaking in the bath.

It's not about how utterly satisfied I am, both physically and mentally.

It's the fact that a bridge has been built between us. Before, we were only ever forced to be beast and prey.

Now it's different.

Now, a new emotion has blossomed between us and I have every intention of exploring it. That's part of the reason why I woke up in an excellent mood.

All I want is to go to school and see his face.

Maybe kiss him, too.

Maybe watch him practice.

Maybe provoke him so he'll chase me.

My wild train of thoughts scatters when the sound of arguing comes from the living room.

Mom is talking rapid-fire as two male voices try to interrupt her. I usually wouldn't bat an eye at the sound of people in the house since she brings her staff over for meetings all the time.

The fact that they're all speaking in Japanese is what makes me pause.

"I said no." Mom's voice is hard—more than usual, that is—and I can sense tendrils of her anger simmering to the surface.

"You don't have a choice Sato-san," a man says with a hint of suppliance.

"Never have, for that matter," another one speaks, and the calm in his tone somehow causes sharp needles to erupt at the base of my neck.

"Get out of my house," Mom shrieks. "Both of you, out!"

"You're making a grave mistake, just like you did twenty-two years ago," the first one says. "Be rational, Sato-san."

"I lost that part of me the day I lost that last name. It's Chester now, and I will not be intimidated by you or *him*. Tell him that the days of me running away are over. Do you hear me? They're *over*."

"That's not very wise, Sato-san," the second man emphasizes.

"She said her last name is Chester." I step out of the shadows, my fists balled at my sides. Mom and I have our differences, but I would beat anyone who bullies her the hell up.

Not that I thought anyone was able to bully my mom, who's always been larger than life and just as intimidating.

Three pairs of eyes slide to me. Mom's are frantic. The two men's are contemplative at best.

One is short and older, around his mid-thirties. The other is taller, leaner, and looks way younger, probably around my age. Both men are Asian and are wearing dark suits with a white shirt and no ties. The taller one has black button earrings and what appears to be a tattoo of a snake peeks from his collar up the side of his neck. His looks are discreet, like some sort of a smart accountant who somehow turns out to be a serial killer.

A shiver rattles me at the way he's watching me with an intent that could break stones. His gaze is sharper than that of the other one, who has a round face and a bland stare.

I inch closer to Mom so we're both facing them and whisper, "Who are these people?"

"No one you should worry about," she says in English, then switches to Japanese. "Leave right now or I'll call 911."

"If you could, you would've done that already," the short one replies in the same language.

"I'll call them if you don't leave us in peace," I say in Japanese while I point my phone at them as if it's some sort of a weapon.

The taller man smiles, but it's predatory at best. Or maybe it's amused. I'm not sure which way to read the glint in his eyes.

He offers me his hand. "My name is Ren. Pleased to meet you, Hito—"

Mom steps in front of me like a mama bear ready to cut a bitch down. Her words are growly and deep. "Leave. Now."

"You're making a grave mistake," the shorter one tells her.

The tall one, Ren, peers over Mom, which isn't hard since she's short, and smiles at me. The feeling of being targeted hits me again. "We'll meet again…Naomi-san."

Mom looks ready to grab a bat—or better yet, her gun—and shoot them down, but they bow, perfectly demonstrating Japanese manners, and then waltz out the door.

Neither Mom nor I bow back, which is considered rude. Our feet remain caged in place as we watch the front door until their car, a black van, leaves the property.

Wait.

A black van?

Images of the van that followed me a few weeks ago slip back in my mind, but I quickly shoo them away. I'm making up stories again and that's never a good thing.

Mom's posture relaxes a little, but she doesn't lose the sharp look in her dark eyes or stop breathing harshly through her teeth.

It's the first time I've seen her beside herself since the red night. She has always acted cool and collected, and I actually started to doubt if she has a heart or if it was replaced by ice at some point.

"Who were those men, Mom?"

"No one."

"They were clearly someone. Are they from your past?"

Her gaze snaps in my direction and her pupils are so dilated, it's like she's on drugs. "Why are you saying that?"

"They called you by your old last name."

"Right. That."

"What other reason would there be for me saying that?"

"It's nothing."

"There's obviously something going on. Why did Ren say 'pleased to meet you, Hito'? Do I have another name?"

She purses her lips. "Your only name is Naomi Chester. That's all you need to know. And erase that motherfucker's name from your memories. You didn't meet a Ren."

"But—"

"Go to school, Nao. You'll be late."

I want to argue and be mad. I want to demand being in the know about things happening in both our lives, but the weary look on her face stops me. Dark circles line the bags under her eyes and her face is a pale shade of white.

It's been that way for a few weeks now. Is she even sleeping properly?

I should get her one of those sleep aids from the pharmacy later.

While I don't want to make a big deal out of it, I also can't pretend as if nothing happened. "I'm not a little girl anymore, Mom. I can sense when things are wrong, no matter how well you hide it. So instead of keeping me in the dark, how about you just…talk to me?"

Her expression softens a little, her voice softer, lower. "How about you?"

"Me?"

"Will you talk to me, Nao-chan?"

"About what?"

"About why you no longer look me in the eyes for more than a second and how you don't kiss me goodnight anymore."

"I'm not a little girl."

"I can see that." She smiles a little. "You even have a boyfriend."

"Sebastian isn't my boyfriend."

"Is that why you make out when you think I'm not looking?"

My cheeks flame as images of what we did rush back in. "You saw that?"

She nods. "He looks like a good kisser."

"Mom!"

"Fine…fine. I won't tease you about your first boyfriend."

"I had Barry from middle school."

"The one you dumped because he didn't like anime and manga?"

"Barry made fun of me for reading manga."

"Sebastian doesn't?"

"No." I kick an imaginary rock. "He…even thinks my sketches are cool."

"That's because he has a good eye."

"Thanks," I say awkwardly, lowering my head as I make my way to the door.

"Nao-chan?" she calls after me in an affectionate tone that she hasn't used since I was young.

I stare at her over my shoulder. "Yeah?"

"Come home early. I need to tell you something."

I pause at the vulnerability in her voice and the way she grabs the cigarette pack and fingers it, but then I whisper, "Okay."

I've been wanting her to talk to me for a long time, but why do I have a feeling that this might not be what I bargained for?

At all.

TWENTY-NINE

Naomi

I'M STILL THINKING ABOUT THE WEIRD ENCOUNTER WITH those two men during my morning classes.

It's impossible not to, considering all the facts that line up.

They knew Mom's old name.

They're Japanese.

They drive a black van.

Oh, and one of them was so pleased to meet me that he called me a different name altogether.

I hope I'm just being paranoid and that whatever Mom will tell me doesn't have anything to do with them.

The moment I dismiss any thoughts of them, they rush back in. Especially Ren.

There's something about Ren.

But what?

"Nao! Are you listening?" Lucy waves a hand in front of my face.

"Oh, sorry." I grimace as I shove my books into my bag after the professor leaves. I'm ready to get to lunch and lose myself in Sebastian. "What did you say?"

Lucy rolls her eyes. "I was asking if you were too busy boning to answer my text."

"Luce!" I cast a glance at our surroundings before I murmur, "Who even says boning anymore?"

"I do. Besides, everyone knows you and Sebastian are…a thing."

"We're not a thing."

"What are you then?"

I weigh my words as we step out of the lecture hall. Really, what are we? Mom called him my boyfriend and Lucy implied we're a thing. Is that what we are? A couple?

We might not have started under traditional circumstances, but we started. We're…there. Or here, or whatever.

Our relationship is no longer only sexual. Maybe it has never been only sexual from the beginning.

"We're just us," I tell Lucy with a grin.

"Nao…" she trails off, then clears her throat. "Maybe you shouldn't get too comfortable in Sebastian's company."

"Why?"

"Well…he's a Weaver and the quarterback, and all of that comes with attention."

"I'm fine." *So far.*

"Are you sure? Because he's popular and has that whole limelight thing you hate so much."

"Oh, come on, Luce. Spare me the hypocrisy. I hate Reina and her mean girls, but I didn't ask you to not be comfortable in their company. I never whined about how you spend most of your time at her house, playing dress-up and worshipping the goddess of beauty to keep you forever young. I respected your choice, so please respect mine."

"You're right." She gulps. "I was out of line. I'm sorry."

"It's okay. I didn't mean to be bitchy."

"I'm just worried about you, Nao. I've never seen you this lost in a man before. I thought it was just a crush, but it's turning into something a lot deeper than that."

"Don't worry, it's just a crush." *With depraved sex.* But I spare Lucy the details.

My phone vibrates and I smile when I see his name.

Sebastian: I'm running late because of Coach. Wait for me before you start eating.

Sebastian: I have something of yours.

He attaches a picture of his veiny hand holding a bottle of apple juice.

I grin like an idiot as I type.

Naomi: I had juice this morning.

Sebastian: Not my special type. Prepare that mouth for me.

Naomi: Stop it.

Sebastian: I was talking about the juice. Where did your mind go, baby?

My cheeks catch fire as I shove the phone back in my pocket and listen to Lucy talking about our upcoming exams. There's still a big game for the Black Devils this Friday, so we'll lose an entire evening—and the days leading up to it.

Scoffs and groans echo in the air as Lucy and I approach the table where the cheer squad and the football players sit.

My guess is that it's more about me rather than my best friend, who awkwardly sits down.

I join her, too, pretending to be oblivious to the animosity as I swing my bag to my side.

They wouldn't be this obvious about it if Sebastian was sitting me on his lap. Lucy said whenever anyone attacks me, he'll level them with a look from behind my back and it's enough to shut them up.

Well, at least, most of them. Brianna, Reina, and Owen are rogue.

Prescott, too, though he's not as talkative as the rest of them.

Now that Sebastian is caught up with his coach, I'm all alone on the battlefield. It's not that I need his protection, considering I was doing just fine before he came along, but it feels good to not be in a constant state of war with the world.

Brianna is still as nasty as ever, but everyone else isn't. It's as if they're finally acceptant of me, and as a result, I haven't been as venomous or as sarcastic as I was in the past.

Besides, I'm in a good mood today and no one will ruin it.

"Um, excuse me?" Brianna taps her glittery nails on the table in front of me.

"To what do I owe the pleasure, Bee?" I mock.

"It's Bree!" she screeches, her veins tightening in her red neck, seeming to be on the verge of popping. "And your ass is not welcome here, you skank."

I stare around the table, pretending to search for something. "I don't see your name anywhere here, so I can sit my ass anywhere I like."

"You must think you're all that just because Sebastian looked in your trashy direction. Bitch."

"Bree," Reina calls while stroking circles on her temples. She's been silent, almost meek lately, no longer tormenting me as if it's her favorite sport.

"I'm done playing, Rei. It's time this fucking bitch learns her place."

"It's gone on for long enough," Josh says through a mouthful of French fries.

I stare at everyone present at the table. Some snicker, others smirk, and most are elbowing each other and murmuring under their breaths.

As if they're all in on a joke I'm not privy to.

I stare at Reina because, with Sebastian out of the picture, she's the one who calls the shots. "What's going on?"

"Over here." Brianna taps her long finger in front of me again. "Game over, Naomi."

"Bree." Prescott shakes his head at her and Lucy's lips part in pure shock.

"Is someone going to tell me what's going on?" I don't recognize the spooked tone in my voice or the premonition of something horrible rushing my way.

Brianna's shrill laughter echoes around us, and for some reason, my limbs lock. "Did you really think Sebastian would be interested in someone as unimportant as you just because? Are you that dumb to believe that's possible? The only reason he ever approached you is because we dared him to fuck you, take your V-card, and make a show of it. But you went ahead and fell for the bet like the stupid little bitch you are."

I'm so stunned for a second that I don't speak. My ears feel like they're closing and the shatter around me seems like it's coming from underwater.

Something feels off.

Me. I feel totally off.

It's like I'm frozen and there's nothing to unfreeze me or even allow me to move.

"Uh-oh." Someone laughs, and for the life of me, I can't figure out who. "She's broken."

The snickers and laughter rise in volume, and all I can do is sit there, staring numbly ahead of me.

At Reina.

"That's not true," I murmur.

Somewhere deep inside me, I know it is. Everything makes sense. The way he was insistent about courting me. The way he inserted himself into my life and refused to leave, no matter how much I tried to kick him out.

"Oh, it *is* true." Josh licks his upper lip. "It should've been me, not him. Come on, Rei, let it be me this time."

"Say it," I whisper to Reina. "Say it's not true."

She releases a sigh, letting her hands drop on the table. "Do you really believe that?"

No. No, I don't.

But if she says it, there won't be anything to compete against. It's Reina's word against all their nonsense.

Surely, there's an alternative reality where all of this is a distasteful joke.

You're the only distasteful joke here, Naomi.

"It was so cute watching you act like a puppy in love when we all knew Sebastian was playing with you." Brianna laughs. "Didn't she look like a perfect fool?"

Many agree and laugh, some point their fingers at me as the whispers erupt.

"What a joke."

"Look at her. She's still broken."

"Someone call the doctor."

"Even her friend knew…"

My gaze snaps to my side to find Lucy staring at her lap, zipping and unzipping her bag at a rapid speed. Her face is red, her freckles dark, and her lips are pursed.

Tears I never wanted to shed in front of these assholes fill my lids. When I speak, my voice is so low and pained, it's like it's coming from a dark corner I didn't know existed inside me. "You knew?"

She slowly stares up at me with tears clinging to her lashes. "It's not that, I…"

"You knew."

It's not a question, but a mere statement of facts from the way her brows are knitted and her nose is scrunching.

The girl I called my best friend was well aware of the game played against me and didn't say anything.

I stagger to a standing position and grab my bag with stiff fingers. My arm feels as heavy as my tongue inside my mouth.

The need to cry is so strong that all I see is blurry lines. All I hear is the taunts and whispers, the jabs and mockery. All I taste is the salty bitterness of my tears. All I feel is the need to crawl somewhere no one will see me and sob my heart out.

A shadow falls over me, and I don't have to look to see who it is.

The man I thought was made for me.

The man I was thinking of being in a stupid relationship with.

When the facts are, he's been using me to chase away his boredom.

I believed the depravity he painted and I thought we were playing a mutual game when he's been playing me all along.

He stops a small distance away, probably reading the atmosphere. But it's not far enough to block his scent.

It's not far enough to stop the fit of rage I've never experienced before.

Forget red.

My vision turns pitch fucking black.

"What's wrong?" he asks slowly.

I don't think as I grab a glass of water and throw its contents at him, dousing his face and T-shirt.

A collective gasp echoes in the group and our surroundings.

But I don't wait for them to direct their malicious intent toward me. I don't wait for the humiliation of what I just learned to sink in further.

Holding my head high, I rein in the tears stinging my eyes and march out the door.

As soon as I'm outside, I let them flood my cheeks.

I let the pain wash over me.

And just like that, it feels as if I'm back to being that helpless girl I was twelve years ago.

THIRTY

Sebastian

I REMAIN STILL AS I WATCH NAOMI'S RETREATING BACK. Her movements are stiff at best, her legs carrying her with a force that rattles her bag and makes her short dark hair swish in the air.

She dressed differently today. Her pink dress stopping at the middle of her thighs in a girly kind of way. While I hate the idea of anyone looking at her like that, I can't help being sucked into the view.

Even as the droplets of water slide down my chin and collarbone. Even as laughter and mockery echo in the space.

My first instinct is to run after her, catch her and kiss her. Maybe fuck her.

It doesn't matter what I do as long as I'm near her, breathing in her peachy scent and having her by my side where she fucking belongs.

But I can't leave when the whole campus's attention is veered in the wrong direction. It'll keep escalating from now on and I'm possibly the only one who can fix it.

It took fucking it up for me to step up.

So while everything in me is itching to follow after Naomi and grab her by the throat, I can't.

The door rattles from its hinges as she slams it shut on her way out. The murmurs and jabs echo louder in the air, mixing and heightening until her name is on every fucking tongue.

My teammates are laughing like whores without clients. The cheerleaders are whispering and giggling. Brianna's mouth is open in a shit-eating grin that I want to jam Josh's nonexistent balls inside of.

Reina massages her temples while Lucy and Prescott have some sort of a mojo silent communication thing going on between them as they stare at each other from across the table.

Naomi's friend, or ex-best friend, judging from the way her cheeks are streaked with tears, stands up. Probably to follow Naomi.

"Sit down, Lucy," Brianna orders with a venomous tone. "Or else you're out of the inner circle."

"I don't care about that." Lucy's chin trembles as she turns around.

I wipe my face with the palm of my hand and let the bottle of juice drop in my backpack. "Sit down."

"I need to make sure she's okay." Lucy sniffles.

"You should've thought of that before the whole show took place. You might not have been present when the bet was on, but you suspected it, yet you chose to turn a blind eye because of your position and your privileges. So don't pretend you're all worried now that the deed is done. Shut the fuck up and sit the fuck down."

Fresh tears flood Lucy's cheeks as she drops to her seat with a whimper. She sniffles in that involuntary way people do when they're flooded with emotions. Or that's what Nate told me once as we watched a boring movie with great acting.

Prescott jumps up and stands by her side, then places a hand on her shoulder. A red hue covers his cheeks as he glares at me. "Why the fuck are you taking out your anger on her? It's not Lucy's fault that you accepted the bet and Naomi finally found out your intentions toward her."

"My intentions toward her?" I repeat with mock laughter. "You couldn't begin to figure out my intentions toward her even if you and the whole campus spent sleepless nights trying."

"What the hell?" Brianna's brow furrows. "It was just a bet and it's over. The bitch finally learned her place."

My gaze falls on her and she stiffens. I don't even glare. People spend energy to express their anger because it's foreign to their nature.

Not me.

All I have to do is drop the mask and let my true self shine through. I stare and allow the rage I've been stifling since I was six years old to pour out in somber doses.

Even my voice has the lethal, calm edge I often alter so that I don't appear to be a psycho. "Call her that again and I'll make sure *you* learn your fucking place, Brianna."

"But she's right. It was just a bet." Josh comes to her rescue like the little bitch he is.

"Whether it's a bet or a game, it's none of your or anyone else's business. If I catch anyone, and I mean *anyone*, trashing her or bullying her, I'll fuck them up until they wish for death. And I don't mean physically. I'll find the fault in their existence and screw their lives over with it so they'll never be able to be functioning pieces of shits again."

All the murmuring, laughter, and jabs come to a halt, and for good reason.

I'm not the type who makes idle threats.

Or any threats at all, really.

Being raised in the heart of power didn't teach me to abuse it or to make use of it whenever necessary.

On the contrary, it made me more aware of my resources.

Having that type of influence at the tip of my fingers is a guarantee, but not if exercised poorly.

I only make threats when absolutely necessary. To protect myself, for instance.

And her.

Because at some point, Naomi has become an undivided part of my being and I'd use all the power I have to make sure she stays safe.

And happy.

And fucking mine.

"Relax, dude." Owen laughs, trying to lighten the mood. "No one will bully her."

"Or make any bets about her again." I meet Reina's blue gaze.

She's stopped drawing circles on her temple and is watching me with a slight smile. It almost appears...victorious.

What the fuck is she celebrating when Naomi is already out of reach?

"I mean it, Reina," I say. "Fuck with me and I'll fuck with you."

"You can't fuck with me, Bastian."

"Asher is coming home this weekend, so I very much can. You're well aware of how he loves making your life hell, so don't put me in the fucking mood to instigate it."

Her smile drops and she sucks in a breath. It's not as noticeable as Bree's huffing or Lucy's sniffling or Prescott's hushed soothing words, but it's there.

Naked for my eye.

Our own queen bee has a weakness and I'll use it to make sure she leaves Naomi in peace.

Because this might have started with a bet, but it was never the beginning of us.

And it sure as fuck isn't going to be the end.

We have a bond now. A sacred connection that people spend their entire lives searching for.

We found it together.

I found *her*.

Someone who accepts me just the way I am without trying to fix me or any of that bullshit.

In fact, she gets off on my real nature as much as I get off on hers.

And there's no way in fuck I'm letting her slip from between my fingers now that's she's finally close.

If I have to chase her, so be it.

I'll run after her until she realizes there was no escaping me in the first place.

Because there's one thing my toy doesn't realize yet. Or maybe it's buried too deep for her to recognize it.

She's mine.

Body and fucking soul.

And it all started the day she got off on having me chase her in the woods.

Or maybe it started the first time I saw her three years ago when she smiled while she was crying.

THIRTY-ONE

Naomi

I FOOLISHLY BELIEVED IN SOMETHING.

The fact that I'm strong.

That's nowhere near the truth. Otherwise, I wouldn't still be crying hours after I learned the biggest lie of my life.

It's a pain I've never felt before, not even during the red night.

It's like free falling to the sun and burning before hitting the bottom.

It's like dying while being unable to express any pain.

As I sit in my unmoving car, hugging the steering wheel, I mourn a part of me that only saw the light for a while before it was snuffed out.

A part that wasn't even supposed to see the light. Sebastian wrenched it out just so he could burn its wings and leave it to drop to its death.

But what I mourn the most is my naivety. Since I was a kid, I've made it my mission to build a wall between me and the world. And yet, I let him sneak in ever so easily.

I didn't fight him enough.

But it's not because I didn't want to. It was more because I couldn't. We share a twisted relationship, after all, and not in my wildest dreams did I ever think that type of connection could be faked.

Apparently, it can.

And I'm a fool for believing otherwise.

By the time the afternoon rolls by, I'm done having a pity party on one of the forest's secluded roads.

I'll have to get past this somehow.

I need to. Otherwise, it'll break me beyond the point of no return.

After cleaning my face with some wipes, I hit the gas and head home.

Every time I think of the scene in the cafeteria, a fresh wave of tears assaults me, and I have to take deep breaths to stop them from flooding my face.

Maybe I was only ever meant to be alone and I'm just fighting a losing battle.

When I take the road to my house, I notice a black van behind me.

My heart thumps as I squint, but I still can't make out any faces through their tinted window.

The memory of the two men from this morning rushes back in. I wish I'd memorized their plate so I'd know if it was the same people.

I step harder on the gas and speed around some other cars. But I don't lose them.

In fact, they become more insistent about staying in the same lane as me, right behind me.

Oh, God.

They *are* after me.

My throat closes and my heart beats faster until all I can hear is a low buzzing. My fingers shake around the steering wheel and I keep attempting to escape them. I'm contemplating calling 911 as I'm nearing the exit that leads to my house, but they speed past me.

I release a long, tortured breath even as I watch my rearview mirror all the way home. I stop in our driveway and retrieve my phone. Despite everything that's happened, the pieces of my broken heart jolt when I find several missed calls from Sebastian over the past couple of hours.

It's useless to think of myself above this if my heart is yearning for a word from him.

Anything.

But I'm not that idiot. I never will be.

Ignoring his calls and also several from Lucy, I opt to turn off my phone. Just as I'm about to, my screen lights up with another one.

Kai.

After what he told me about the possibility of my father's death, we've barely talked. I assumed he didn't want to tell me more bad news.

In return, I didn't push; therefore, I didn't receive any further news.

Clearing my throat, I answer, "Hello."

"Hey, Naomi." His voice is light, not as serious as the last time.

"Is everything okay?"

"Yes. Actually, I might have some good news for you."

I perk up in my seat, my throat dry with the tangible taste of excitement. "What?"

"I had a meeting with a few other people who were present the night that picture was taken. Apparently, your mother left the club with a different man than the one who owned the car we previously identified."

"And…do you know who he is?"

"I'm getting there. Give me some time and I'll be able to locate him."

My chest feels lighter, even if all of this could be smoke and mirrors. After all, Kai could locate this man and find out he's dead, too. Or maybe my father is, in fact, the man who already passed away and I'm just chasing an illusion.

But I don't care.

As long as there's hope to reunite with Dad, I'll hold on to it with both hands.

"Thanks," I murmur.

"Don't thank me until I bring him to you. Or maybe I'll take you to him if the circumstances allow for it."

"That would be great." I swallow as I stare through the rear-view mirror to make sure no one is there. "Kai…"

"Yes?"

"I have a friend who thinks she's being followed by a car, should she call the police?"

He pauses, no sound coming for several seconds until I think he's no longer there, but then he asks in his serious tone, "Did she see the face of who's following her?"

"No."

"A license plate?"

"No…" I was too nervous to focus on that.

"Anything specific?"

"It was just a black van. It's the second or third time she's seen it around."

"Calling the police is pointless unless she has something to back her claim. A license plate number is the very least she has to provide."

"I see."

"Is your friend scared? Feeling threatened?"

"A little." *A lot.*

"Does she suspect anyone?"

"It could be people from her parents' past."

"Maybe you should distance yourself from her then."

"I...will." I scoff internally at the thought of distancing myself from myself. I'd love that option more than anything right now.

After I finish the call with Kai, I step out of my car and drag my feet to the house.

I want to collapse and sleep until tomorrow.

Or next week, if that's possible.

Then I recall Mom's dark circles and I jog back to the car, get the sleep aid I bought this morning, and go inside.

I head to her room, which is rare as hell for me to do. But I guess I just need my mom right now.

Just like that red night.

It's ironic how we're not really that close, but she's the one person I turn to in my darkest moments.

Her bedroom is filled with model sketches and she has a mannequin in the middle that's wearing half-black and half-white like the evil guy in Batman.

Countless copies of her couture house's brochures are spread out on the coffee table and I can't help my smile as I reminiscence about how far she's come.

She started with nothing and built her way to the top by the sheer force of her determination and ambition. And that alone is awe-inspiring.

A few wedding dresses lie on the bed as part of her new collection, I assume. Chester Couture has the most sought after wedding dresses and not just anyone can afford them. Mom pays special attention to their design more than anything else.

I pause when I see red droplets on one of them.

Please tell me she didn't prick her fingers again. Or worse, she overworked herself until she had a nosebleed.

I head to the bathroom and raise my hand, about to knock. The sound of heaving stops me in my tracks. It's so raw and haunting that my ears prickle.

My unsteady palm pushes the door open and the scene in front of me cuts me in half.

Mom is crouching in front of the toilet, vomiting. But that's not the part that causes my fingers to unclench, letting the bottle crash to the floor.

It's the blood marring her hands while she grips the toilet. It's the trails of crimson on her cheeks as she vomits blood.

"Mom!" I run toward her and crouch beside her. "What's going on? Are you okay?"

She heaves a few more times, the sound getting louder and uglier with each passing second.

I place a shaking palm on her back, unsure how I'm supposed to react in such a situation. She's vomiting straight out blood and it splashes all over the white ceramic toilet.

I retrieve my phone with a shaky hand. "I'm…I'm going to call an ambulance."

She shakes her head once and motions at a towel. I drop my phone before I grab it and give it to her. She slowly wipes her face, her trembling hand barely holding the towel.

I help her get up, and she leans on me to reach the sink. She washes her face and brushes her teeth clean while I stand there watching her close as if I'm seeing her for the first time.

Since when did my mom become so thin that her collarbone is protruding through her tank top?

Since when were her dark circles so prominent that there's a shadow beneath her eyes?

Also, why is she so pale and her lips chapped?

A gloomy halo falls over the bathroom, festering in the corners and triggering an ominous sensation inside me.

"Mom… Should I take you to a doctor?"

"No. I'm fine." Her voice is low, exhausted, like her appearance.

"But you were vomiting blood just now. That doesn't look fine to me."

She wipes her face, and even though the blood is gone, it doesn't look healthy.

It's wrong.

Everything is.

"Come with me." She motions at the room with her head and I follow after, my steps hesitant and my limbs barely keeping me standing. Why do I feel like I'm a death-row inmate being led to the guillotine?

Mom sits me down on the sofa beside her and grabs both of my hands in hers. "I'm sorry you have to find out this way, Nao-chan. I wanted you and myself more prepared."

"More prepared for what?" I can hardly speak past the lump in my throat.

"I have stomach cancer. Late-stage. The doctors said I have a few months at best. A few weeks at worst."

My lips part and I want to laugh.

I want this to be a distasteful joke so I can laugh, but the sound doesn't come. My vision becomes blurry and Mom turns into a shadow as I stare at her through my tears. "Please tell me you're kidding, Mom."

"I'm so sorry, Nao-chan. I found out recently, and I didn't want to worry you, but maybe I was just being selfish. You were finally having fun and living and I didn't want to ruin that for you. But you were right, this is your life and you should know what's going on in it."

I shake my head frantically, causing the tears to cascade down my cheeks. When I was five years old, I had my first experience with death when one of our neighbors in Chicago, Mr. Preston, passed away in his sleep.

I asked Mom what it means to die and she said it's when people go to the sky and no one can see them again. She said she will die, too. We all will. I remember crying and screaming at her to take it back, because Mom's words were law in my head. She never lied to me and never gave me misguided truths. She didn't even let me believe in Santa, the boogeyman, or the tooth fairy. She never painted the world in bright pink colors for me.

So when she said that she would eventually die, I believed it and I hated it. I spent days crying in my sleep, thinking about how she would die like Mr. Preston from next door.

I'm that little girl now as I shake my head over and over again, not wanting her words to be true. "Take it back, Mom."

"Nao-chan…"

"Please, *please*, take it back. Please don't say that you're leaving. Please tell me it's not your time yet and that the doctor made a mistake."

"Honey…" She wraps her arms around me, her voice brittle. "I'm so sorry."

My head lies on her chest and she's trembling. Or maybe I am. Maybe it's the both of us.

I don't even know whose sniffles are echoing in the air or whose salty tears I'm tasting.

All I know is that I can't stop the wave of grief that confiscates me until it's the only thing I can breathe.

Sebastian's betrayal mixes with the news of Mom's illness and drags me under. The sound of my breaking insides echoes so loudly in my ears that I'm momentarily deafened. Noises and motions blur in the background and it's hard to focus.

The pain slashing through my chest is so strong, my bleeding heart is unable to take it all in and shatters into a million irreparable pieces.

Mom strokes my back like she did during the red night. She whispers soothing words in Japanese and tells me she loves me. Just like that night.

And I want to scream.

I want to stab fate in the face for being this cruel.

"I already notarized my will," she speaks softly, though her voice is a little bit broken, a little bit tired, a little bit…dead. "You'll inherit the couture house, my properties, and any stocks I purchased over the years. I asked Amanda to help you if you want to lead Chester Couture, but if you don't, you can appoint an acting CEO and just judge them by their performance. But no matter what you do, don't disappear from the executive board, they will think of you as weak and clueless. Some of those directors know nothing about art and fashion, so don't let them have a say in any creative decisions. Believe me, they would try to intimidate you and—"

"Mom…" I pull back to stare at her. She's having her serious mask on, the business one that's always thinking one hundred years into the future.

"What is it, Nao?"

"I don't care about any of that. Can't we…can't we get a second opinion?"

"I had a third and my options keep diminishing."

"Can't you have surgery or something?"

"The tumor can't be operated on due to the low survival rates associated with it."

"How about chemo?"

"I'm afraid it's too late for that, too."

A sob tears from my throat. "How…how can you be so calm about this? How can you talk about the will and the business and fuck knows what?"

"Because you're staying, Nao. And I want to make sure you have everything you need."

"Everything I need to live without you?"

She strokes my hair behind my ear and smiles a little. "You're old enough."

"I'm never old enough to be without you, Mom."

"I used to think that, too. When I was pregnant, you were this naughty fetus who kicked me day and night to make yourself noticeable. One time, a bunch of strangers surrounded me in the supermarket just to see the entertaining ways you moved in my belly and I wanted to ward them off you, to take you and run away. And I did. I tried my best to protect you from the world. It might have to do with being an immigrant and having to adapt to a culture so much different than mine, but I found it hard to trust anyone, even your babysitters. After what happened with Sam, I decided that I couldn't be parted from you, and that might have turned a tad too suffocating for you. It's because I thought you would be too vulnerable in the world without me, and in a way, I still believe that. But I also see how fiercely independent you are. How genuinely you love and care, even if you don't show it much. You remind me of myself when I was younger and if that's of any indication, I'm sure you'll do just fine."

An onslaught of tears covers my cheeks. "I don't want to, Mom. Please...please don't go...you're all I have."

Her lips thin before she releases a long breath. "There's also the father you've been searching for since you were a little girl."

"You...knew?"

"Of course, I did. You put it in a lantern when we went to China last year."

"I...don't need him if you stay. I'll stop looking for him, I promise."

"You don't need him even if I don't stay."

"Is he alive?"

"Unfortunately."

"Why are you saying that?"

"Because he's a dangerous man. Nao-chan, the reason I re-located from Japan to the States isn't because of social circumstances. I did it to escape him and his influence. If I'd stayed, you would've been brought up in a corrupted way where you have to fight for your life every day."

"Then why were you with him? Why did you give birth to me?"

"Back then, I was this simple girl from a conservative family. My parents had me at an old age and worked tirelessly in their small convenience store to make ends meet. Then your father walked in, threatening their business and their poor old hearts. My parents weren't his only targets. Everyone in our neighborhood was. I was so sheltered and oblivious to the world that I had a false sense of grandiosity and thought I could stand up to him and his tyranny. I believed in the stupid myth that the good always outweighs the bad, but I was in for a life lesson. People like your father only know how to take and take until nothing is left behind. But he knew how to play with my young and foolish emotions, I'll give him that.

"Thankfully, I was beginning to learn his ways and I realized I wasn't safe with him. As soon as I knew I was pregnant with you, I didn't think twice before I left. Not only Japan and my elderly parents, who couldn't handle what I became, but also him. You gave me my fresh start, Nao. I regained the strength he'd slowly purged out of me. I stood above his gaslighting and abusive behavior, thanks to you. Keeping you was a no-brainer. After all, you're the only thing I can call mine."

The tears don't stop as I listen to her nostalgic retelling of the old days. I wish I could reach out to her younger self and hug her, but since I can't, I wrap my arms tighter around her in a silent show of support.

Normal people don't survive what my mom did. They don't use it as a strength to climb to the top, despite many odds being against them.

A sense of guilt hooks with my grief and drags me under. If I'd known my father was her nightmare and that he hurt her, I wouldn't have searched for him. I wouldn't have hurt her by constantly asking about him.

"Point is, your father is not a good man, Nao, and he's nowhere near the perfect image you built of him in your head. If you ever loved me, you'll forget about him and stop searching for him."

"Do…those men from this morning have something to do with him?"

She hesitates before making an affirmative sound.

"Why were they here?"

"They're your father's men."

"He has men?"

"Lots of them, and those two might have been the most so-phisticated of the bunch."

"Did they come to bother you?"

"To intimidate me so I'll admit you're his."

"He doesn't know about me?"

"I lied to him and faked a DNA test that shows you're not his daughter, but he still suspects me, even after all these years. He still wants to get his filthy hands on you, but I will fight until the day I die."

"Do you hate him so much because he's dangerous or be-cause he…hurt you?"

"Both."

"How badly did he hurt you?" My voice breaks with crash-ing guilt.

"Badly. He didn't do it physically, but he destroyed my naive heart. Though I guess I should be thankful for that. If it weren't for his emotional abuse, I wouldn't have gotten to where I am today. Still, I would never allow him near you. That's why I moved us all the time and even suggested going to California next. I tried to escape his clutches, but he always found you."

"But he doesn't think I'm his daughter."

"Oh, he does. I don't know why, but the more I deny it, the more he's hellbent on having you. Especially these last couple of months."

"He…he wants to meet me?"

"He already did, Nao-chan. You just don't remember him."

THIRTY-TWO

Sebastian

I SEARCH FOR HER EVERYWHERE.

Which isn't a lot of places. She's usually either in her house, or in the forest.

With me.

I was so sure she'd be at that rock. No idea if it's my ego trying to play it down or if I really thought I'd find her in our place, waiting for me.

At any rate, that's not the case.

So I went to her house right after, but her mother told me she wasn't there.

I tried calling her a thousand times. Then I sent a series of texts.

Where are you? Call me back.

If you haven't read my earlier text, this is a reminder to call me.

I know you're hurt and I don't want you hurt. So let me explain. The situation isn't what you think.

Ignoring me is not going to solve the issue, Naomi.

If you think giving me the cold shoulder will make me back down, then you're terribly mistaken. I'm coming for you whether you like it or not.

Where the fuck are you? At least tell me you're okay.

This is starting to piss me off and you know how crazy I turn when I'm angry. Stop testing me and answer the fucking phone.

If I find you hurt in any way…

Baby. Come on, just let me know you're all right and I'll stop bugging you. For now.

This will just keep escalating and you better be ready for the consequences, Tsundere.

She didn't answer any of my texts, but she did read them at some point, which should mean she's all right.

Or maybe she's been kidnapped and whoever took her is reading her messages.

I shove that thought out of my head as I hit the gas until I reach the highest speed possible. I've been driving so recklessly all day that I'm surprised I haven't gotten into an accident.

The day has turned into night, and I've already done the tour of the fucking town. Twice.

Maybe she went to another town. Or another state.

Maybe even another country.

She's crazy enough to do it, but I'm betting on the fact that she wouldn't just leave her mother behind.

No matter how much she says she's mad at her, she still cares for her.

But maybe her mom knows and she asked her to hide her whereabouts from me.

The ringing of my phone drags me from my chaotic thoughts. Mrs. Weaver flashes on the dashboard.

I inhale deeply as I answer in the cheerful tone she expects, "Grandma."

"Sebastian!" she coos, her tone honeyed, which means she has company.

Sure enough, chatter reaches me from her end.

"I'll be right back, darling," she tells someone. "My grandson is on the phone…yes…the star."

There are some gleeful remarks that I want to shut the fucking door on, but I can't, because no one hangs up on Debra Weaver. It's the other way around.

Soon after, the sounds disappear and she hisses, "Where the hell are you?"

"Huh?"

"We have a gathering this evening. You and your uncle were supposed to show up."

Fuck. We do.

I completely forgot about it in my attempts to find Naomi.

My mind speeds in different directions, searching for a plausible solution. "I have a late class. I can't make it."

"Late class with the seamstress's daughter?" Her tone is deadly, and if we were face-to-face, I'd see the twin flames in her eyes.

"How do you know about that?" There's no use denying it, and if I do, she'll just use it as an invitation to strike harder.

"You really thought we would let our only heir on the loose after you kissed the girl on TV?"

A miscalculation on my part. I should've known that Grandma would grab hold of that behavior like a magnet. She doesn't focus on what's normal, but more on what tries to be normal when it, in fact, isn't.

"She has nothing to do with this," I say in my most neutral tone.

"You just proved that she does by defending her to me."

I tighten my hold on the steering wheel. My grandparents are like sharks to blood, the moment they smell weakness, they latch on to it until they bring you down by using it.

That's what they did to Dad and have been trying to do to me and Nate.

We held on for so long.

Or at least, my uncle did. Looks like I allowed them to smell my blood after all.

"You have two options, Sebastian. Drop the seamstress's daughter as gently or as cruelly as you prefer, or watch as she breaks her neck. Be here in fifteen."

Beep.

I slam the breaks so hard, the car nearly topples over. My fist drives into the steering wheel and I'm surprised it doesn't come off.

Pain reverberates in my knuckles, but it doesn't compare to the warring state in my chest.

When my parents died in that car accident and my grand-parents adopted me, I learned something.

In order to survive, I needed to play their sadistic games. I needed to act a certain way, speak a certain way, and even smile a certain way.

It's all part of the social play the Weavers have excelled at for generations. To be able to carry on with the legacy, I had to be strong-minded enough to lead the family, but I wasn't allowed to step out of the norm.

Up to this point, I've been the perfect Weaver neither Dad nor Nate could be.

But the image I've spent years perfecting is slowly crumbling in front of me. And that brings on one urge.

The only urge I have.

The need for violence.

I kick the car in gear, driving at a crazy speed until I'm back at Naomi's house. Fuck Grandma's gathering. If she's holding a guillotine over my head, I might as well indulge.

I fully expect Naomi's mom to tell me she still hasn't come home, but I pause when I find her car in the driveway.

A small space in my heart lights up as I step out of the vehicle the fastest I ever have.

My feet come to a halt as soon as I cross the distance to the porch. A lone yellow light shines on a small figure sitting on the outside steps.

Naomi.

Her head is in her hands as she stares out at the distance. A quick sweep of the driveway shows only her car, so her mom must be at work late, as usual.

There's always some shipment going wrong or a design that didn't meet her standards. Naomi often grumbles about how much of an unhealthy workaholic her mom is.

She doesn't notice me as I slowly approach her. It's not until I'm a small distance away that I notice the shaking in her shoulders and the defeat bowing her usually upright posture. Goosebumps cover her bare arms from the slight chill and I want to hurt an invisible being for causing her discomfort.

My Naomi looks so breakable, so fragile, almost like she could be ruined with a mere touch.

I came here charged with anger and the need for violence, but as I observe her state, all those thoughts vanish from my system.

"Baby."

She stiffens as she slowly lifts her head. I expect to find tears in her gaze, but there are none.

I wish she was crying, kicking, or screaming. I wish she'd jump up and strangle me and knee me in the balls.

Any of those options are better than the blank stare in her eyes. They're dark under the lack of light, but it's as if no soul resides behind them.

Washed away.

Just like the rest of her expression.

"You didn't answer my calls," I say quietly because any other volume would probably have the exact opposite effect.

She jerks up suddenly. The motion happens in one go, I expect her to come at me, but she simply turns and stomps to her front door.

Not so fast.

I grab her by the arm and swing her around. She slaps me across the face, and a muscle works in my jaw at the force of it.

She sure as fuck knows how to put all her weight behind her hits.

"Leave me alone." Her voice is guttural, raw, almost like she's used up all her other emotions and all she has left is anger.

I know that feeling all too well. I've lived it since I lost my parents, and I don't want her to experience the same emptiness.

Not on my fucking watch.

"You should know by now that I won't. We're bound together, Naomi."

"Bound together?" She scoffs. "By what? Your lies? Your fucking games? Reina's bets? You already won. You fucked me, depraved me, and humiliated me to your heart's content, so go gloat about it to your stupid friends and leave me be."

The apathy behind her words pisses me off. People think hate is the worst emotion, but it's not.

Indifference is.

The fact that Naomi could write me off so easily provokes my ugly monster to rear its head.

"That's where you're wrong, baby. I can't leave you when I'm not done with you."

"Well, I fucking am, Sebastian! I played your game, however unwillingly, and it's time to end it."

"Unwillingly? Fuck that. You enjoyed every chase as much as I did. Your cunt strangled my dick with the intensity of your excitement and fear, and you came more than either of us could count. So don't stand there and utter the word unwillingly."

"That was only physical. I never signed up to be emotionally abused! So, yes, Sebastian, it's over. The next time you come near me or attempt to touch me, I'm going to file for a restraining order."

"And you think a restraining order would stop me?"

She swallows, her pretty little throat working with the

motion and I wrap my hand around it hard enough so she knows who's in fucking charge here.

"I told you not to play with my beast if you can't handle it. I told you to use your safe word, but you didn't. You squealed and ran for it. You gasped and moaned and begged me to use you. That's our reality, Naomi. It's what we are, you and I. Beast and toy. Monster and prey, so don't you fucking dare threaten me with staying away from you, because that's not going to happen."

For the first time tonight, moisture glistens in her eyes even as she glares at me, her dark eyes drawing holes into my soul. Her voice comes out as a strained whisper, "You *ruined* all that when you lied to me from the beginning."

"I never lied to you."

"You hid the truth, which is worse than lying. You only made a game out of my feelings and turned me into the laughingstock of campus."

"No one will bother you."

"You really think that's the problem here?"

"You're worried about people bullying you, which won't be happening if they want to see another day."

"You don't even see it, do you?"

"See what?"

She punches me on the chest so hard, I falter, and she uses the chance to free herself from my hold.

"What you did to me! The way you played me! Do you not realize how wrong it was?"

"No, because I got to have you. The method doesn't matter, the result does."

She slowly shakes her head, her lips parting in a small whisper, "You're crazy."

"Oh, baby, you've only ever seen a portion of my crazy. Don't provoke me or I'll show you the rest."

Her chin trembles, but she doesn't break eye contact as she

reaches behind her and fumbles with the handle of her front door until it opens.

"We're over," she emphasizes, and then she's dashing inside and locking the door.

Usually, she doesn't do that when her mom isn't around. It's some form of an invitation so I can startle her and take her by surprise.

This is a clear sign of her rejection, but it's not going to work.

I don't care what I have to do, but I'll get my Naomi back.

Even if I have to drag her out kicking and screaming.

THIRTY-THREE

Akira

Dear Yuki-Onna,

I don't know why you feel the need to defend your fucked-up fetish, but that's what all people with egotistical problems do, don't they? They instantly attack the opposing party because God forbid if they're wrong.

And you are. Wrong, I mean.

Stop your nonsense and get some help instead of trying to accuse me of things that would never measure up to your actions.

So what if I watch breath play porn? You don't see me going around and practicing it. So what if I fantasize about it? I'm not the sick one who thinks about doing it in real life while ignoring every safety procedure under the sun. I'm sure your mom taught you to be cautious. Remember who you were before this madness and do better.

I'm far from being your morality police, Yuki-Onna. I'm just the small angel on your shoulder who's desperately trying not to be shoved down by your demons (yes, plural, because you have a lot of that shit).

Am I trying to help? Negative. Do I take pleasure in your torment? Also negative.

Which brings me to the question I've been thinking about since I read your letter. Why the hell do I look forward to your every letter when I despise your actions and choices?

Is this toxic? Probably. Will I stop? Probably not.

Here's a sliver of the truth that you'll never learn about me otherwise. Your mundane letters, no matter how tedious and self-centered, distract me from my head and my life.

And for that alone, I can't stop this chain of exchange. I have no clue why you won't, though, since I've been calling you every colorful name under the sun.

But, hey, they say birds of a feather flock together so maybe this, whatever the fuck this is, was always meant to happen.

I was meant to send that letter and be excited like a kid. You were also meant to write back and distract me.

My life is everything I don't want and you're the only thing I actually have control over in it.

So no, I won't be closing my windows or getting a talisman. Yuki-Onna is welcome anytime as long as you drive away the boredom.

insert something witty I don't have the energy to think of that doesn't mean love here
Akira

THIRTY-FOUR

Naomi

LIFE IS UNFAIR.

But if I keep pondering on that, all I'll be having is a pity party with chips and apple juice as an audience.

So I don't.

It's been three weeks since Mom dropped the bomb about her cancer.

Three weeks of trying to be there for her even while she insists on continuing to work as if nothing has happened. She said she wants to keep everything perfectly organized and ready for when it's time. Besides, it's not like Mom to flounder about and think about death.

When I begged her to go on a trip with me, she said we'll go to Japan because that's where she would like to spend her last days.

Fortunately, she's not in much pain, thanks to her meds. It's probably because she didn't undergo any surgery or chemo.

But the fact remains that the cancer is eating her from the

inside, festering in her while she goes through her meetings as if the end isn't near.

I've tried to see it from her perspective and respect her wishes like the doctor advised me to. But it's hard to pretend. It's hard to cook together, watch movies, and take hikes while knowing these activities may be the last I have with her.

It's even harder to have no one to talk to about it.

I can't forgive Lucy, even though she came begging, telling me she suspected there was something going on but didn't know what it was.

She also stood up to Brianna in public and got called names and was shunned out of the inner circle. Not that it makes up for what she did, but I'm glad she left that toxic bunch.

It's been getting crazier in that circle.

That same week, after Friday's game, Reina was assaulted in the forest and lost her memory. So now, she's this completely different person who smiles and laughs and cares about people.

Even me.

The other day, she apologized to me after she learned that she bet Sebastian to fuck me, and I choked on my spit. After I told her to fuck off, that is.

The guy himself has been relentless.

There hasn't been a day where he didn't corner me, approach me, or talk to me.

Sometimes, it's a joke about how his dick misses me. Other times, it's intense, where his chest flattens against mine and his face is mere inches from my mouth.

He absolutely has no fucks to give about my decision or the fact that I told him we're over. In fact, he still thinks we're together and that sooner or later, I'll cave in to the connection we have.

I've held on to my anger as much as I could. Add in my constant grief about my mom and I've been in no state of mind to even think about him.

But I do.

God, how much I do.

I think it's because of the loneliness. The lack of friends and the need to burst bubbling inside me.

Besides, I'm well and truly an addict now. No matter how much porn I watch, there's nothing that resembles the intensity of what I felt from Sebastian's hands.

There's nothing out there that matches the raw chase and the raw hunger I experienced with him.

Sometimes, I lie in my bed and think about his huge cock, rough hands, and wicked tongue.

Sometimes, I let my fingers slip beneath my panties in a hopeless attempt to recreate the sensations.

It doesn't work. Not really.

How long will it take before I get over it? Because I've been on the brink lately, snapping at anyone who moves.

Coming to campus has become a nightmare. Surprisingly, no one bullies me or throws jabs in my direction, but looks don't lie. They regard me like I'm a pest.

Besides, Brianna has been making it her mission to turn me into an outcast—even more than before.

Now that Reina has lost her memories and is no longer her bitchy, authoritative self, Brianna has been spreading her venom all over the squad. She's been actively trying to make my and some of the other girls' lives hell.

I've been at the point of rage-quitting for a long time, but I haven't. I won't upset Mom when she doesn't have much time left.

Sighing, I head to the parking lot while checking my messages. I don't know why I wish to find one from the PI, Kai.

I know I won't. After Mom begged me to stop searching for my father, I did.

It took all I had to call Kai and tell him to abort the mission. He asked me why and I told him it's because having Mom was enough.

And it is.

Holding on to the anger more than I should have has kept me from realizing that fact.

Kai simply told me to call him if I needed anything and that was that.

And yet, I still think he'll one day call me and tell me he found my father or send me his address in a text message.

None of those texts appear. But my screen overflows with messages from someone else.

Sebastian.

He now has this habit of telling me all about his day and giving me a monologue with the weirdest things, even when I never reply. And when I do, it's to tell him to go fuck himself. To which he replies that he'd rather fuck me.

The messages of this day include:

I'm meeting Nate later this week. You were practically drooling when we had dinner together, so do you want to join?

On second thought, no. I don't want you drooling over him. It's best if you don't ever see him again.

Though if you insist on going, I can make him wear a mask. What do you think?

As much as I enjoy my one-sided conversation, you can at least give yes or no answers.

And before you ask, no, fuck you, leave me alone don't count as an answer. As much as I love it when you're Tsundere, the cold shoulder is getting tiresome.

Anyway, date tonight? Or a chase? I'm open to both as long as I get to bite and suck your tits while your tight cunt clenches around my dick.

Or your ass. It feels as good as your cunt.

And don't even try to pretend that you don't miss the chase as well. You're fucking torturing us both and it's not fun. At all.

But I'll wait.

Now, see what you do to me and feel guilty.

He's attached a selfie from the chin down that looks to have been taken right out of the shower.

And he's naked. Fully.

My eyes fly open as I lean on my car. I try focusing on the droplets of water sticking to his six-pack or to the tattoos in Arabic and Japanese, but my eyes immediately stray down.

His eight-inch cock stands erect between his legs. It's big when it's flaccid, but it's huge when hard and ready.

The veins pop on the side and the crown is purple and swelling, leaking with precum.

Fuck.

This is really not the image I need to see in my sexually-frustrated state of mind.

"Is that Sebastian?"

I startle and shove the phone in the pocket of my jeans at Lucy's sheepish voice. Thank God she's a safe distance away and she couldn't have seen me ogling a dick pic.

"Why are you talking to me?" I sound like a bitch, but I really couldn't care less at this point.

Maybe I'm indeed a bitch.

Lucy's mouth turns downward. "I'm just trying to make convo."

"Well, don't."

She sighs heavily. "I'm sorry. I'm ready to apologize for the rest of my life if you want."

"Maybe I just need you to leave me alone."

"Stop being an asshole." Reina joins Lucy and crosses her arms.

She might have lost her memories and done a one hundred eighty-degree shift in personality, but apparently, she still likes Lucy.

And she still has that glare no level of amnesia can erase. "She already apologized to you."

I place a hand on my hips. "Doesn't mean I'll forgive her."

"You don't have to, but that will only hurt you both in the long run. Weren't you supposed to be best friends?"

"Best friends don't stab each other in the back." My voice breaks and I hate it. I hate the weakness.

"I didn't mean to." Lucy's lids shine with tears. "I swear I didn't want to hurt you, but I admit to being too blinded with the glamorous side of being popular and I let that get to my head, and for that, I'm terribly sorry."

"It doesn't matter whether you're sorry or not. It changes nothing."

"Of course, it does." Reina sighs heavily. "Listen, the whole Sebastian thing is fucked up, but it's all on me. Lucy had nothing to do with it, so if you want to blame anyone, blame me."

"Blame you?" I laugh with no humor. "You don't even remember why the hell you did it."

"I'm sorry for that, too." She lowers her gaze. "If I could, I would've found out why so I could give you closure."

"Who says I need closure?" My voice breaks again and I curse myself for it.

Reina smiles and it's weak—haunted, even.

She's been making these types of expressions more often than not since she lost her memories and her estranged fiancé, Asher, returned to town.

"It's okay if you do, Naomi," she says. "We all do."

Well, I don't.

I *really* don't.

Maybe if I repeat that long enough, I'll start to believe it.

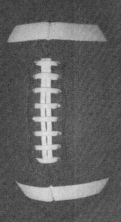

THIRTY-FIVE

Sebastian

Naomi's had enough time.

To reject me.

To pretend that she's moving on.

But I know she isn't.

How do I know? It's simple.

The rage in her eyes that she projects onto the world is so similar to mine. Her need to snap at anyone and anything, then retreat into her bubble speaks volumes more than her scathing words.

They're only armor she chooses to hide behind.

Because no matter how angry she is, no matter how much she hates me for succumbing to a stupid bet, she still looks up at me with those big brown eyes. She still has that spark only I can recognize.

I still feel her shudder whenever I corner her somewhere hidden on campus or near her favorite fountain where she usually has lunch.

After Grandma's unveiled promise of retribution, I made it

my mission to not be alone with Naomi. I take Debra Weaver and her threats seriously. The last time she made one to my dad, he and Mom ended up dead.

There's no way in fuck I'm letting history repeat itself with Naomi. So in a way, I've been using this down period to make a case against Grandma's theory. If she believes that I'm no longer interested in Naomi and that I caved to her threat and stopped seeing her, she'll retract her claws.

That decision has had its own repercussions on me, though.

Not fucking my pretty toy for weeks has turned me into a bitter, raging asshole. I'm even worse than Asher now and have been punching Josh and anyone who even looks in Naomi's direction.

I can't help it.

The moment one of the guys has made any remarks toward her, no matter how innocent, I've had the need to pummel their faces to the ground. And not only in fantasy but also in harsh, unyielding reality. I had to do it outside of everyone's view so I don't tarnish the Weaver name and have my grandparents breathe down my neck.

But I reveled in every second of punching those assholes. Now, I understand why Asher broke his knuckles punching a guy who was flirting with Reina in high school.

It feels fucking euphoric.

Owen usually peels me off the fuckers before I break their faces.

Since Asher came back, he and Owen take me for drinks as if that will loosen me up. It's made me even more volatile and I can barely stop myself from starting fights for no reason other than sheer fucking frustration.

That's what happens when addiction is taken away.

Or obsession.

Or fucking companionship.

Naomi has become a huge part of my life that I can no longer survive without.

I don't know how it got so serious so fast, but it did.

I even asked Nate to look for the fucking asshole, Sam Miller, who dared to put his hands on my Naomi when she was nine. After she told me the story in Owen's party, it took everything I had not to release my rage and pummel everything in sight.

The thought of her being hurt and scared cut deeper than any fucking thing I went through.

I don't know what I would do to the bastard when I find him, but it's probably something more violent than anything I've committed so far.

Truth is, I have no clue how far my limits stretch when it comes to Naomi. Especially if it has to do with the low fucking life who traumatized her.

My uncle pulled some strings with his detective friends, and they found that Sam was filed missing in records. Nate said he could've run away or living in another country. But that doesn't mean I'll give up. I'll find the bastard and make him pay.

With his life, if need be.

I'm honestly not above that when it comes to Naomi.

Owen told me to find a pussy to wet my dick in and relieve some tension. I punched him. As if that would be possible or I'd be interested in anyone else after I had my Naomi.

No one can match up to her fire, her fight, and even her adorable innocence, and it's not for lack of trying. Countless girls, cheerleaders included, throw themselves at me at every game. I only let them to gauge Naomi's reaction.

Often times, she glares before she lowers her head and leaves. At that exact moment, I push away whatever girl is clinging to me.

I have no interest in fucking anyone but her.

Which brings me to the reason why I'm here.

In front of her house.

I shouldn't be, not when Grandma could be having someone watching this place.

But it's been four weeks already. Even my grandma wouldn't keep up for this long.

Besides, it's late and I have my hoodie on.

Ms. Chester's car isn't in the driveway, just as I'd hoped. The front door is closed, but I'm not going through there, anyway. Naomi already gave me the alarm code a while back, when I snuck in. Here's to hoping they didn't change it.

I round the house and climb the tree until I'm near Naomi's balcony, then jump onto it. My movements are silent as I slide the door open, slip inside, and deactivate the alarm. Same code as before.

Naomi isn't in her room. Not a surprise there either.

I slowly go down the stairs to where the TV screen is shining in the living room. Ominous music from the latest true crime show she's watching fills the air.

That's when I get my first full view of her.

Naomi hugs a pillow to her chest and she holds a bottle of juice, her lips wrapped around a straw. The TV casts a pale blue light on her petite features.

She's so fucking beautiful, it hurts.

Her dark eyes are wide and her lips tremble in complete concentration. I've always loved how scared she gets while watching these shows, but she still seeks them out, anyway.

She still enjoys the thrill they provide.

I sneak up on her from behind just as a retelling of events plays out on the screen. I wrap my hand around her throat and she jolts.

Just when she's about to scream, I slam a palm over her mouth, then lean in to whisper, "Scream and I'll fuck you up."

Her eyes widen and I can feel the exact moment she recognizes me by the slight relaxation in her shoulders and how her breath whooshes into my hand.

But then she stiffens again and throws the pillow back at my face. She follows with the bottle of juice, but I tilt my head to the side and it ends up crashing against the ground.

Naomi kicks her legs in the air and mumbles against my hand. My dick hardens in my jeans in a second as I smell her fight in the air.

I hop over the back of the sofa so I'm on top of her. She doesn't let me pin her down without a struggle, though.

Her nails scratch and her feet kick anywhere she can reach me.

"Fuck, baby. I've missed your fight."

My hand tightens around her throat as I pin her to the sofa. She wheezes for breath and I grunt. "I'll let your mouth go, but if you scream, I'll choke you again."

She doesn't nod; then again, she can't with my firm hold on her throat.

So I remove my palm from her face, only to crash my mouth to hers.

She whimpers against me, then tries to bite down on my lip and draw blood, but I thrust my tongue inside and conquer hers.

I don't leave her room to breathe, let alone fight.

Fuck, how much I missed kissing her, how much I missed her low moans and erotic whimpers. Even her sniffling sounds turn me on more than any other fucking thing on earth.

I kiss her hard, then slow, toying with her limits and blurring her lines. My chest covers her heaving tits and my fingers dig into the soft flesh of her neck.

I kiss her with an urgency that tightens my balls and rushes all my blood to my dick.

She still tries to fight, even as her legs open. She tries to bite, even when her tongue takes tentative strokes from mine.

Then she's mumbling something against me.

Some curse words. Some choice words.

But I take them all.

I'd take anything as long as she's by my fucking side.

"I…hate…you…" she mumbles between pants and sniffles.

I smile.

I fucking smile, because all this time, I thought she was fighting to tell me the safe word.

The one word that I gave her to get rid of me once and for all.

I reach a hand between us underneath her oversized shirt and jam my fingers against her panties. I groan low in my throat when her wetness soaks my skin.

"Hate me for fucking eternity as long as your cunt wants me."

I can feel her glare in the darkness, stabbing me in the chest. "It's only a physical reaction. It means nothing."

"I'll take what I can get."

"I told you we're over."

"I never agreed to that."

"Just leave me the fuck alone!"

"No," I whisper against her throat as I dart my tongue out and lick all the way from her jaw to her earlobe.

She shudders, her legs clenching, and I do it again until I can feel her melting beneath me.

Her fight is still there, I'll give her that, but I don't stop as I pry her thighs open and rub her clit over her panties.

"This cunt is mine, baby. You're all mine. Just because I gave you space doesn't mean we're over."

She whimpers when I lick her lips, then jam my tongue in her wet mouth.

I kiss her more savagely, more hungrily. I kiss her for all the times I haven't kissed her in fucking weeks. My tongue ravishes hers, bruising it, luring it, until she kisses me back. Until her strokes meet mine and her arousal floods my hand.

Her pulse heightens beneath my fingers, turning erratic and out of fucking control.

Just like my own.

Only one woman would extract this reaction out of me and it's her.

My Naomi.

The front door opens and we both freeze.

"Nao-chan, are you still awake? I brought Chinese."

Naomi's eyes widen as I pull my head back, then she mouths, "Go!"

My lips twist in a snarl, but I don't make a move to leave.

"Nao-chan?" Her mother's voice gets nearer.

Naomi digs her fingers into my side, eyes asking, imploring. "Go…"

I lift myself off of her in one swift movement, but not before stealing one last kiss from her swollen lips. "This isn't over, baby."

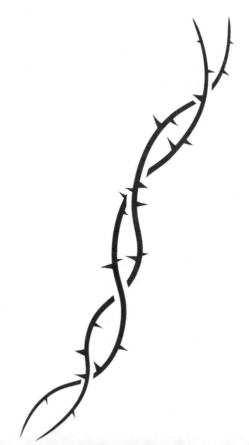

THIRTY-SIX

Naomi

I COULDN'T SLEEP THAT NIGHT.

All I could think about was, what the hell happened and how did I let it?

I still can't forgive Sebastian for what he's done. I still don't want him back.

So why the fuck did my body react in that shameful way?

Maybe it's because the physical and emotional are separated after all.

Maybe it's because I've been sexually frustrated for weeks and I took it out on Akira in the toxic letters we've been exchanging.

At any rate, none of what happened last night should've happened.

If my mom hadn't come in, just how far would I have let him go?

I need to detox from his influence one way or another.

Either that or the bubbling frustration will get the better of me. That and Mom's cancer are too much to handle.

Maybe that's why I cracked and accepted Lucy back, on

probation, as I told her. We're both outcasts anyway, and she basically committed social suicide by going against Brianna. Even Prescott doesn't look in her direction anymore. Reina and I have somehow grown close, too.

I know. Crazy.

So now, the three of us are kind of friends, or colleagues or whatever, but we're not close enough that I'd tell them the whole thing about Mom.

She's keeping it a secret from the board until the last minute and asked me not to say anything in exchange for going on a trip together.

Besides, I don't fully trust Reina and Lucy. It'll take time with those two.

I never would've thought that Reina and I could become close, but here we are. I guess it's all because of her memory loss. It's like the cruel, vindictive Reina has gone and a completely different, honest girl, came in on her behalf.

One who cares and tells Brianna off. One who hates her past actions whenever she's reminded of them.

The fact that her fiancée, Asher, is back, might have something to do with it.

The same Asher who's one of Sebastian's closest friends.

My monster has been bugging me any chance he gets, cornering me and blocking my exits. He sends me texts and talks about himself and me. He still believes there's an us even though I repeated for the thousandth time that we're over.

Stop thinking about him, Naomi.

I repeat that in my head over and over again, and yet, I find myself in the forest at dusk.

At the rock, to be more specific.

My arms lie limp at my sides as I stare at the dirt covering it while the late afternoon sun casts orange hues on the trees.

He must've completely forgotten about this place.

What was I expecting? That he'd make an altar where he used to shove me down and fuck me?

This isn't over, baby.

The sound of his sinister voice in my head sends a chill crawling down my arms.

I internally shake my head as a mocking sound leaves me.

What am I doing here anyway? I should go and bug Mom about leaving work and resting.

It really feels as if she's bringing her death date sooner at the pace she's going.

I'm respecting her every wish, so the least she can do is give me her time.

Or what's left of it.

My chest aches at the reminder and I briefly close my eyes to chase it away.

For the past couple of weeks, all I've done is try to make her comfortable. I even gave up on searching for my father indefinitely.

And I meant it. If he hurt her, betrayed her, I have no interest in making his acquaintance. Like Mom, I know exactly what it means to give someone my all, to be naively genuine, just to be stabbed in the back by the one person I thought was closest to me.

Mom said I met my dad and I don't remember, but she refused to divulge anything else. I only let it go because the subject matter seemed to have bothered her.

I'm about to turn around and leave when something rustles across from me.

It couldn't be…

My pulse thumps in my throat as I squint. There's nothing visible in the bushes, but I know there's someone there.

Waiting…

Lurking…

Did Sebastian follow me from campus? It's possible with the way his aqua eyes promised mayhem when we were practicing across from each other.

My legs itch for a run, and I know, I just know that if I do run, I won't stop.

And neither will he.

If he chases me, we'll just fall back into that black hole that I've been desperately trying to escape, to no avail.

Even with all the bitter emotions, the snap decision in my brain is a lot easier than I thought.

I want to run.

I want to be chased.

Even if it's for one final time.

Just when I'm sucking air into my lungs, a figure appears from behind a tree.

I freeze.

He's wearing black army fatigues and a baseball cap that falls low on his face. He's a bit taller than me and definitely not Sebastian.

Then another taller black figure appears. There are two of them.

I don't think as I turn around and run.

For real this time.

For my life.

Thudding footsteps come from behind me, sounding almost too steady as I sprint the fastest I can.

The hardest I can.

Oh, God.

Who are those men and why are they chasing me? I want to ask that, but I don't trust my voice, not with the amount of panting I'm doing or how hard my chest is rising and falling.

Besides, who cares? They could be one of the freaks who are always in this forest waiting for their next prey.

Someone like me.

I deviate through the narrow paths I used to take when running from Sebastian. I slide down shortcuts that I know will get me to my car faster.

A shadow appears from the side and I shriek as it closes in on me.

I'm about to hit and kick when the familiar bergamot scent fills my nostrils.

My movements come to a halt as I stare up at him. "Sebastian...?"

"What is it?" He removes his white hoodie and grabs my shoulders. "Are you okay? What are you doing here and why were you running?"

"There are...there were two men...they...were wearing black...and they were chasing me...and...maybe they're from the black van that followed me or maybe...they don't even... know me..."

"Hey." He strokes my shoulder. "Deep breaths, baby."

I nearly sob at the sound of that endearment coming from his mouth. I didn't know I missed it so much until now.

"Now, repeat what you said. Slowly. Who was chasing you?"

"Me. Told you we'd meet again, Hitori-san."

I shriek as one of the dark figures closes in on Sebastian from behind. He doesn't even have time to turn around as the man's gun glints and he aims it at him.

Bang!

To be continued...
Sebastian & Naomi's story will conclude in the second and final part of the duet, Black *Thorns*.

Curious about Reina and her fiancé mentioned in this book? You can read their completed story in *All The Lies*.

WHAT'S NEXT?

Thank you so much for reading *Red Thorns*! If you liked it,
please leave a review.
Your support means the world to me.

If you're thirsty for more discussions with other readers of the
series, you can join the Facebook group, Rina's Spoilers Room.

Next up is the conclusion of Sebastian and Naomi's tale in
Black Thorns.

Blurb

A lie turned into a nightmare.

She broke my heart.
Broke me.
Broke us.
Only one thing could mend the gaping wound she left behind.
Her.
Naomi.
All mine for the taking.
All mine for owning.
All mine.

ALSO BY RINA KENT

For more titles by the author and an
explicit reading order, please visit:
www.rinakent.com/books

ABOUT THE AUTHOR

Rina Kent is a *USA Today*, international, and #1 Amazon bestselling author of everything enemies to lovers romance.

She's known to write unapologetic anti-heroes and villains because she often fell in love with men no one roots for. Her books are sprinkled with a touch of darkness, a pinch of angst, and an unhealthy dose of intensity.

She spends her private days in London laughing like an evil mastermind about adding mayhem to her expanding universe. When she's not writing, Rina travels, hikes, and spoils cats in a pure Cat Lady fashion.

Find Rina Below:

Website: www.rinakent.com

Newsletter: www.subscribepage.com/rinakent

BookBub: www.bookbub.com/profile/rina-kent

Amazon: www.amazon.com/Rina-Kent/e/B07MM54G22

Goodreads: www.goodreads.com/author/show/18697906.
Rina_Kent

Instagram: www.instagram.com/author_rina

Facebook: www.facebook.com/rinaakent

Reader Group: www.facebook.com/groups/rinakent.club

Pinterest: www.pinterest.co.uk/AuthorRina/boards

Tiktok: www.tiktok.com/@rina.kent

Twitter: twitter.com/AuthorRina

Made in the USA
Las Vegas, NV
29 December 2023

83638798R00177